PRINCESS DECOMPOSIA and COUNT SPATULA

PRINCESS DECOMPOSIA and COUNT SPATULA

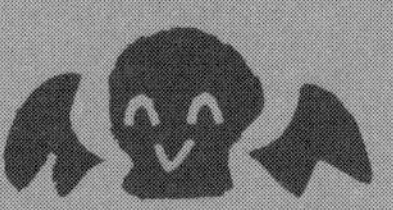

ANDI WATSON

First Second
New York

First Second

Copyright © 2015 by Andi Watson
Published by First Second
First Second is an imprint of Roaring Brook Press,
a division of Holtzbrinck Publishing Holdings Limited Partnership
175 Fifth Avenue, New York, New York 10010
All rights reserved

Cataloging-in-Publication Data is on file at the Library of Congress

Paperback ISBN: 978-1-62672-149-4
Hardcover ISBN: 978-1-62672-275-0

First Second books may be purchased for business or promotional use.
For information on bulk purchases please contact Macmillan Corporate
and Premium Sales Department at (800) 221-7945 x5442 or by email at
specialmarkets@macmillan.com.

First edition 2015

Book design by Colleen AF Venable
Printed in the United States of America

Paperback: 10 9 8 7 6 5 4 3 2 1
Hardcover: 10 9 8 7 6 5 4 3 2 1

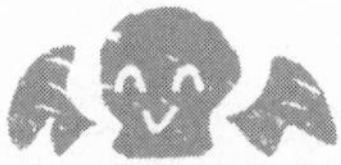

For P,
Princess Decomposia
to my
Count Spatula

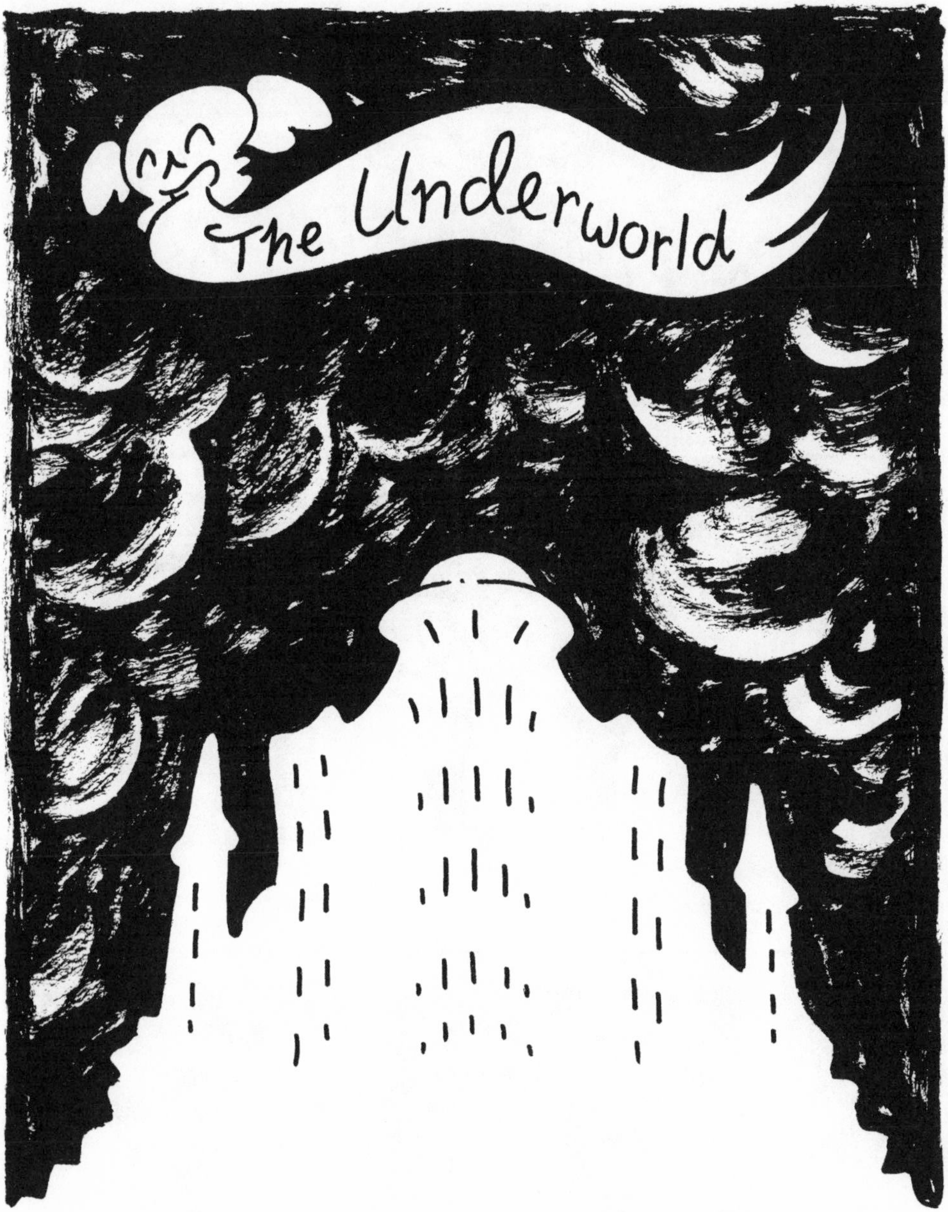
The Underworld

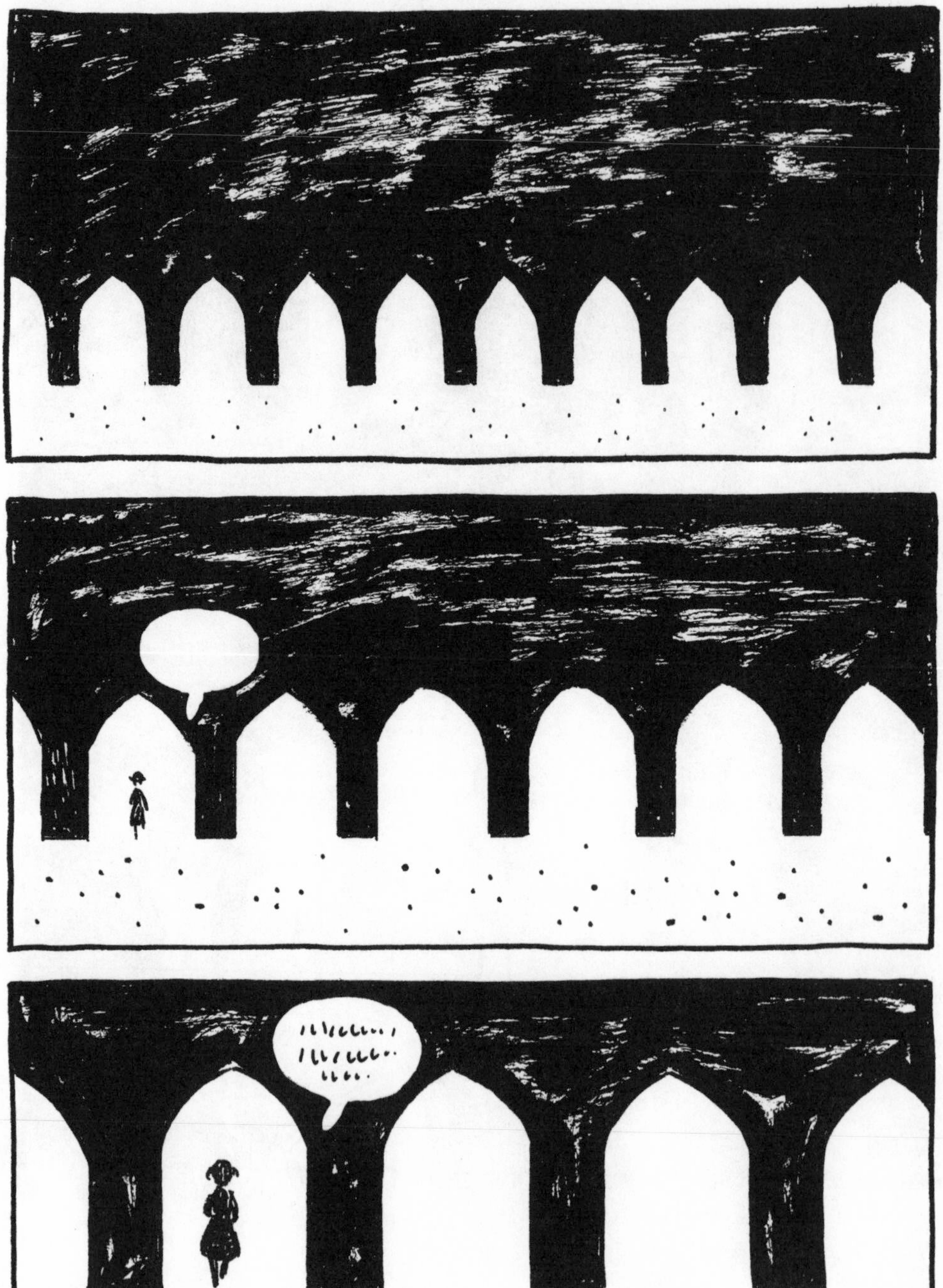

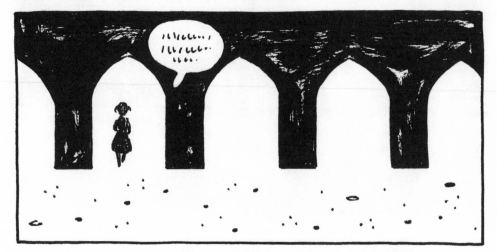

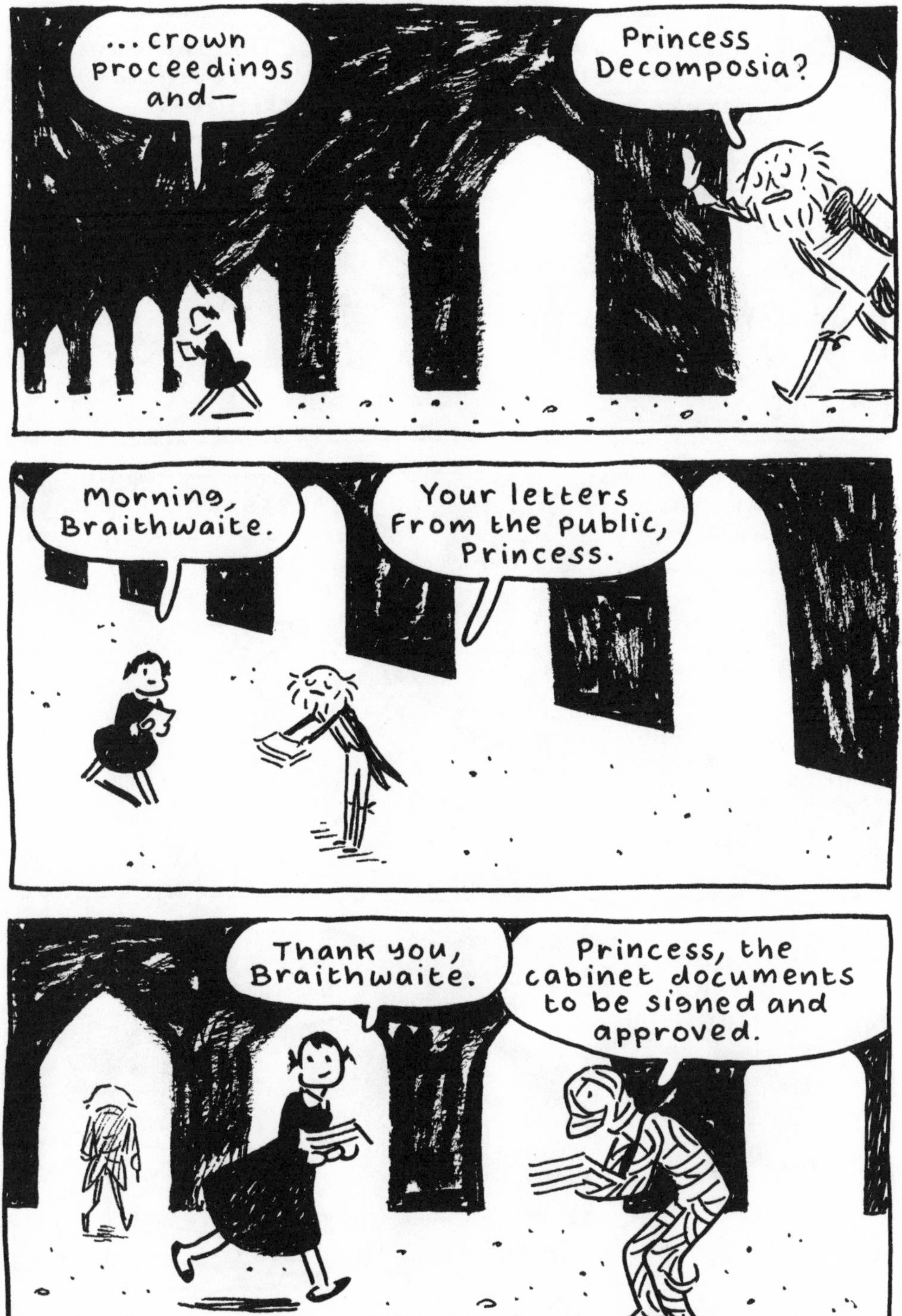
...crown proceedings and—
Princess Decomposia?
Morning, Braithwaite.
Your letters from the public, Princess.
Thank you, Braithwaite.
Princess, the cabinet documents to be signed and approved.

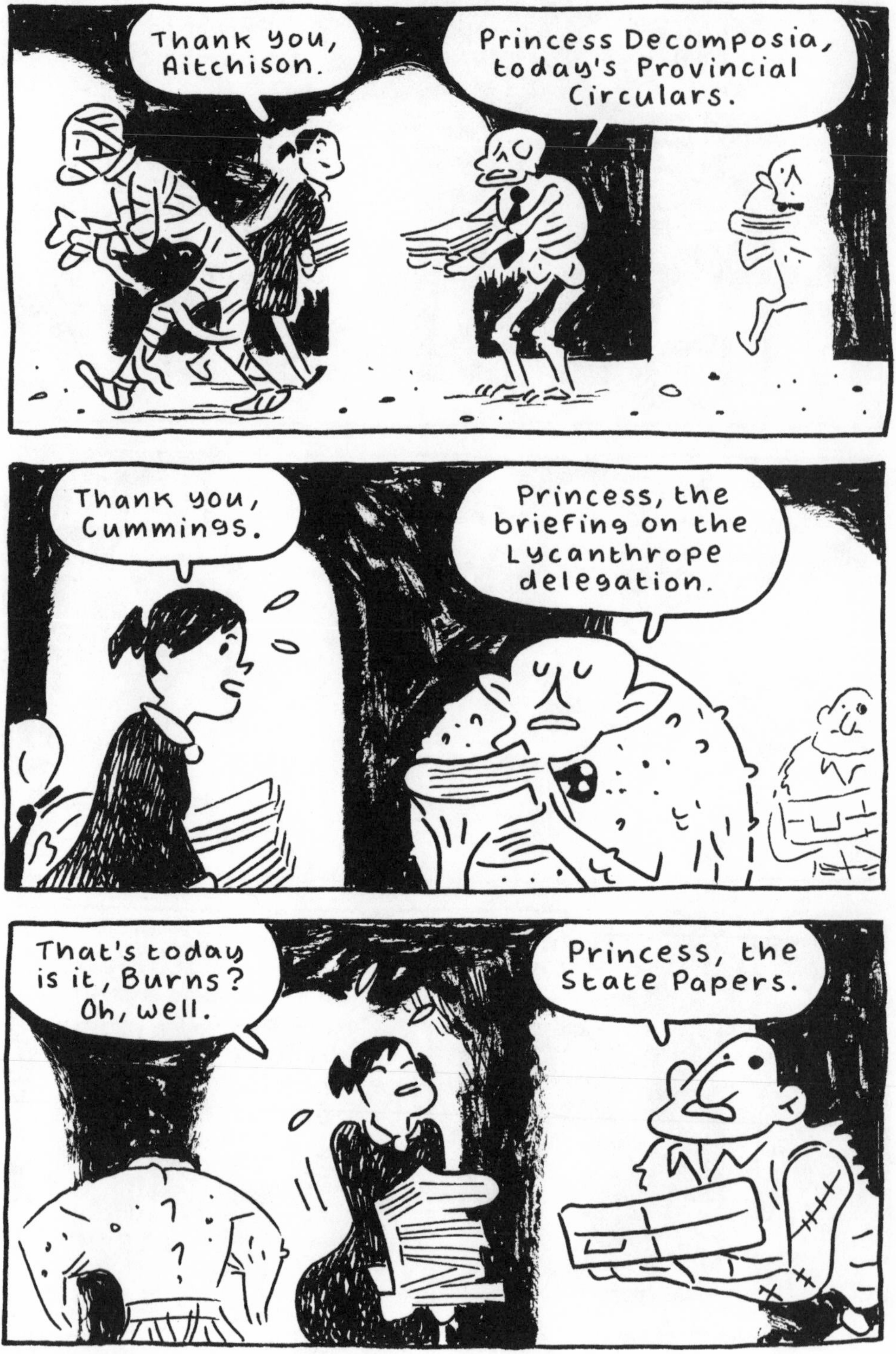
Thank you, Aitchison.
Princess Decomposia, today's Provincial Circulars.
Thank you, Cummings.
Princess, the briefing on the Lycanthrope delegation.
That's today is it, Burns? Oh, well.
Princess, the State Papers.

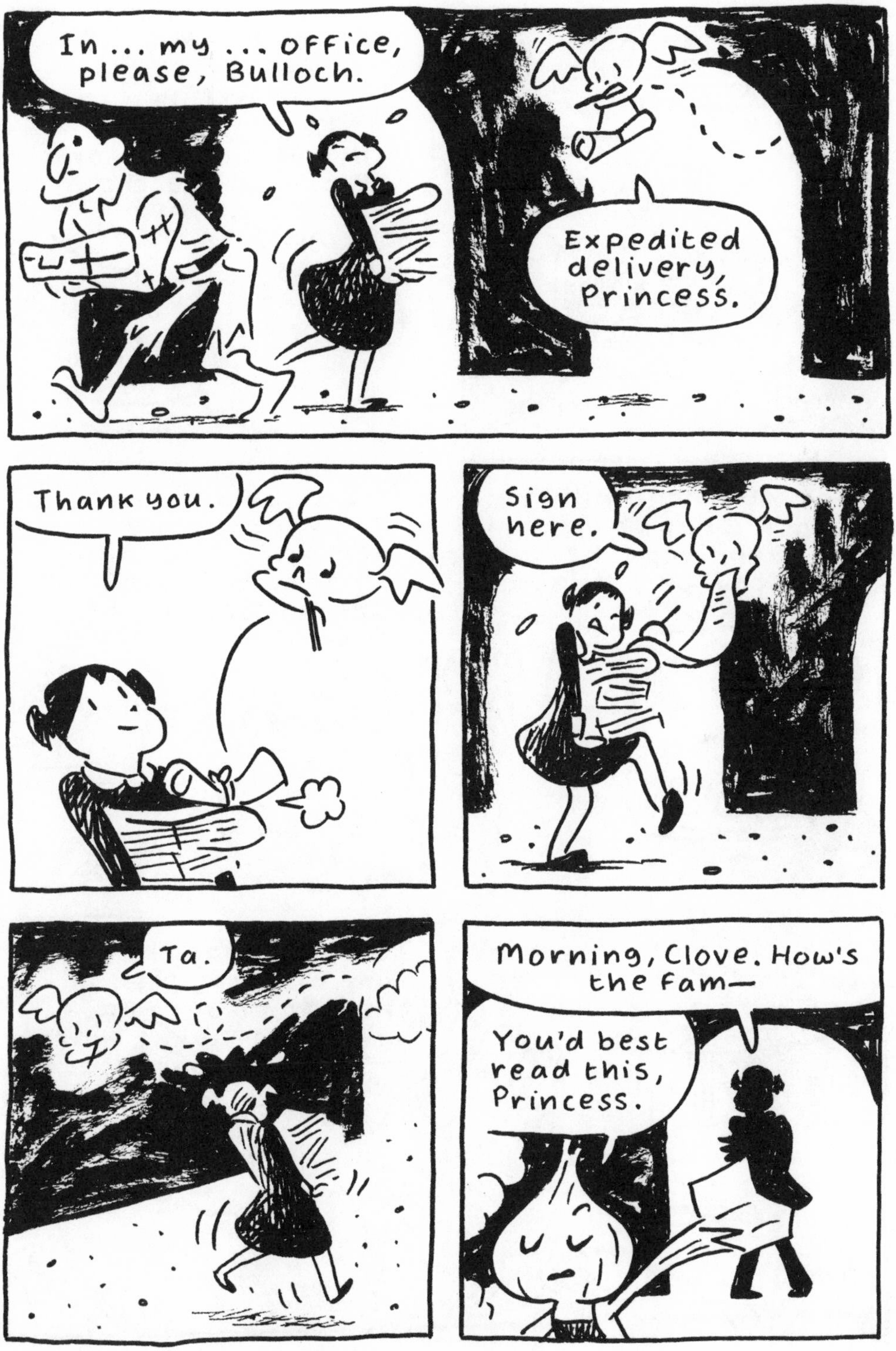
In ... my ... office, please, Bulloch.
Expedited delivery, Princess.
Thank you.
Sign here.
Ta.
Morning, Clove. How's the fam—
You'd best read this, Princess.

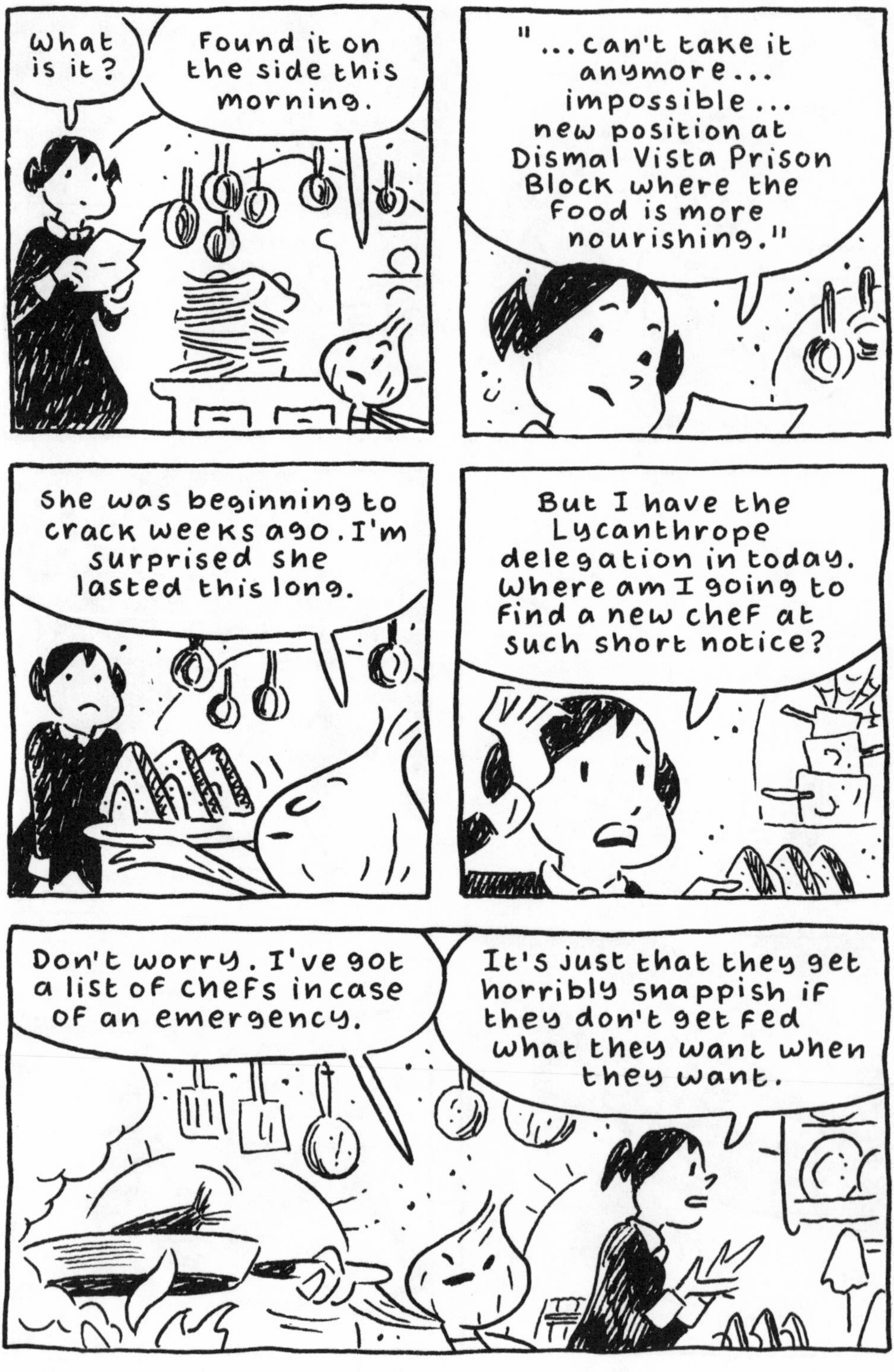
What is it?
Found it on the side this morning.
"...can't take it anymore... impossible... new position at Dismal Vista Prison Block where the food is more nourishing."
She was beginning to crack weeks ago. I'm surprised she lasted this long.
But I have the Lycanthrope delegation in today. Where am I going to find a new chef at such short notice?
Don't worry. I've got a list of chefs in case of an emergency.
It's just that they get horribly snappish if they don't get fed what they want when they want.

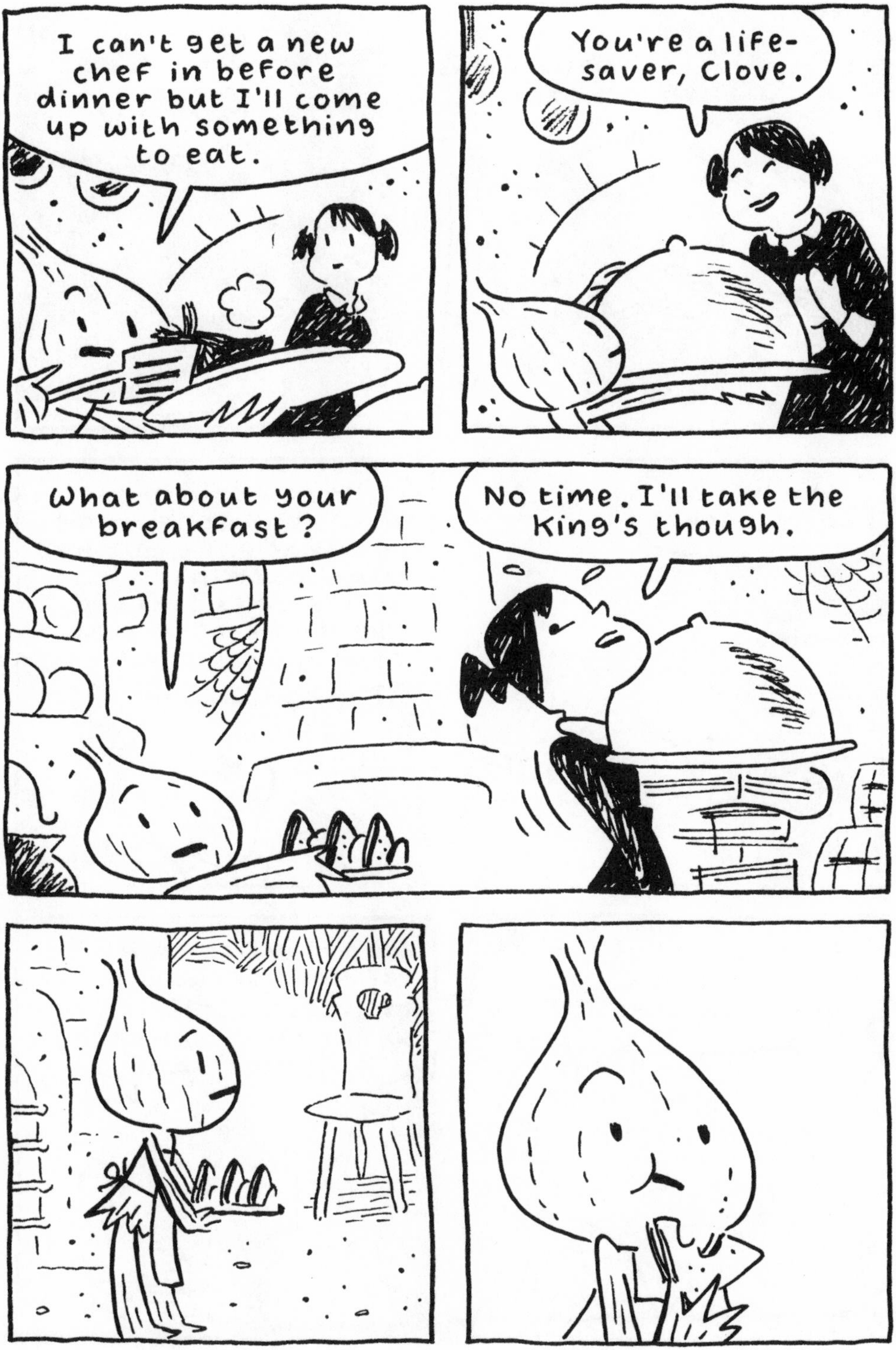
I can't get a new chef in before dinner but I'll come up with something to eat.
You're a life-saver, Clove.
What about your breakfast?
No time. I'll take the King's though.

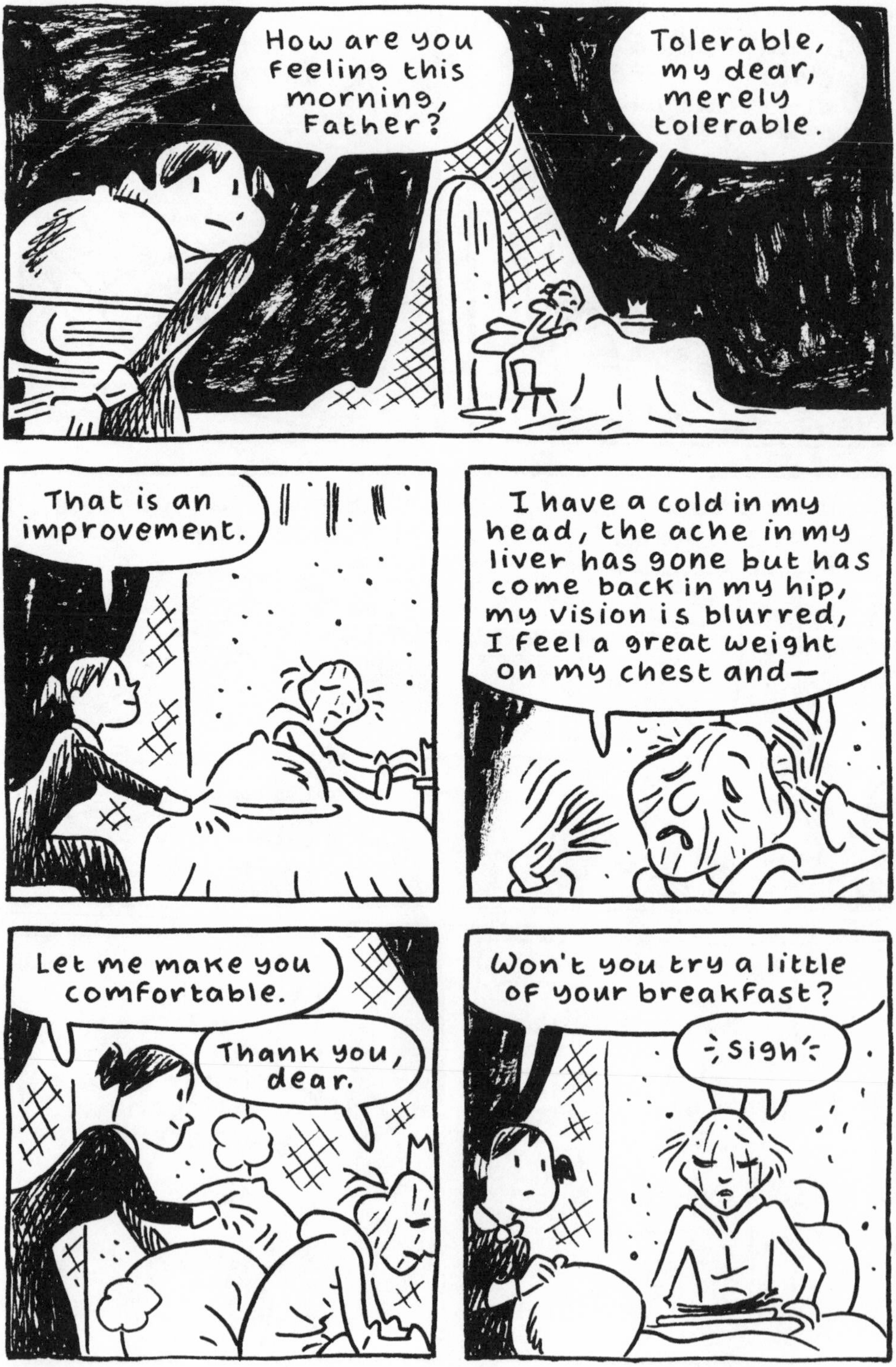
How are you feeling this morning, Father?
Tolerable, my dear, merely tolerable.
That is an improvement.
I have a cold in my head, the ache in my liver has gone but has come back in my hip, my vision is blurred, I feel a great weight on my chest and—
Let me make you comfortable.
Thank you, dear.
Won't you try a little of your breakfast?
Sigh

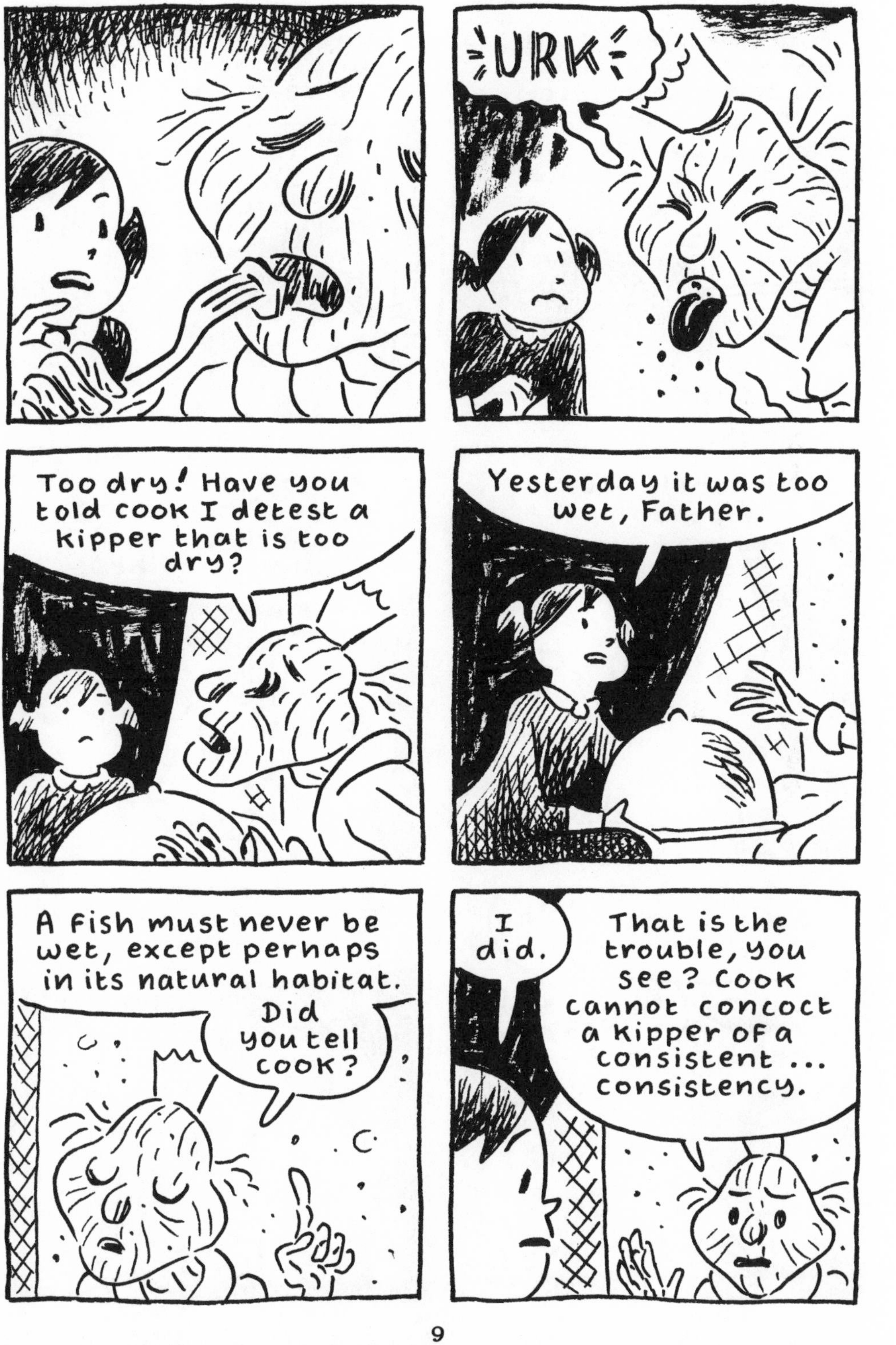
URK
Too dry! Have you told cook I detest a kipper that is too dry?
Yesterday it was too wet, Father.
A fish must never be wet, except perhaps in its natural habitat.
Did you tell cook?
I did.
That is the trouble, you see? Cook cannot concoct a kipper of a consistent ... consistency.

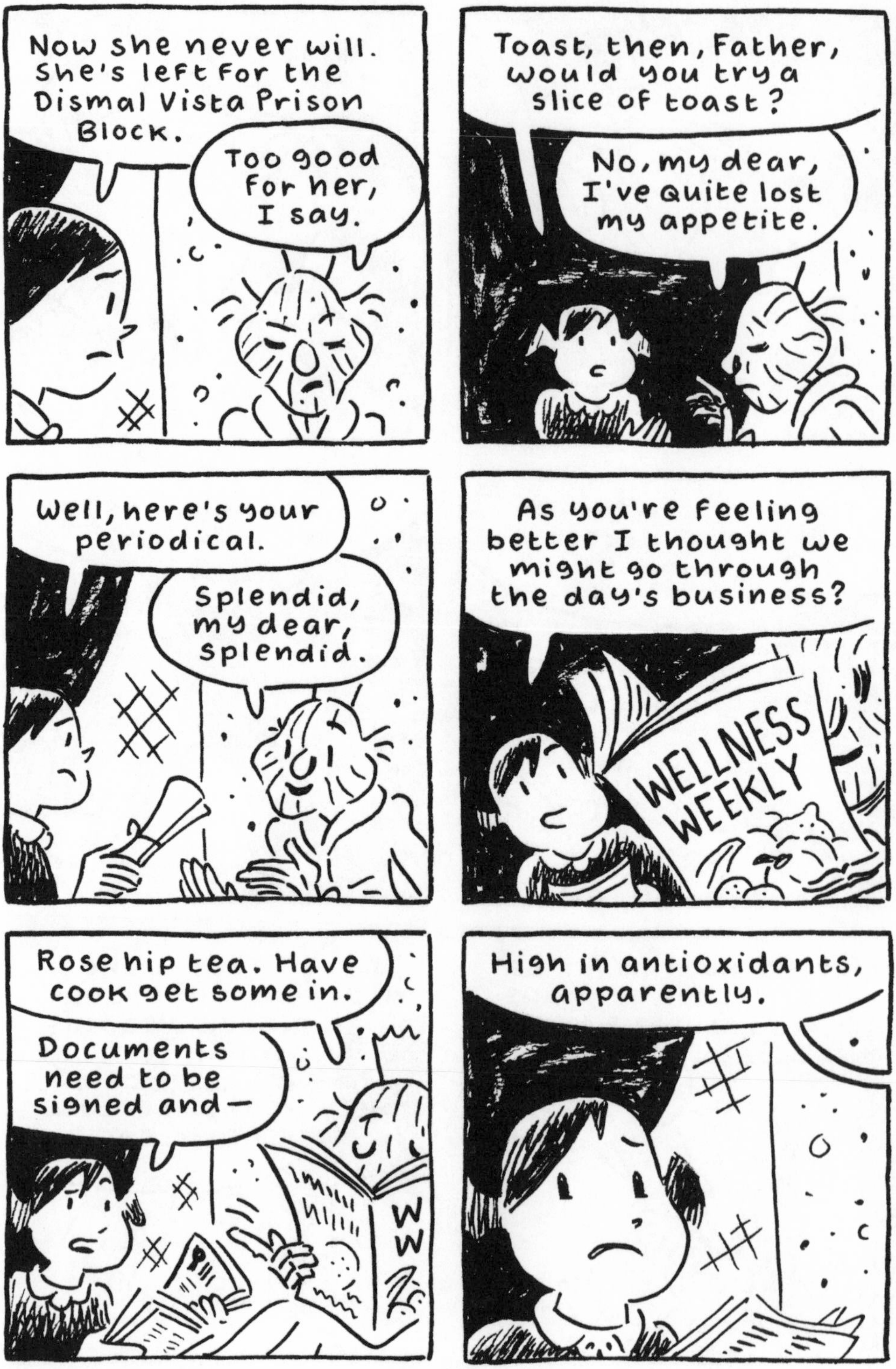
Now she never will. She's left for the Dismal Vista Prison Block.
Too good for her, I say.
Toast, then, Father, would you try a slice of toast?
No, my dear, I've quite lost my appetite.
Well, here's your periodical.
Splendid, my dear, splendid.
As you're feeling better I thought we might go through the day's business?
WELLNESS WEEKLY
Rose hip tea. Have cook get some in.
Documents need to be signed and—
WW
High in antioxidants, apparently.

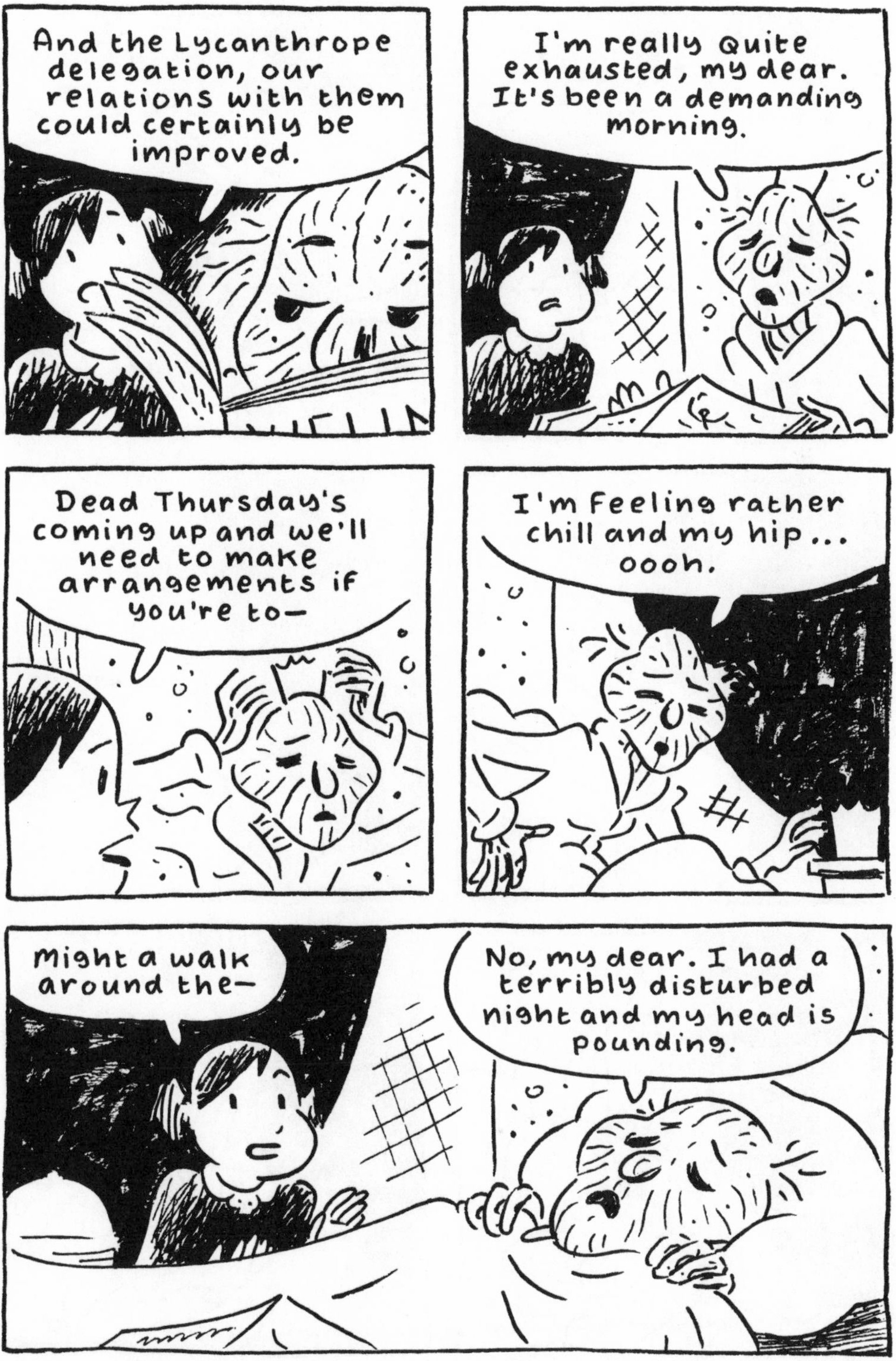
And the Lycanthrope delegation, our relations with them could certainly be improved.
I'm really quite exhausted, my dear. It's been a demanding morning.
Dead Thursday's coming up and we'll need to make arrangements if you're to—
I'm feeling rather chill and my hip... oooh.
Might a walk around the—
No, my dear. I had a terribly disturbed night and my head is pounding.

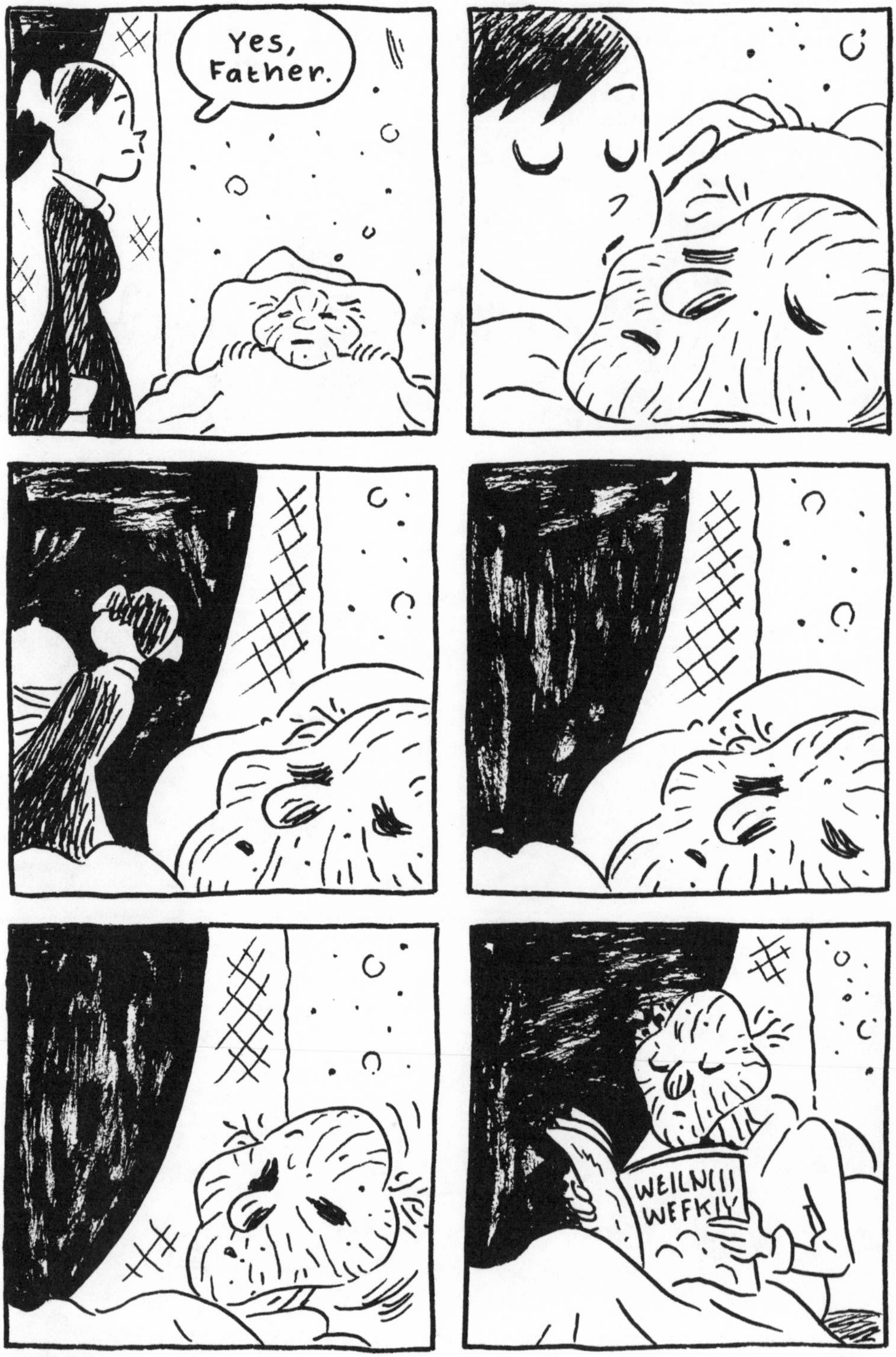
Yes, Father.

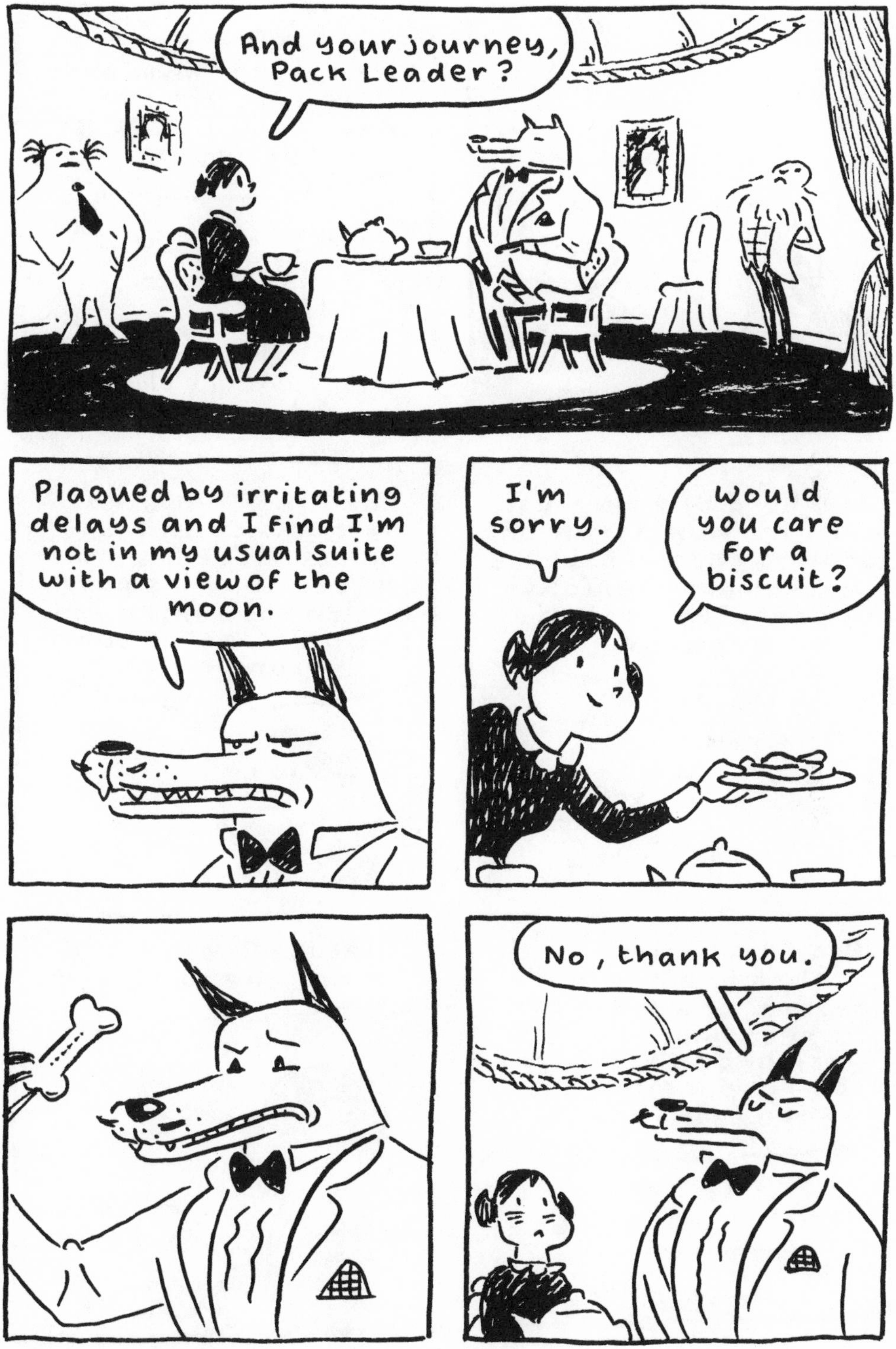
And your journey, Pack Leader?
Plagued by irritating delays and I find I'm not in my usual suite with a view of the moon.
I'm sorry.
Would you care for a biscuit?
No, thank you.

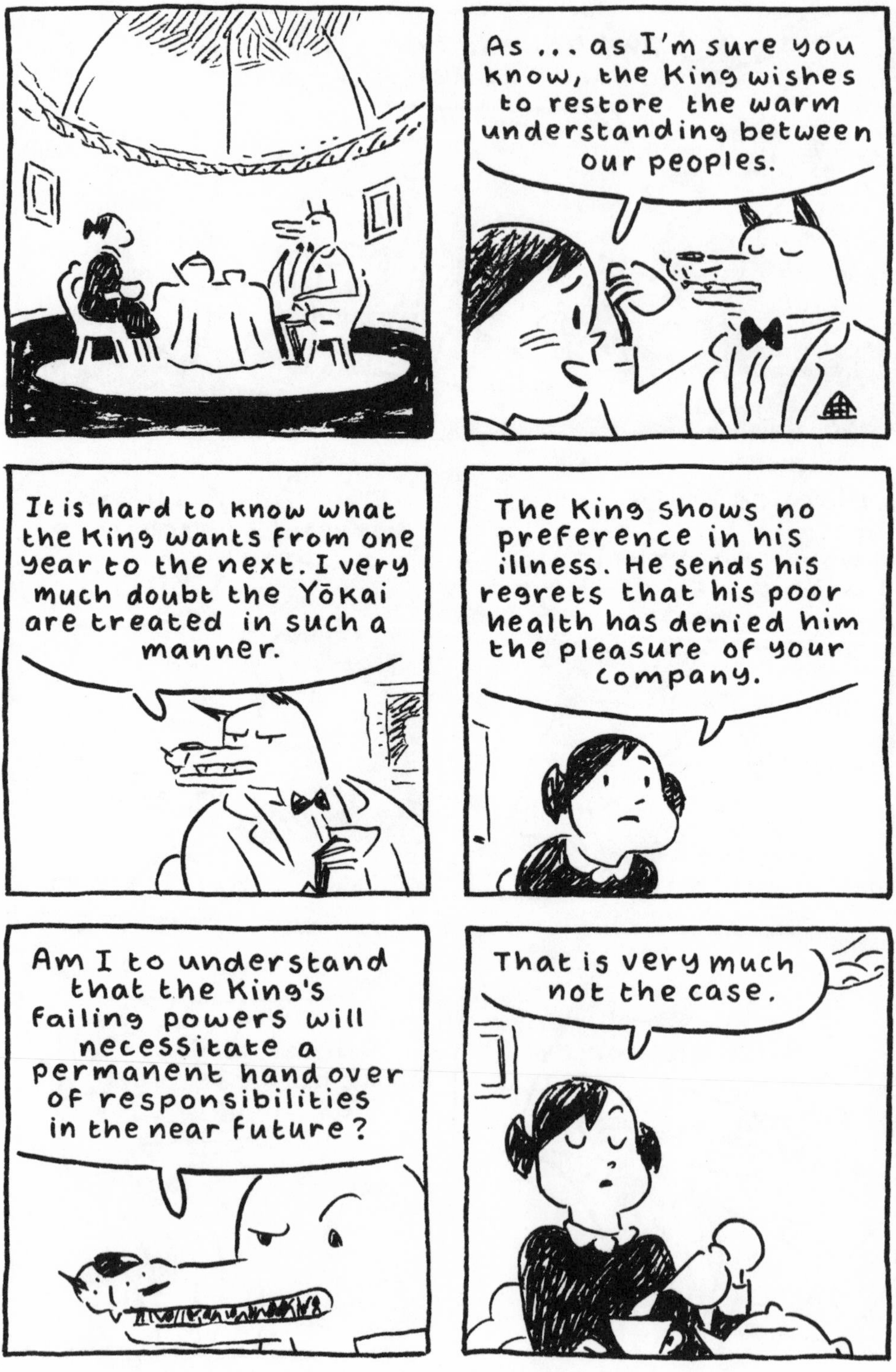
As ... as I'm sure you know, the King wishes to restore the warm understanding between our peoples.
It is hard to know what the King wants from one year to the next. I very much doubt the Yōkai are treated in such a manner.
The King shows no preference in his illness. He sends his regrets that his poor health has denied him the pleasure of your company.
Am I to understand that the King's failing powers will necessitate a permanent handover of responsibilities in the near future?
That is very much not the case.

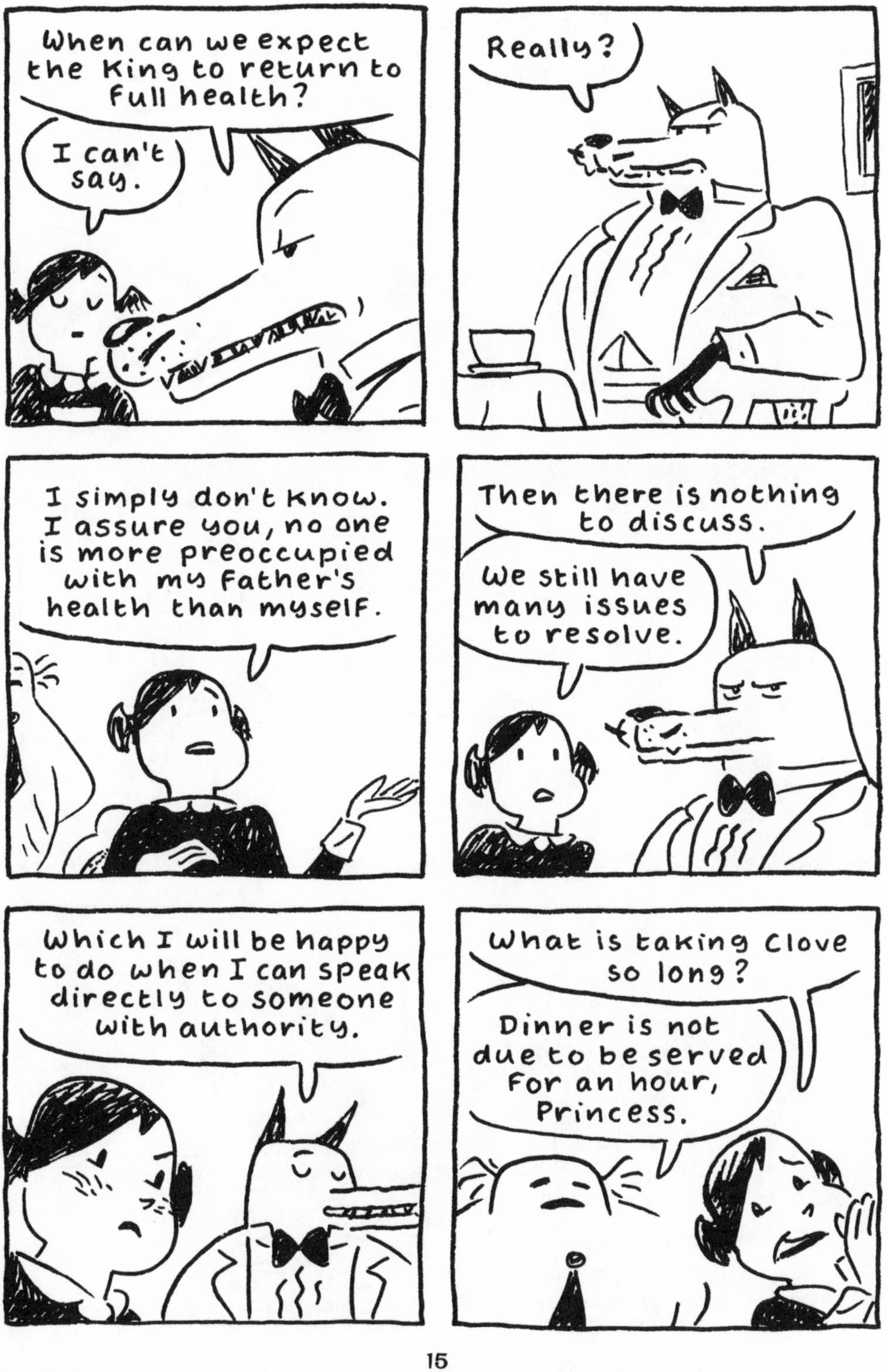
When can we expect the King to return to full health?
I can't say.
Really?
I simply don't know. I assure you, no one is more preoccupied with my father's health than myself.
Then there is nothing to discuss.
We still have many issues to resolve.
Which I will be happy to do when I can speak directly to someone with authority.
What is taking Clove so long?
Dinner is not due to be served for an hour, Princess.

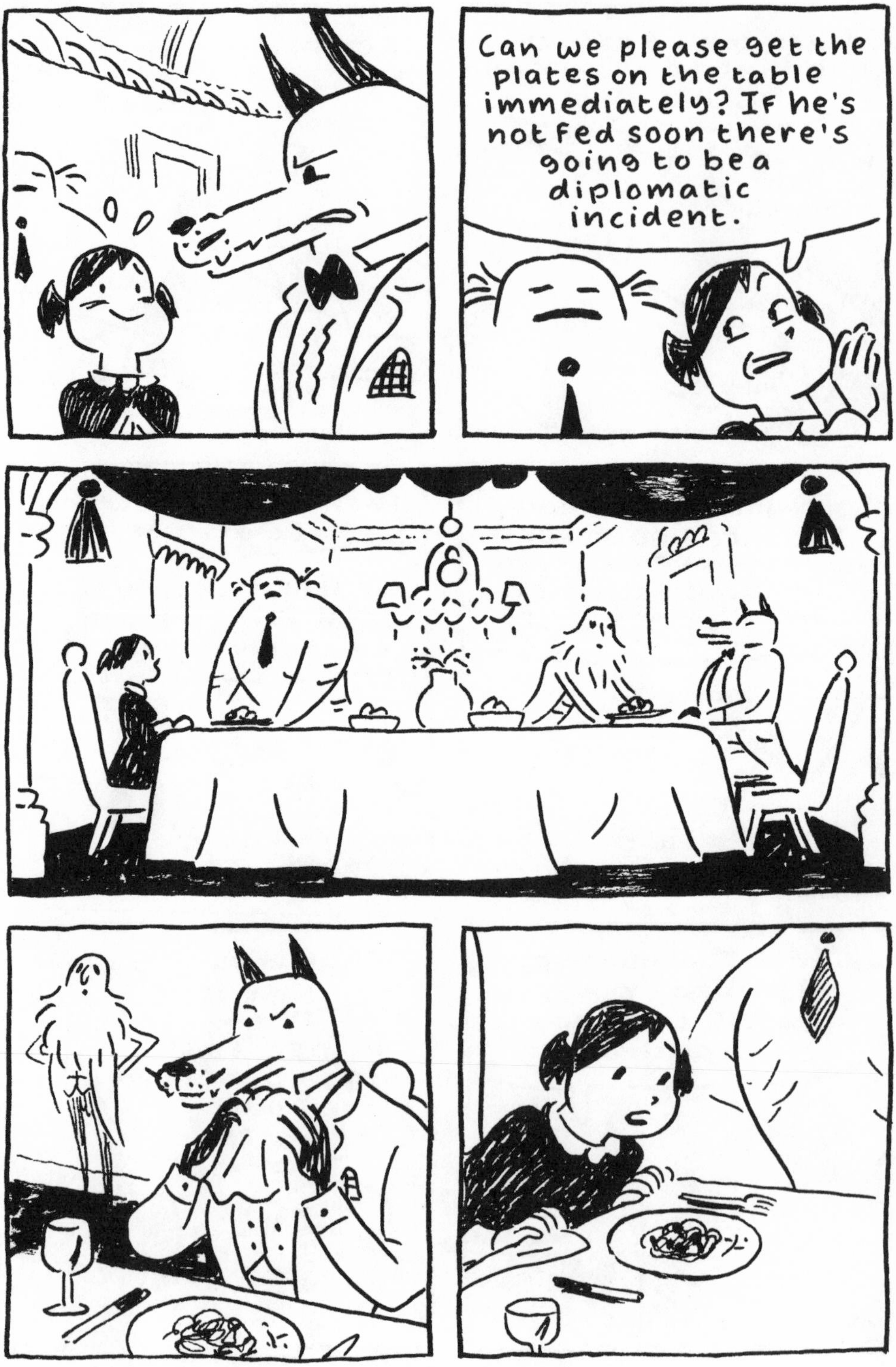
Can we please get the plates on the table immediately? If he's not fed soon there's going to be a diplomatic incident.

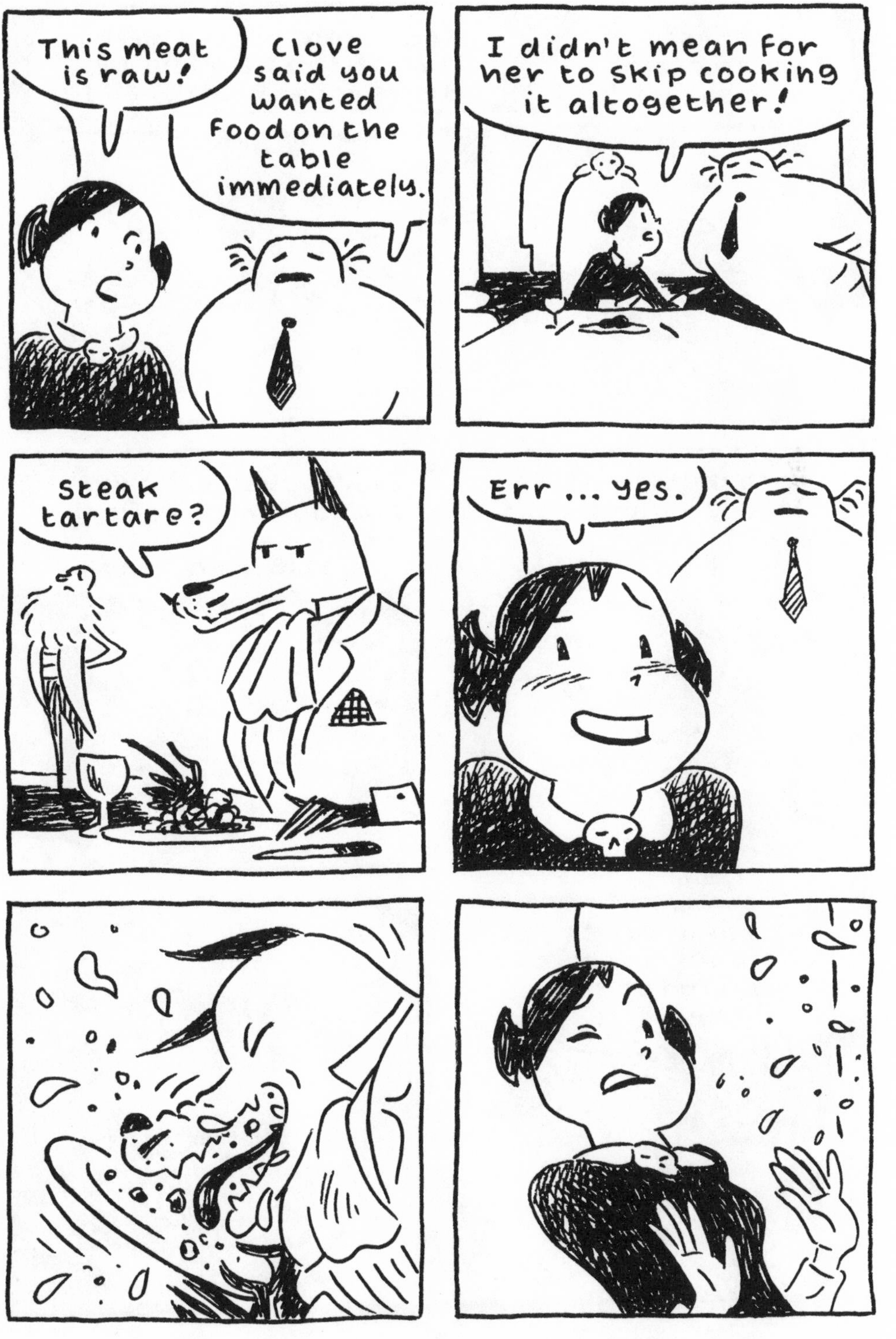
This meat is raw!
Clove said you wanted food on the table immediately.
I didn't mean for her to skip cooking it altogether!
Steak tartare?
Err ... yes.

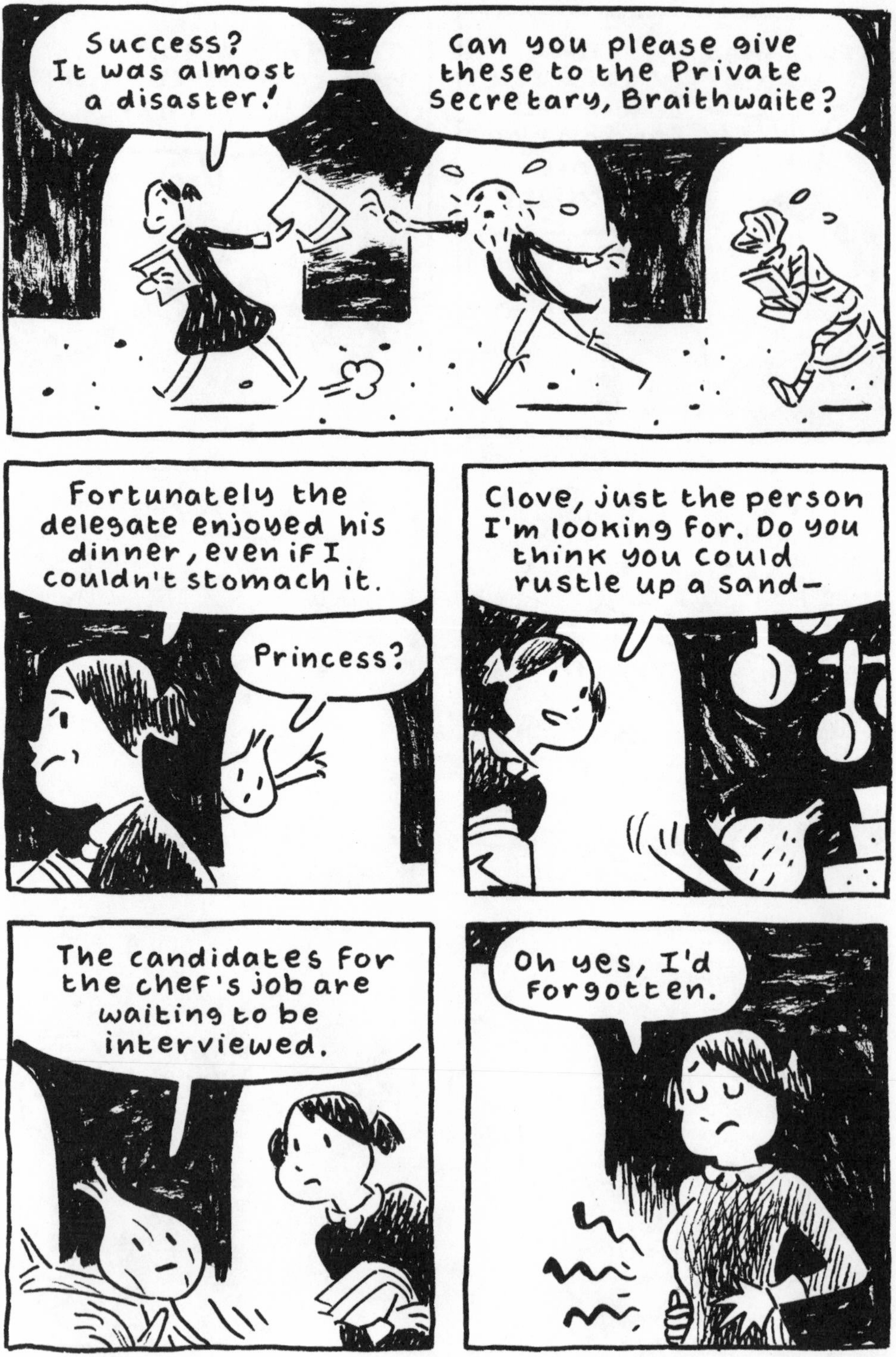
Success? It was almost a disaster!
Can you please give these to the Private Secretary, Braithwaite?
Fortunately the delegate enjoyed his dinner, even if I couldn't stomach it.
Princess?
Clove, just the person I'm looking for. Do you think you could rustle up a sand–
The candidates for the chef's job are waiting to be interviewed.
Oh yes, I'd forgotten.

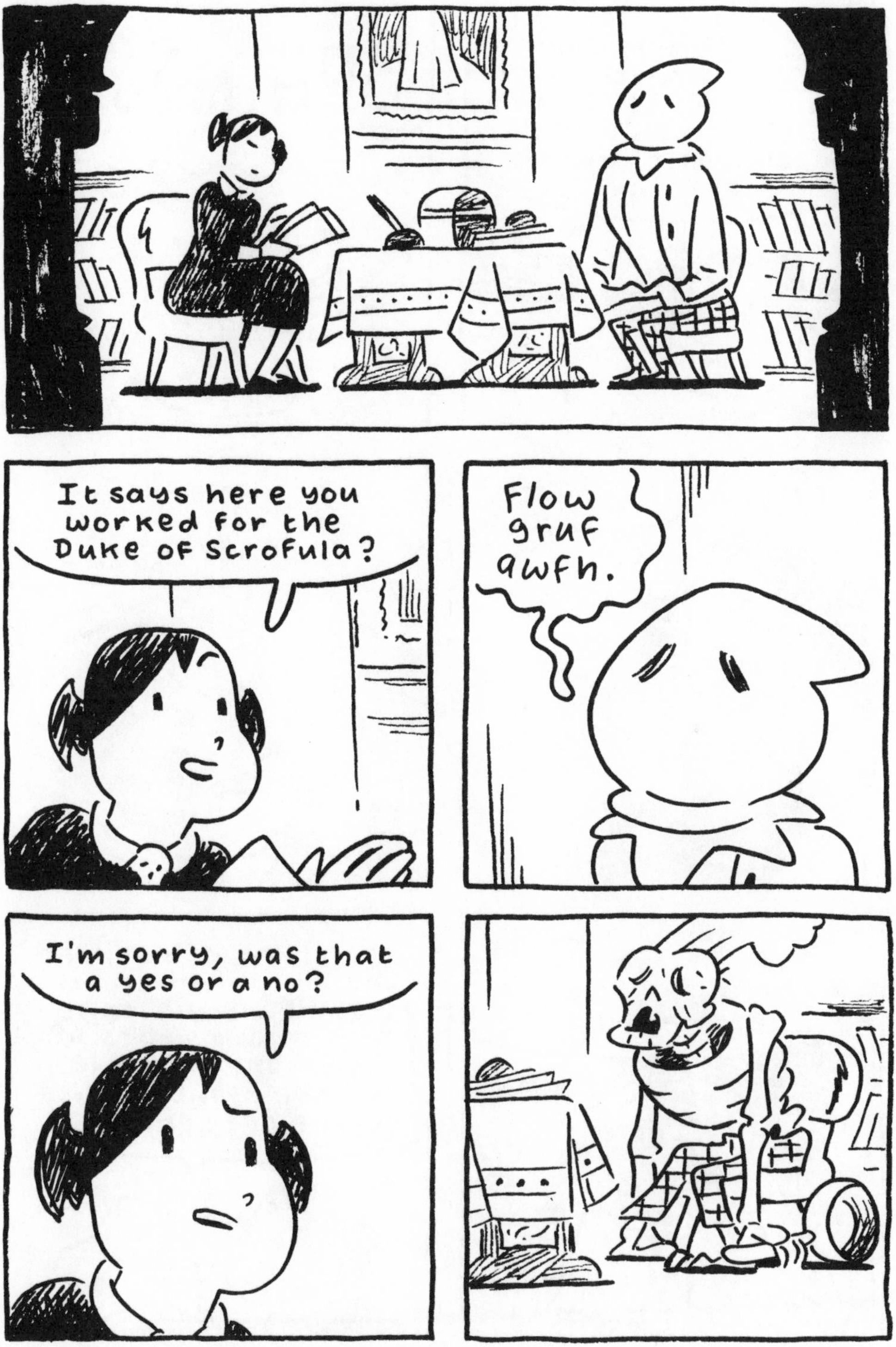
It says here you worked for the Duke of Scrofula?
Flow gruf awfh.
I'm sorry, was that a yes or a no?

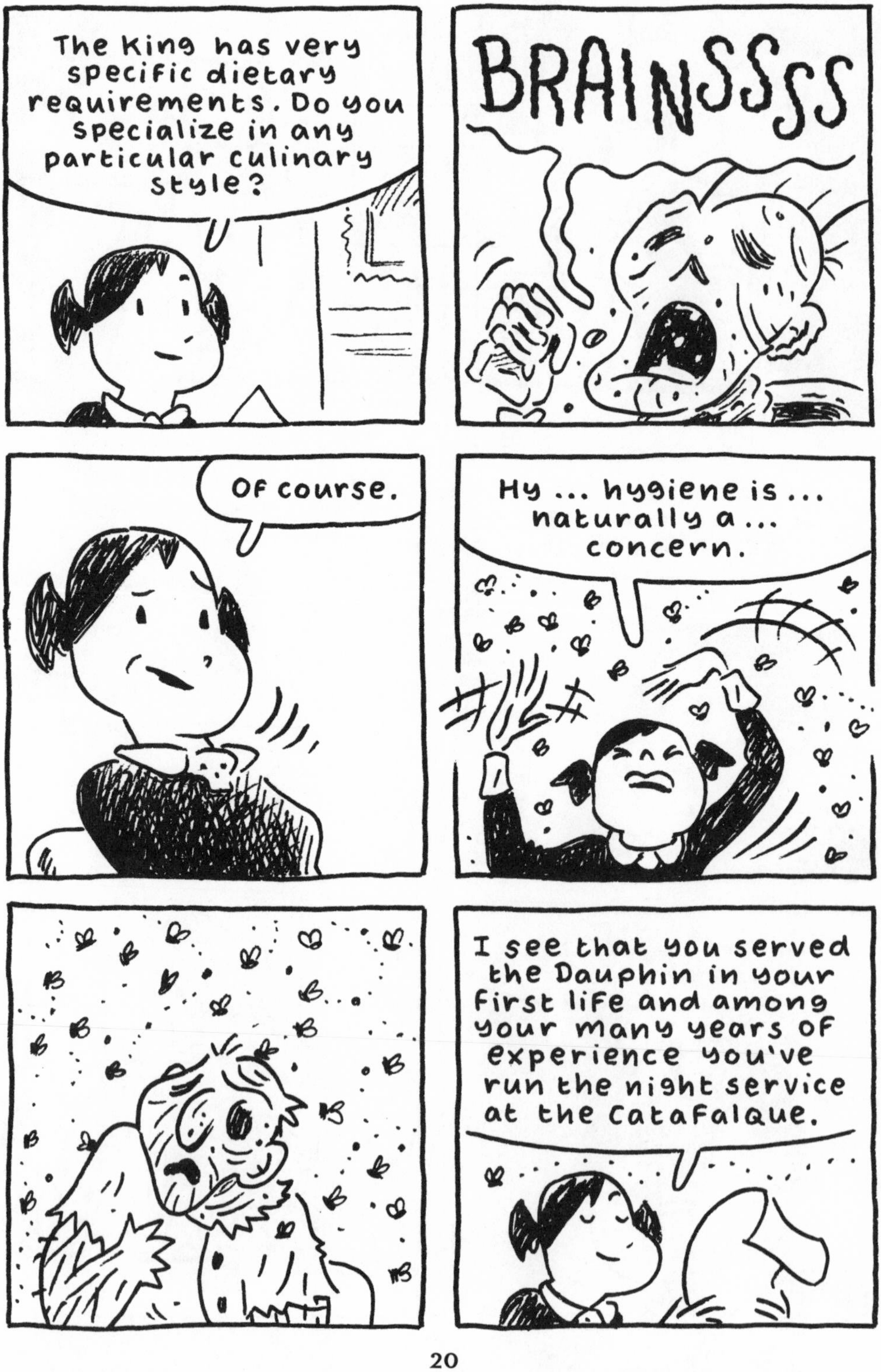
The King has very specific dietary requirements. Do you specialize in any particular culinary style?
BRAINSSSSS
Of course.
Hy ... hygiene is ... naturally a ... concern.
I see that you served the Dauphin in your first life and among your many years of experience you've run the night service at the Catafalque.

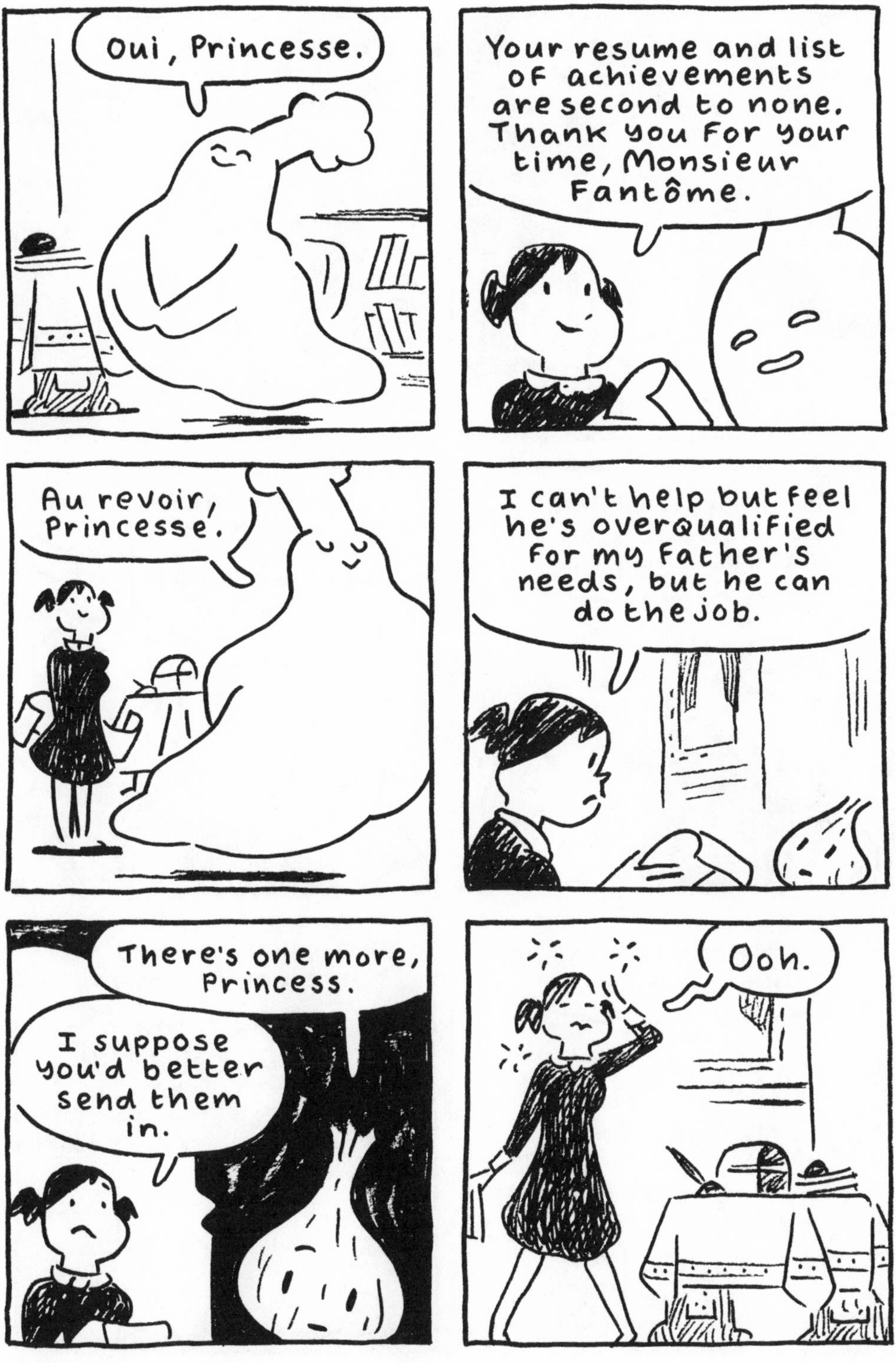
Oui, Princesse.
Your resume and list of achievements are second to none. Thank you for your time, Monsieur Fantôme.
Au revoir, Princesse.
I can't help but feel he's overqualified for my father's needs, but he can do the job.
There's one more, Princess.
I suppose you'd better send them in.
Ooh.

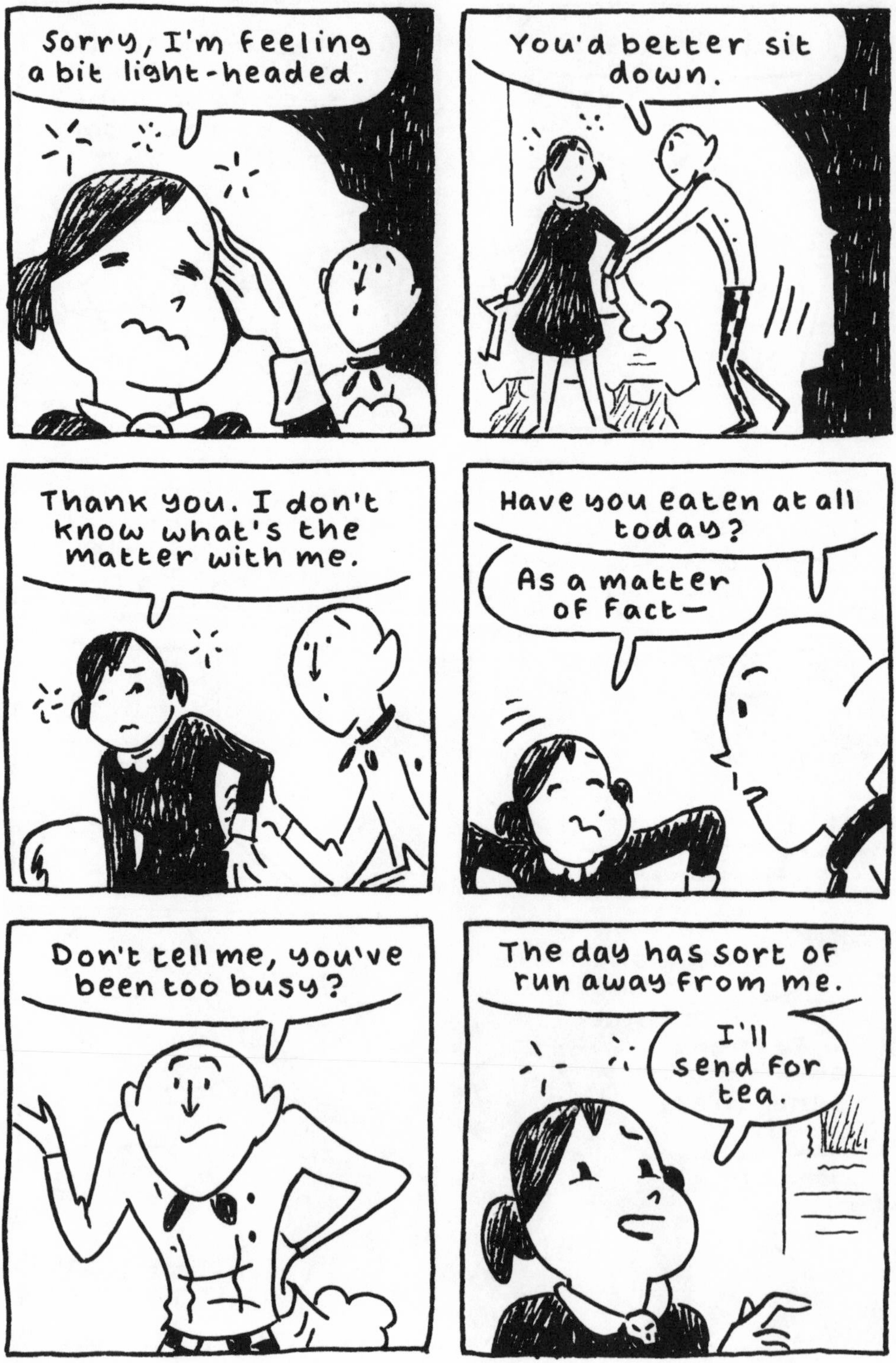
Sorry, I'm feeling a bit light-headed.
You'd better sit down.
Thank you. I don't know what's the matter with me.
Have you eaten at all today?
As a matter of fact—
Don't tell me, you've been too busy?
The day has sort of run away from me.
I'll send for tea.

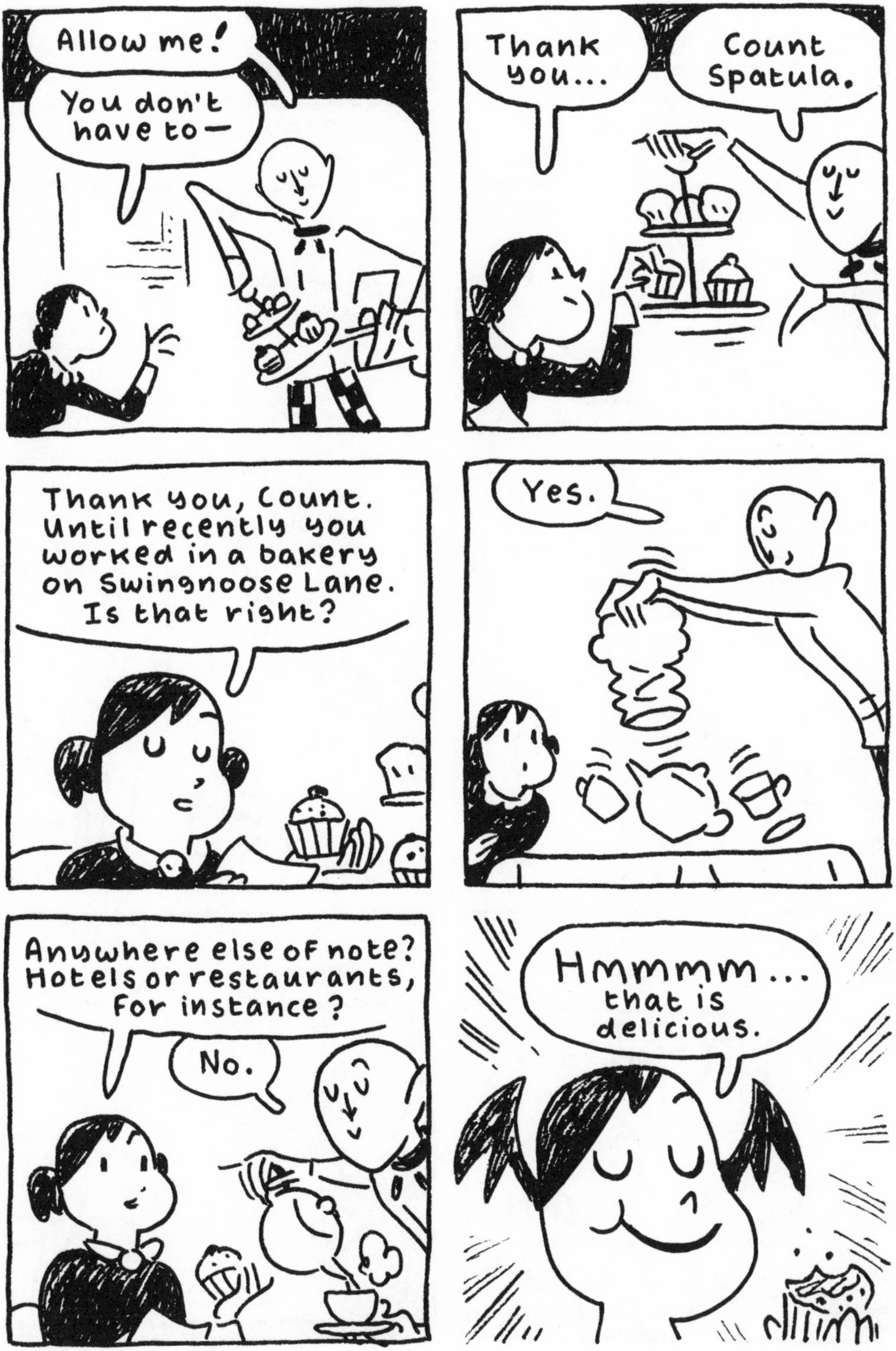
Allow me!
You don't have to—
Thank you...
Count Spatula.
Thank you, Count. Until recently you worked in a bakery on Swingnoose Lane. Is that right?
Yes.
Anywhere else of note? Hotels or restaurants, for instance?
No.
Hmmmm... that is delicious.

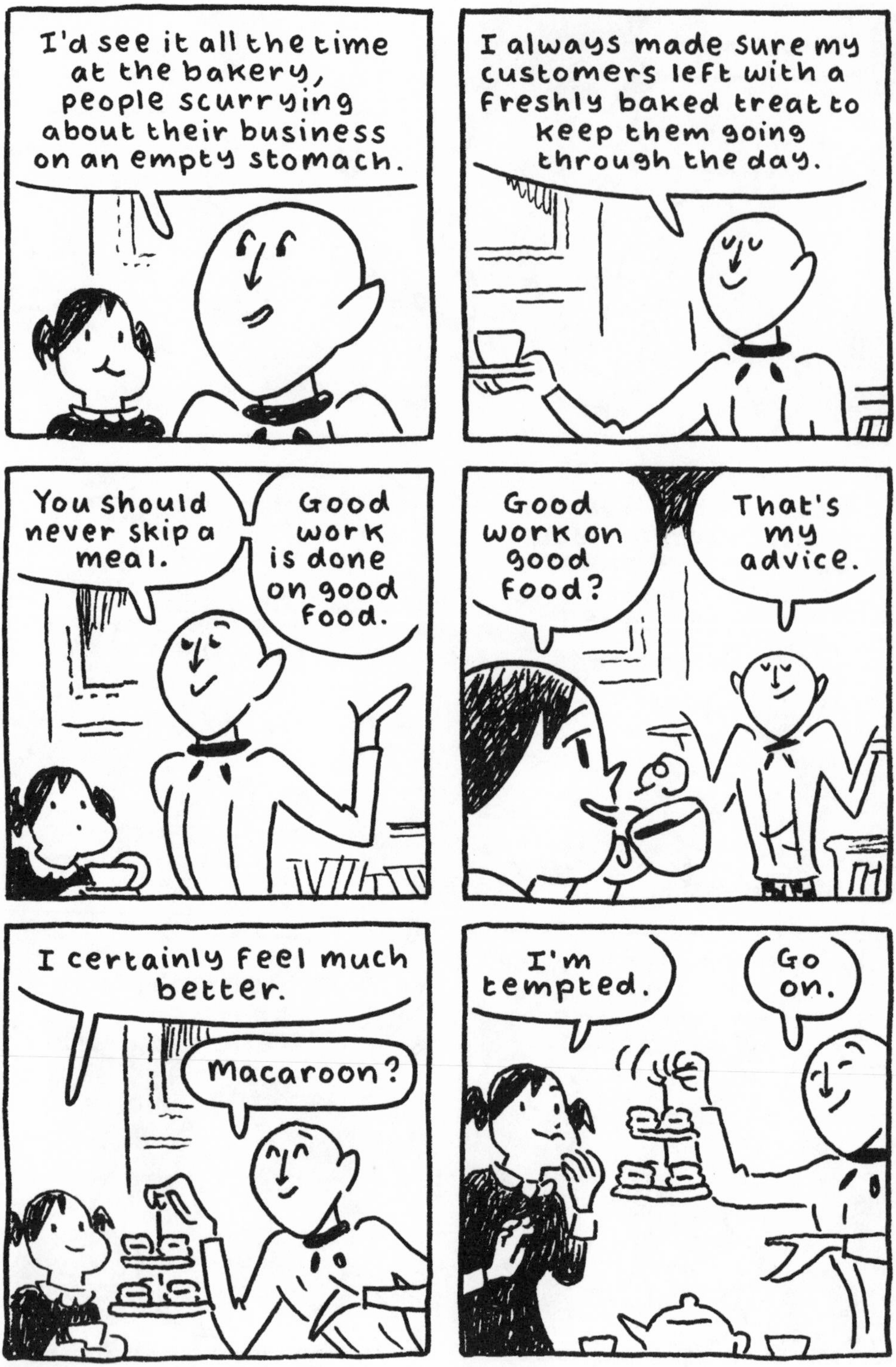
I'd see it all the time at the bakery, people scurrying about their business on an empty stomach.
I always made sure my customers left with a freshly baked treat to keep them going through the day.
You should never skip a meal.
Good work is done on good food.
Good work on good food?
That's my advice.
I certainly feel much better.
Macaroon?
I'm tempted.
Go on.

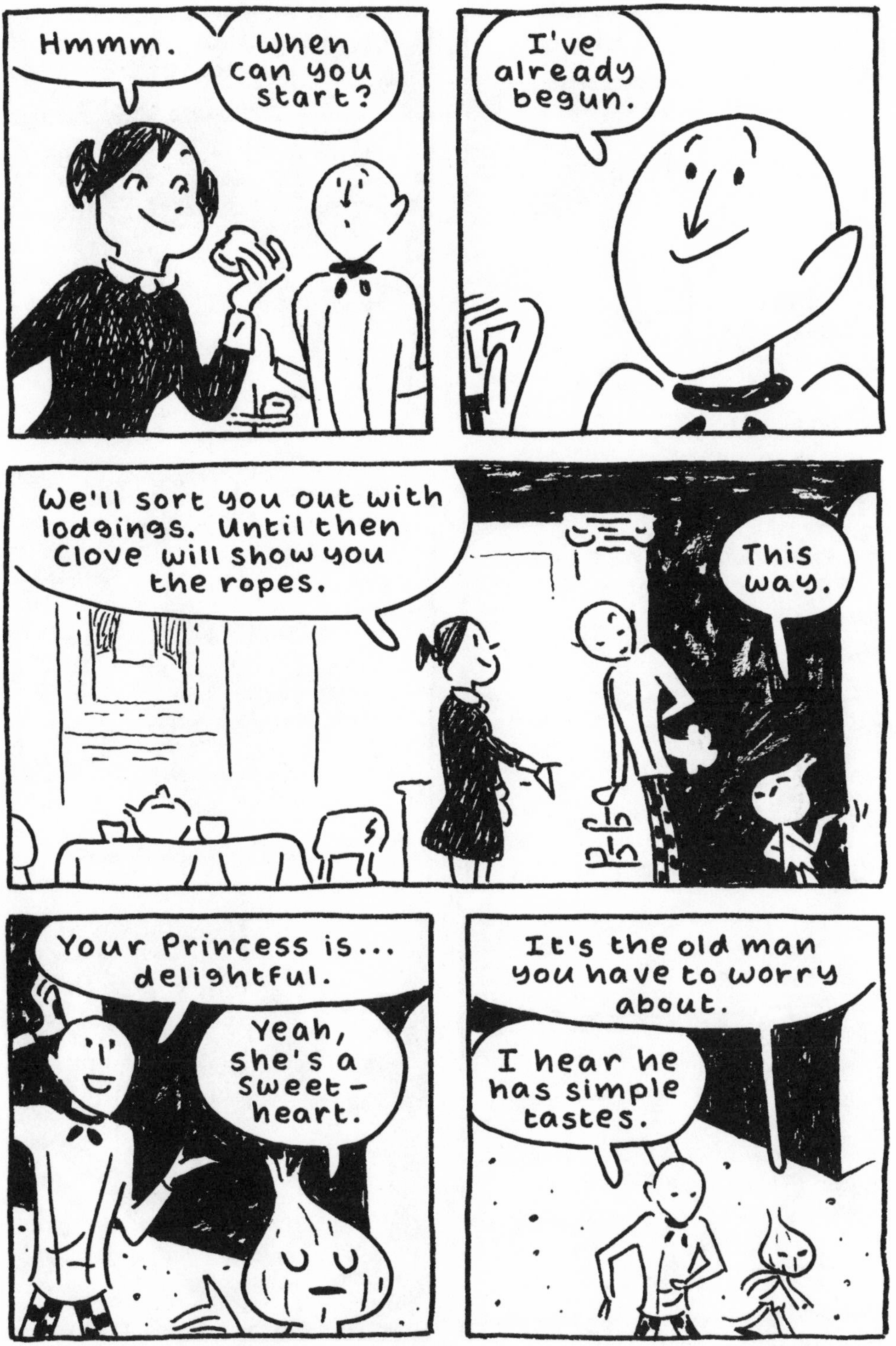
Hmmm.
When can you start?
I've already begun.
We'll sort you out with lodgings. Until then Clove will show you the ropes.
This way.
Your Princess is... delightful.
Yeah, she's a sweet-heart.
It's the old man you have to worry about.
I hear he has simple tastes.

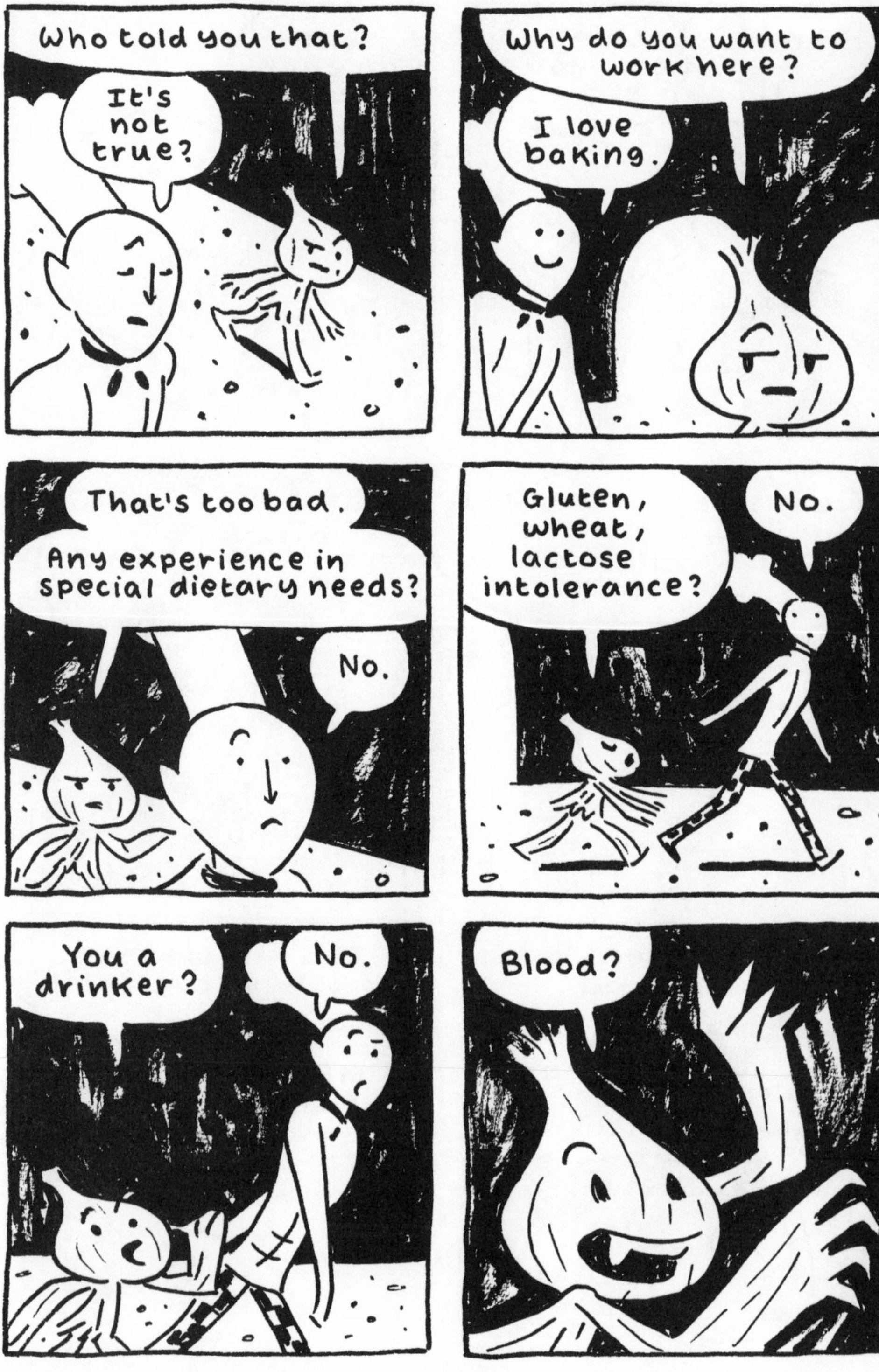
Who told you that?
It's not true?
Why do you want to work here?
I love baking.
That's too bad.
Any experience in special dietary needs?
No.
Gluten, wheat, lactose intolerance?
No.
You a drinker?
No.
Blood?

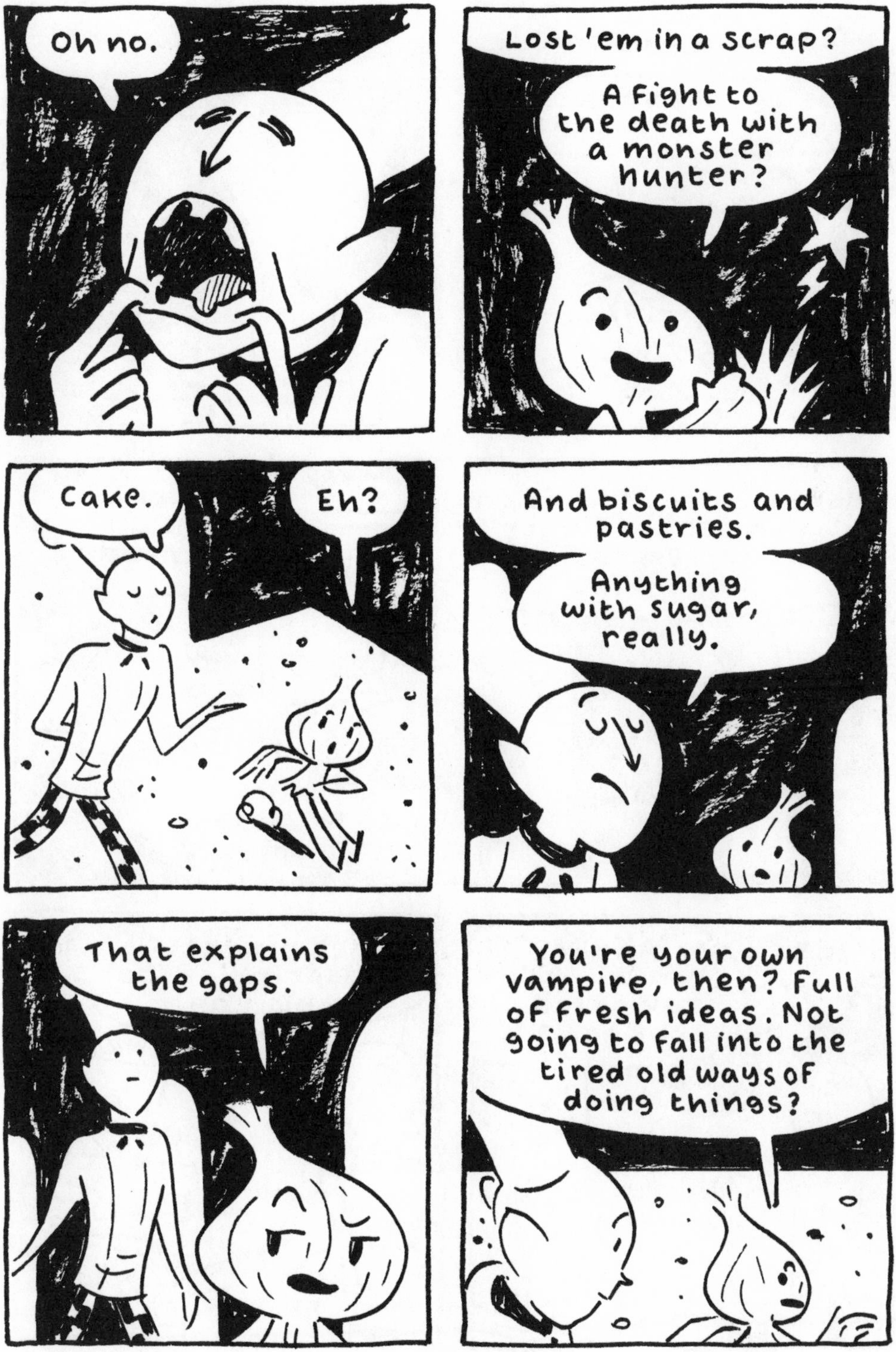
Oh no.
Lost 'em in a scrap?
A fight to the death with a monster hunter?
Cake.
Eh?
And biscuits and pastries.
Anything with sugar, really.
That explains the gaps.
You're your own vampire, then? Full of fresh ideas. Not going to fall into the tired old ways of doing things?

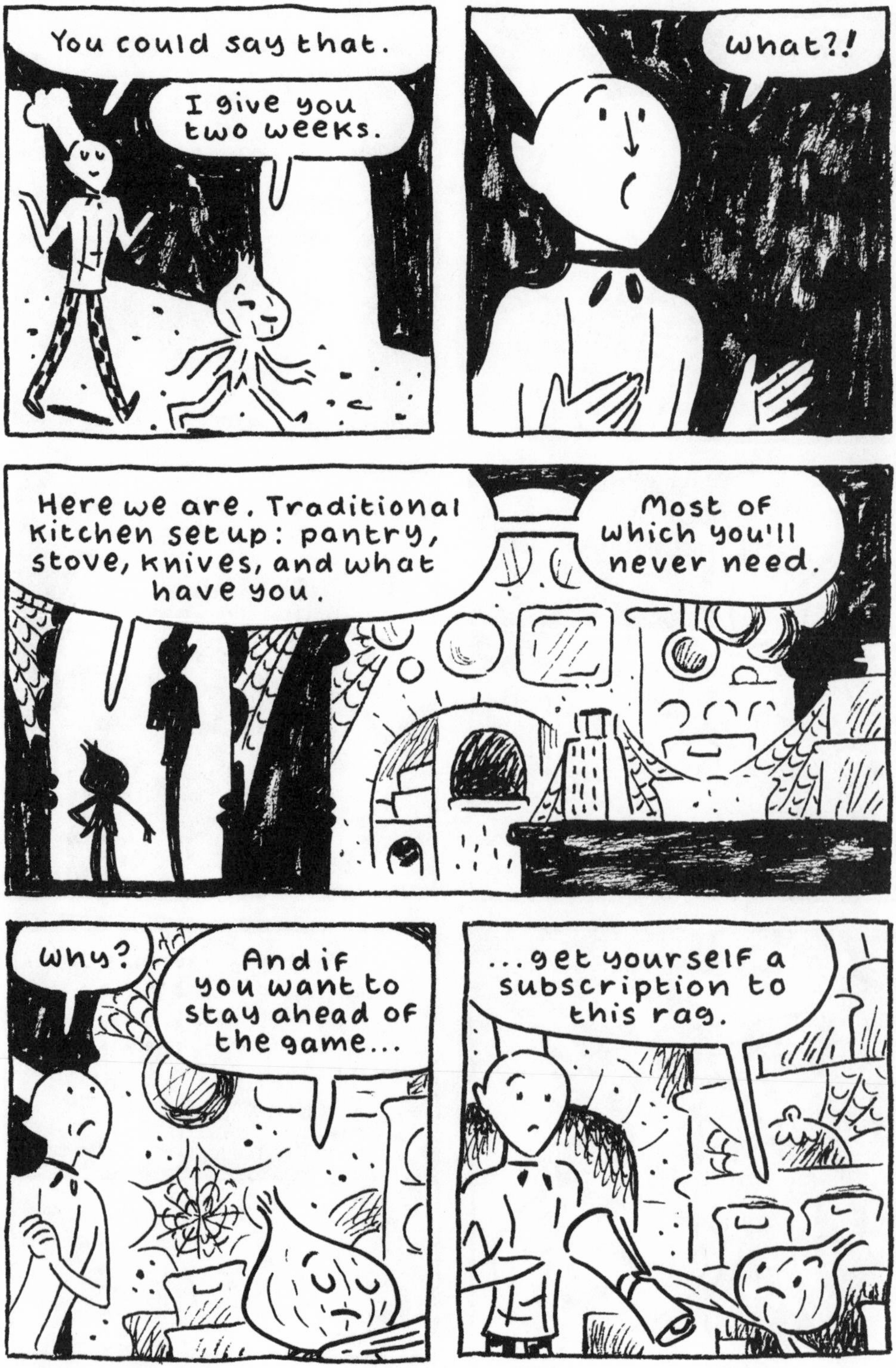
You could say that.
I give you two weeks.
What?!
Here we are. Traditional kitchen set up: pantry, stove, knives, and what have you.
Most of which you'll never need.
Why?
And if you want to stay ahead of the game...
...get yourself a subscription to this rag.

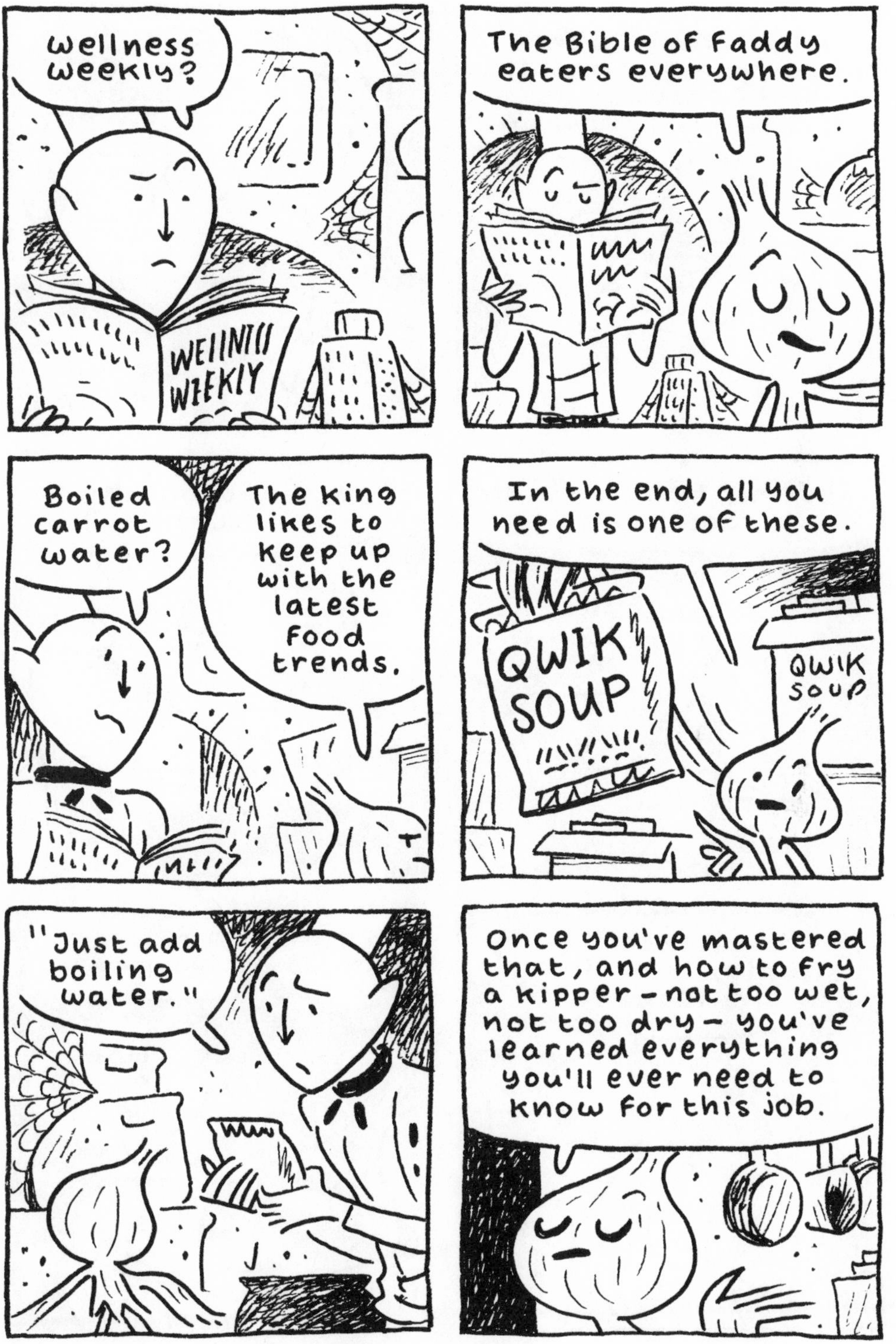
Wellness weekly?
WELLNESS WEEKLY
The Bible of faddy eaters everywhere.
Boiled carrot water?
The king likes to keep up with the latest food trends.
In the end, all you need is one of these.
QWIK SOUP
QWIK SOUP
"Just add boiling water."
Once you've mastered that, and how to fry a kipper - not too wet, not too dry - you've learned everything you'll ever need to know for this job.

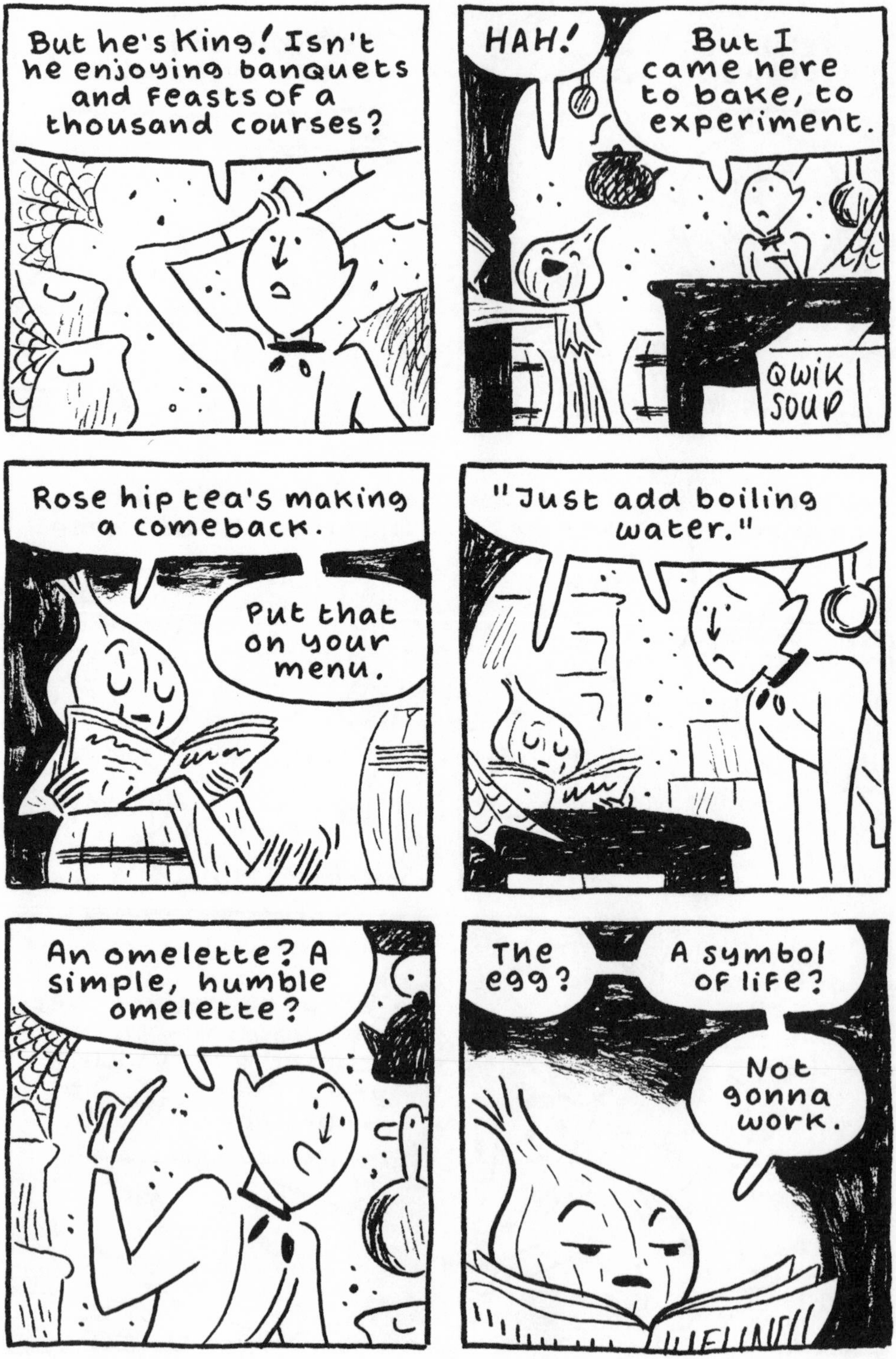
But he's King! Isn't he enjoying banquets and feasts of a thousand courses?
HAH!
But I came here to bake, to experiment.
QWIK SOUP
Rose hip tea's making a comeback.
Put that on your menu.
"Just add boiling water."
An omelette? A simple, humble omelette?
The egg?
A symbol of life?
Not gonna work.

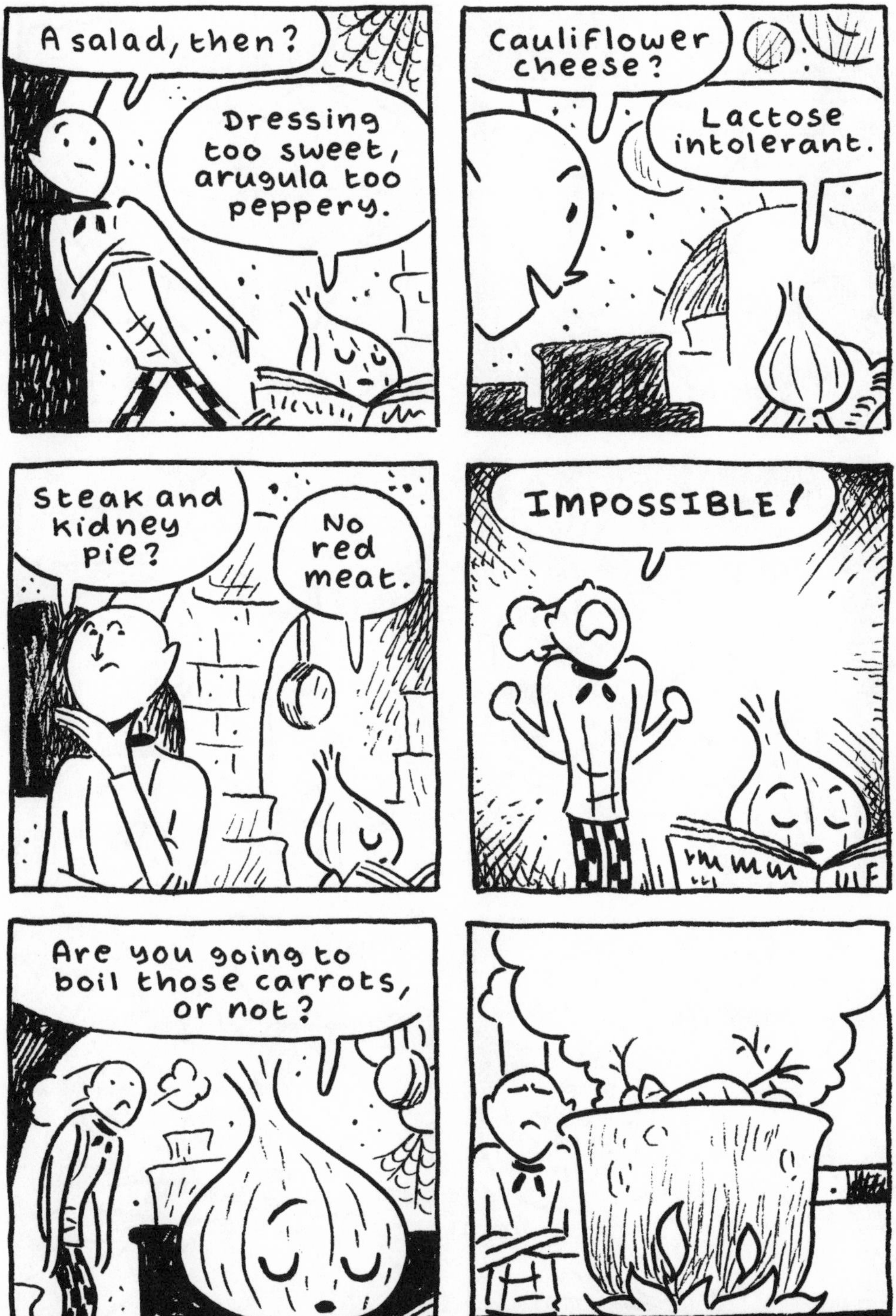
A salad, then?
Dressing too sweet, arugula too peppery.
Cauliflower cheese?
Lactose intolerant.
Steak and kidney pie?
No red meat.
IMPOSSIBLE!
Are you going to boil those carrots, or not?

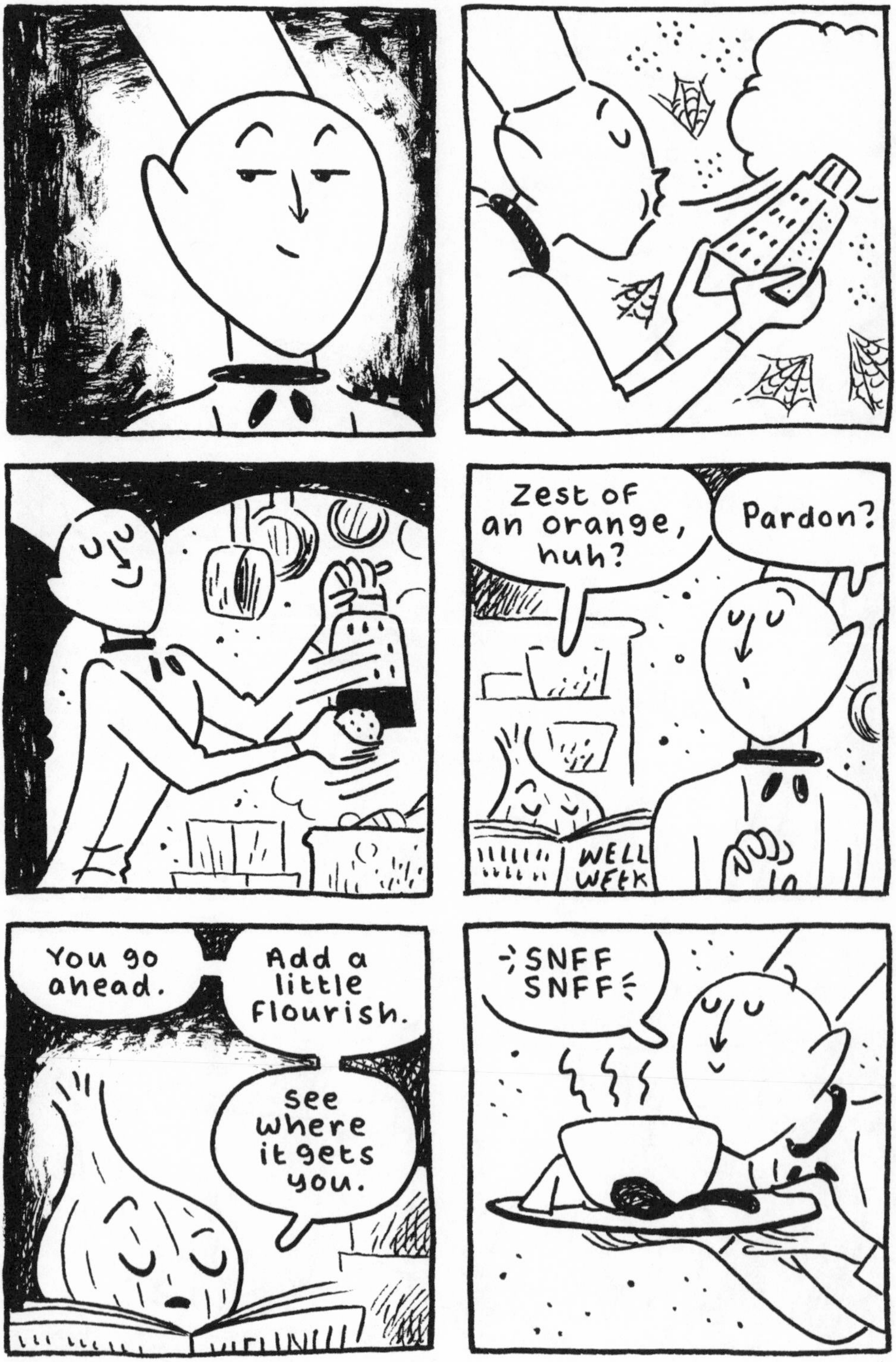
Zest of an orange, huh?
Pardon?
WELL WEEK
You go ahead.
Add a little flourish.
see where it gets you.
SNFF SNFF

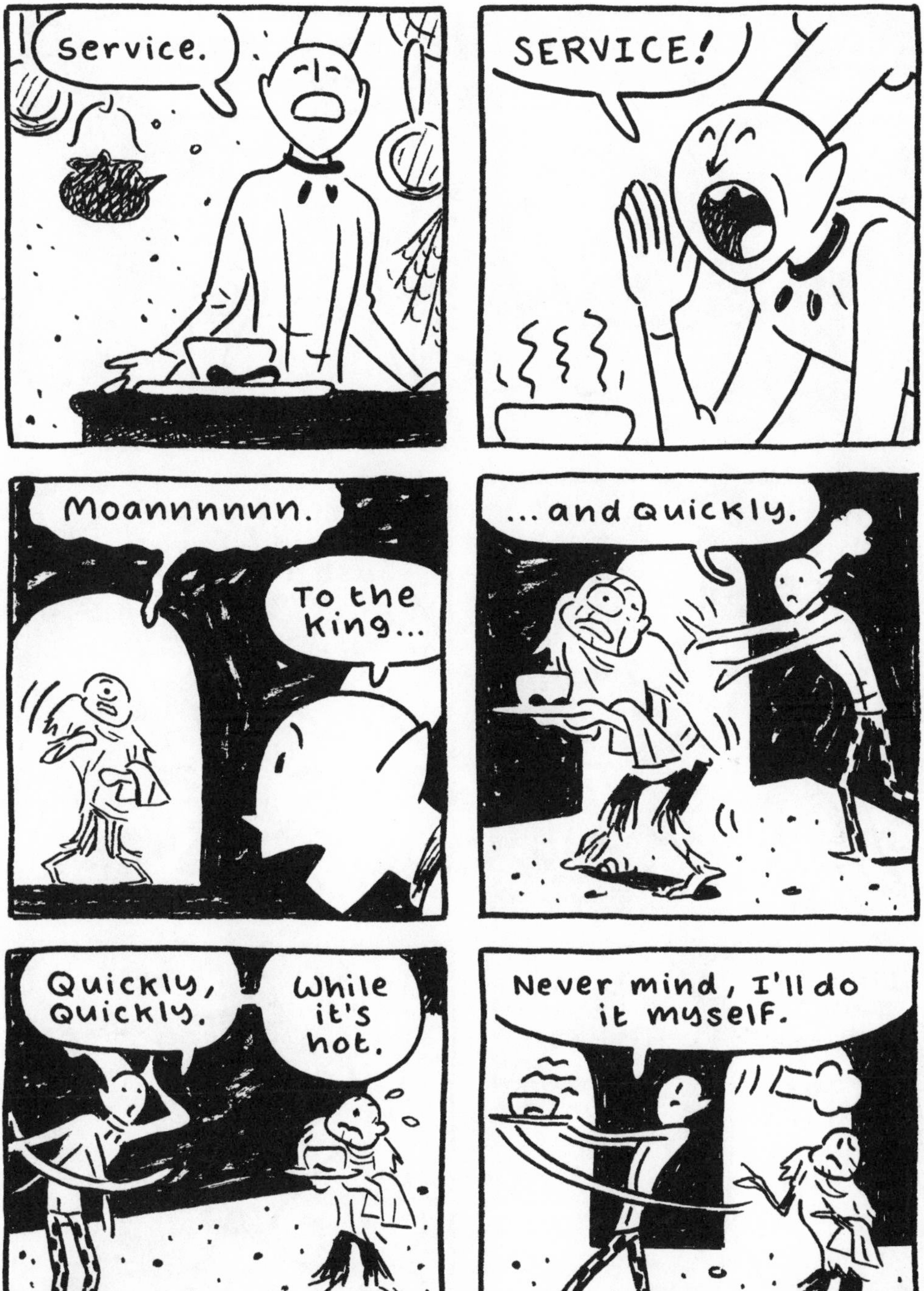
Service.
SERVICE!
Moannnnnn.
To the king...
...and quickly.
Quickly, quickly.
While it's hot.
Never mind, I'll do it myself.

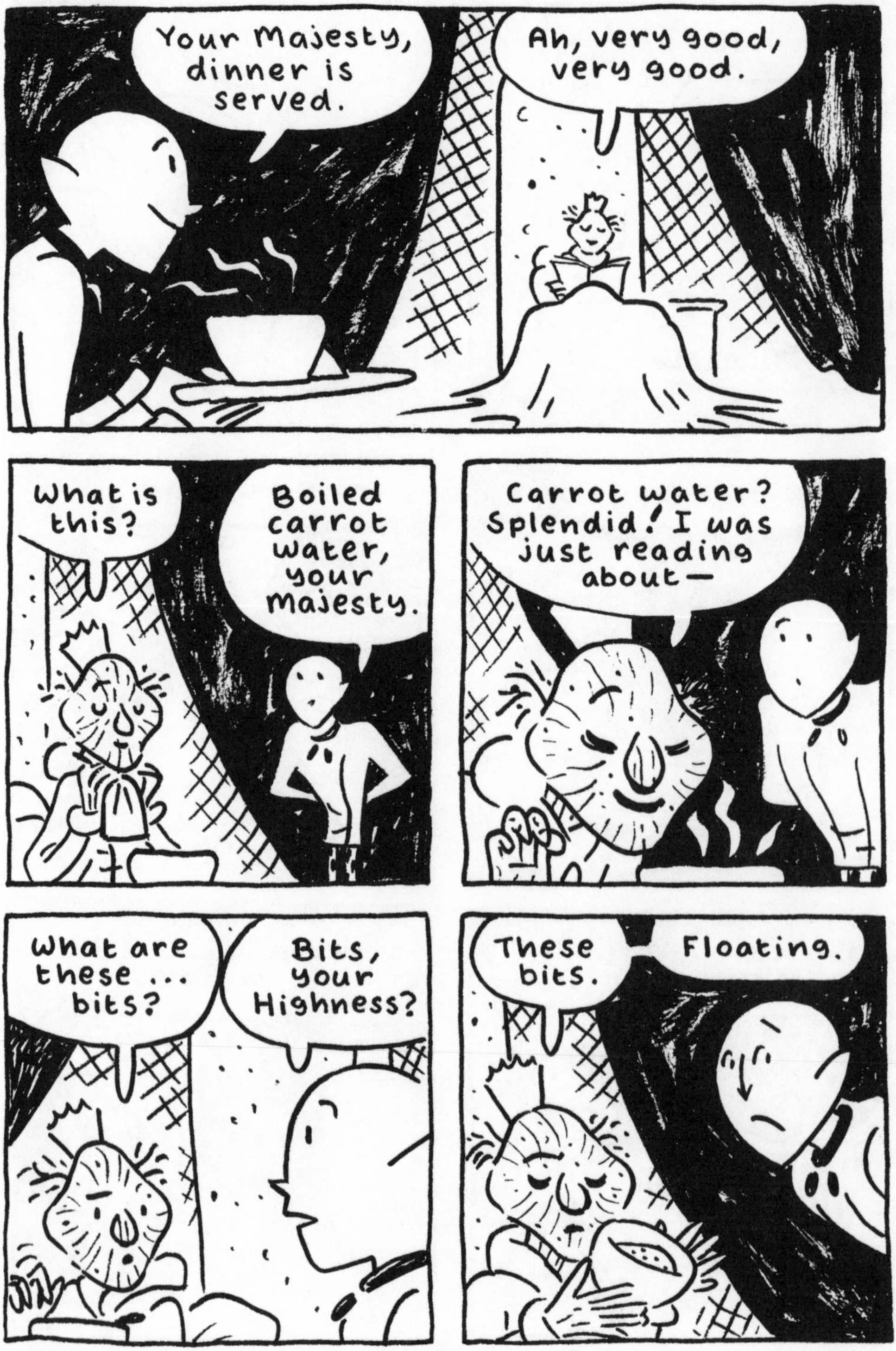
Your Majesty, dinner is served.
Ah, very good, very good.
What is this?
Boiled carrot water, your Majesty.
Carrot water? Splendid! I was just reading about—
What are these ... bits?
Bits, your Highness?
These bits.
Floating.

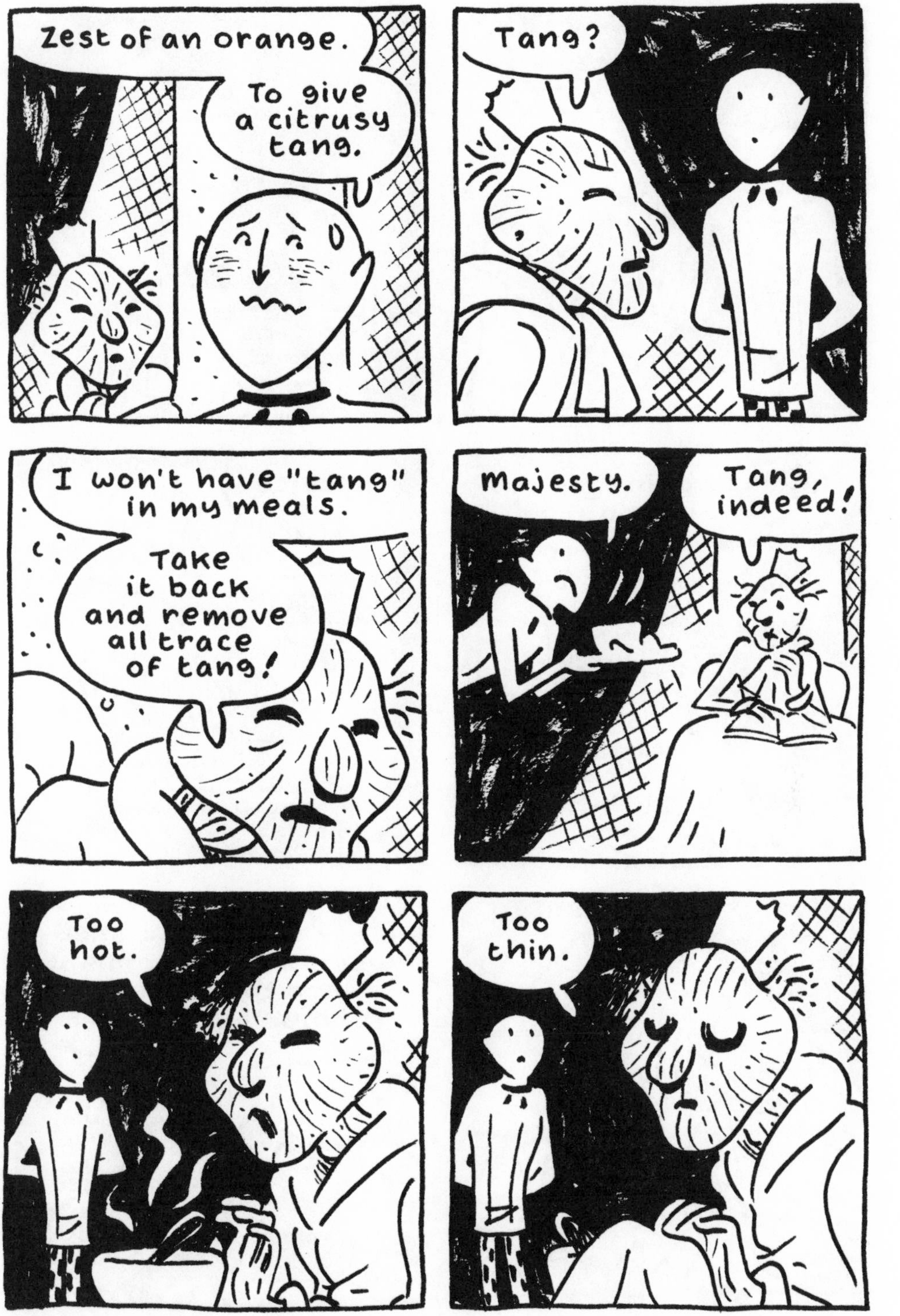
Zest of an orange.
To give a citrusy tang.
Tang?
I won't have "tang" in my meals.
Take it back and remove all trace of tang!
Majesty.
Tang, indeed!
Too hot.
Too thin.

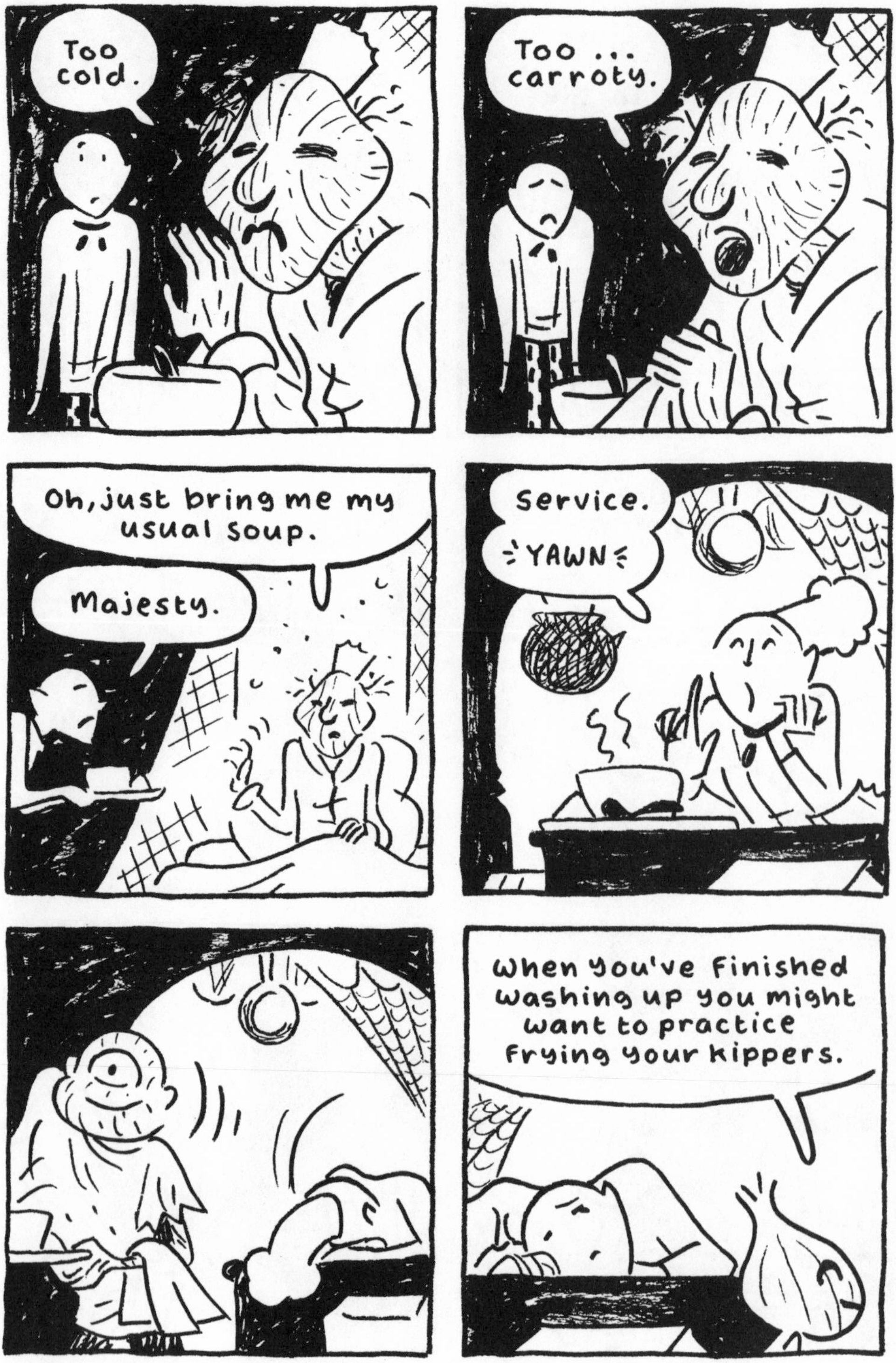
Too cold.
Too ... carroty.
Oh, just bring me my usual soup.
Majesty.
Service.
YAWN
When you've finished washing up you might want to practice frying your kippers.

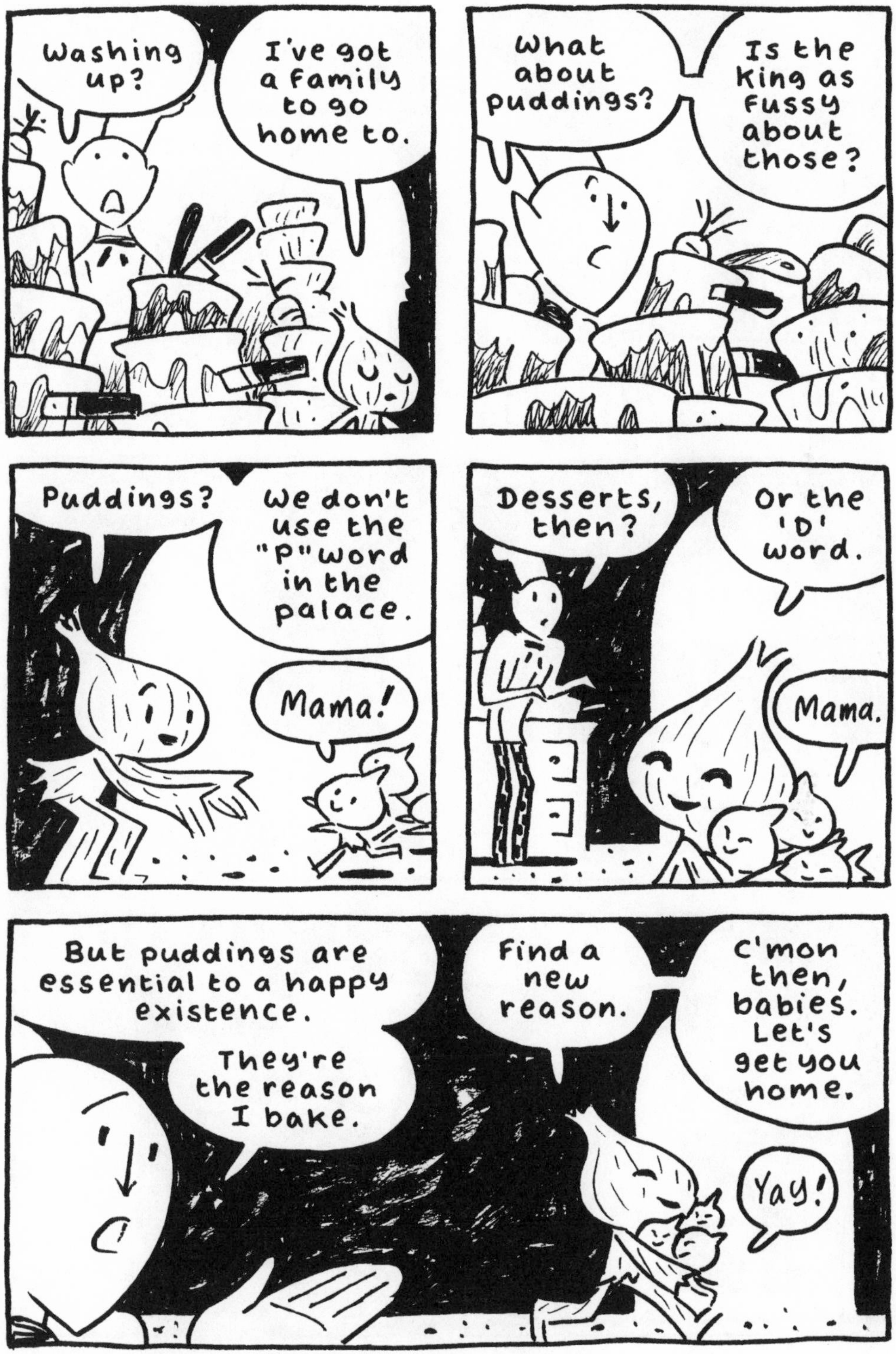
Washing up?
I've got a family to go home to.
What about puddings?
Is the King as fussy about those?
Puddings?
We don't use the "P" word in the palace.
Mama!
Desserts, then?
Or the 'D' word.
Mama.
But puddings are essential to a happy existence.
They're the reason I bake.
Find a new reason.
C'mon then, babies. Let's get you home.
Yay!

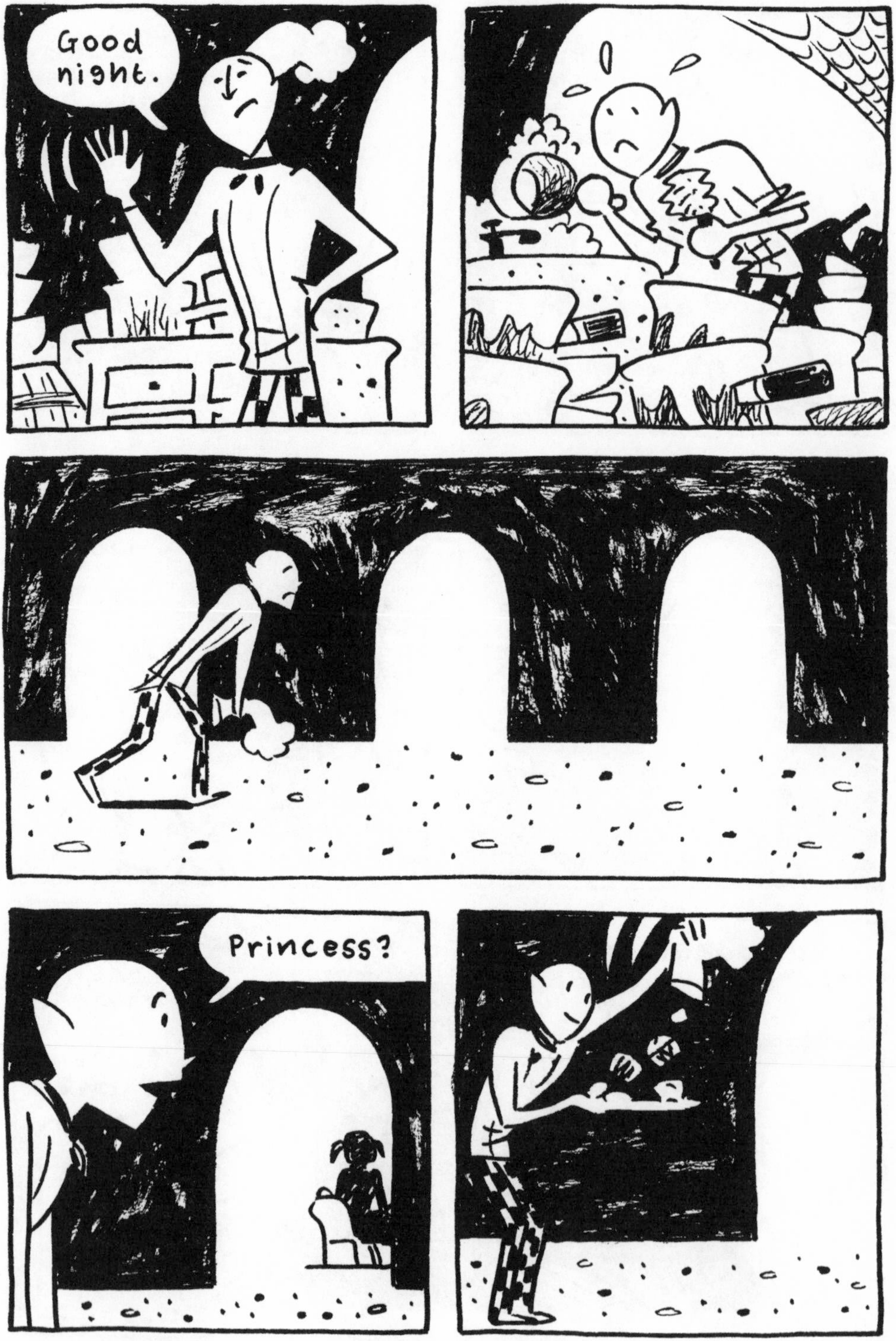
Good night.
Princess?

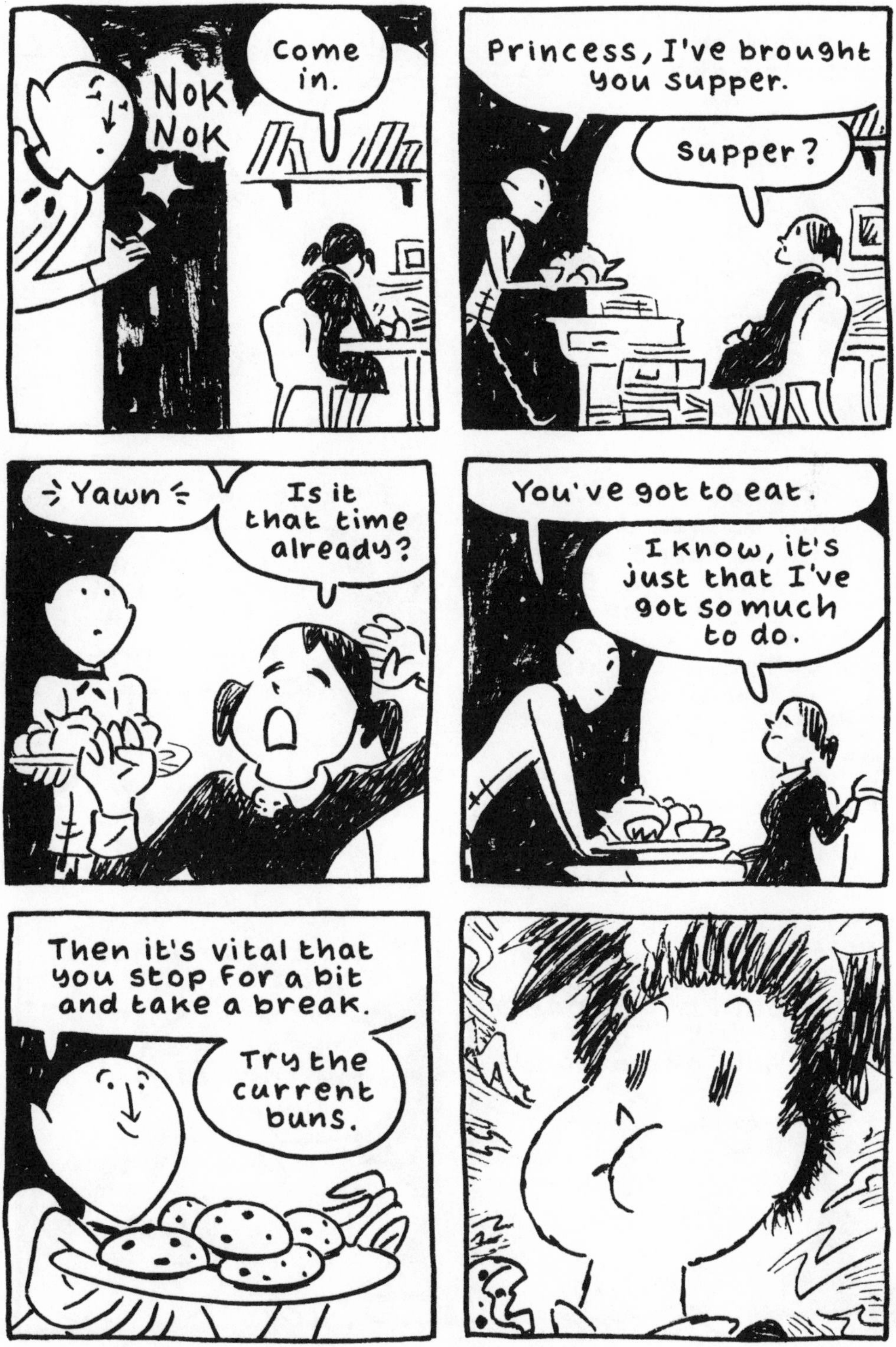

NOK NOK
Come in.
Princess, I've brought you supper.
Supper?
Yawn
Is it that time already?
You've got to eat.
I know, it's just that I've got so much to do.
Then it's vital that you stop for a bit and take a break.
Try the current buns.

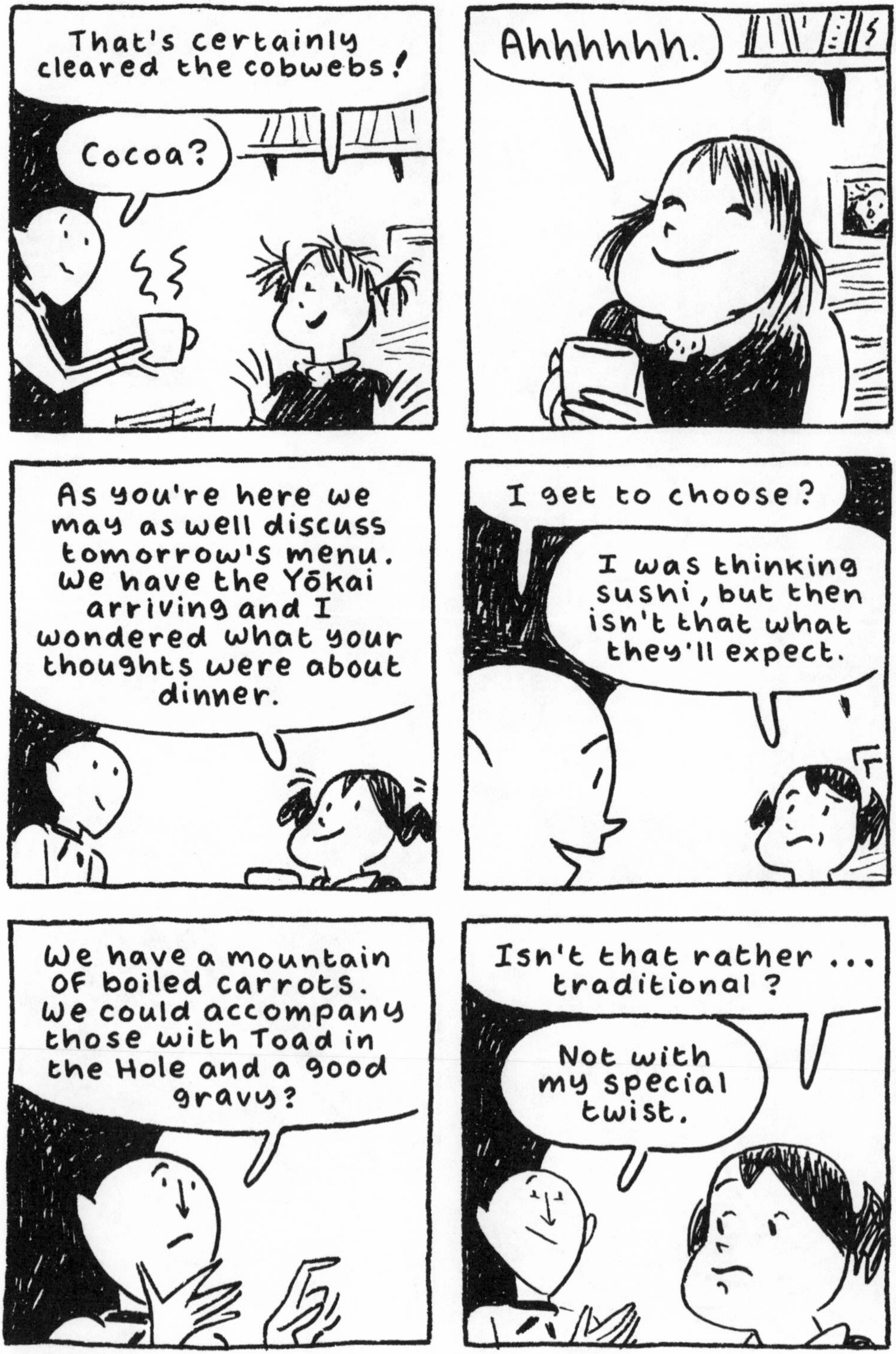
That's certainly cleared the cobwebs!
Cocoa?
Ahhhhhh.
As you're here we may as well discuss tomorrow's menu. We have the Yōkai arriving and I wondered what your thoughts were about dinner.
I get to choose?
I was thinking sushi, but then isn't that what they'll expect.
We have a mountain of boiled carrots. We could accompany those with Toad in the Hole and a good gravy?
Isn't that rather ... traditional?
Not with my special twist.

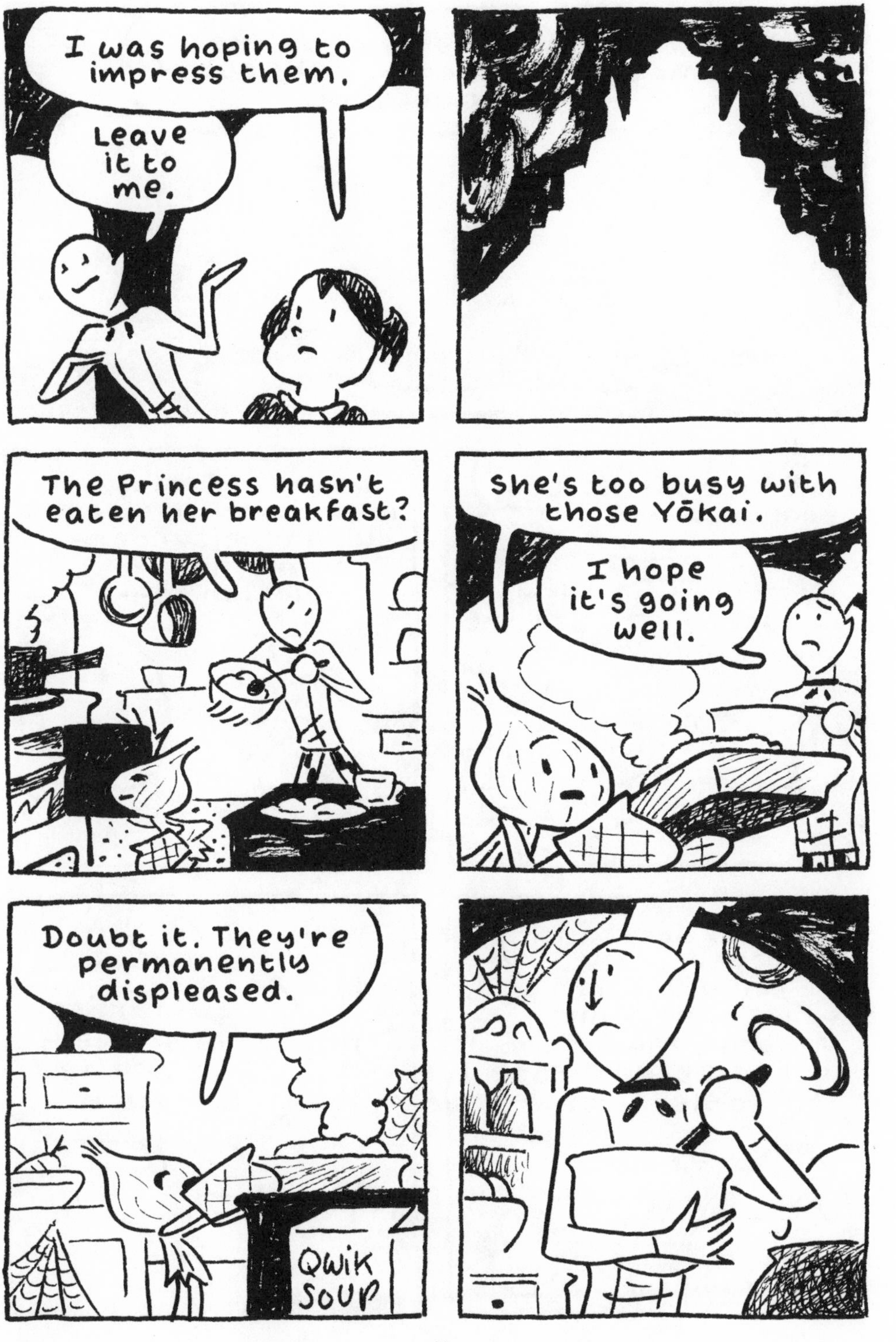
I was hoping to impress them.
Leave it to me.
The Princess hasn't eaten her breakfast?
She's too busy with those Yōkai.
I hope it's going well.
Doubt it. They're permanently displeased.
QWIK SOUP

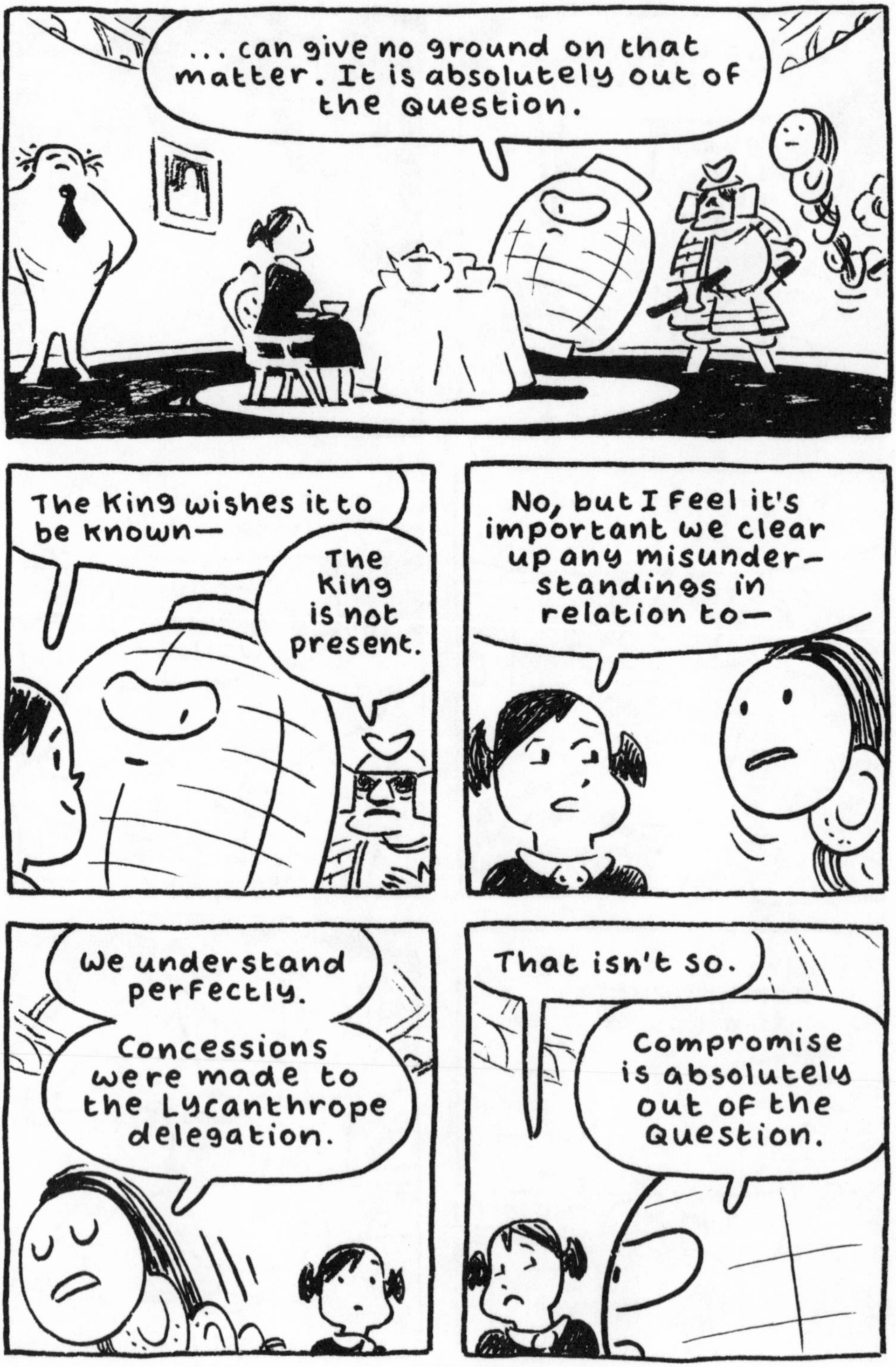
... can give no ground on that matter. It is absolutely out of the question.
The King wishes it to be known—
The King is not present.
No, but I feel it's important we clear up any misunder-standings in relation to—
We understand perfectly.
Concessions were made to the Lycanthrope delegation.
That isn't so.
Compromise is absolutely out of the question.

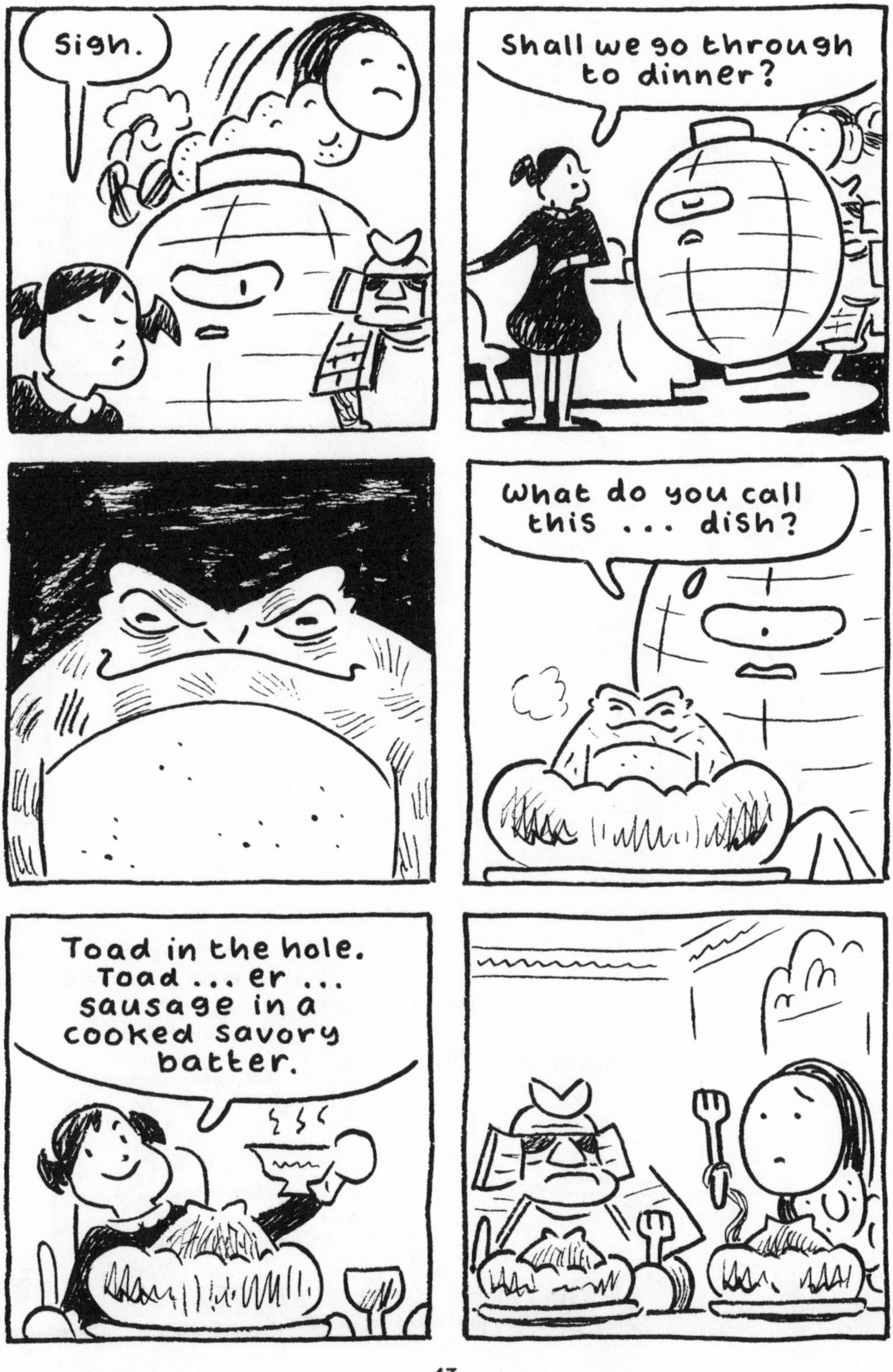
Sigh.
Shall we go through to dinner?
What do you call this ... dish?
Toad in the hole. Toad ... er ... sausage in a cooked savory batter.

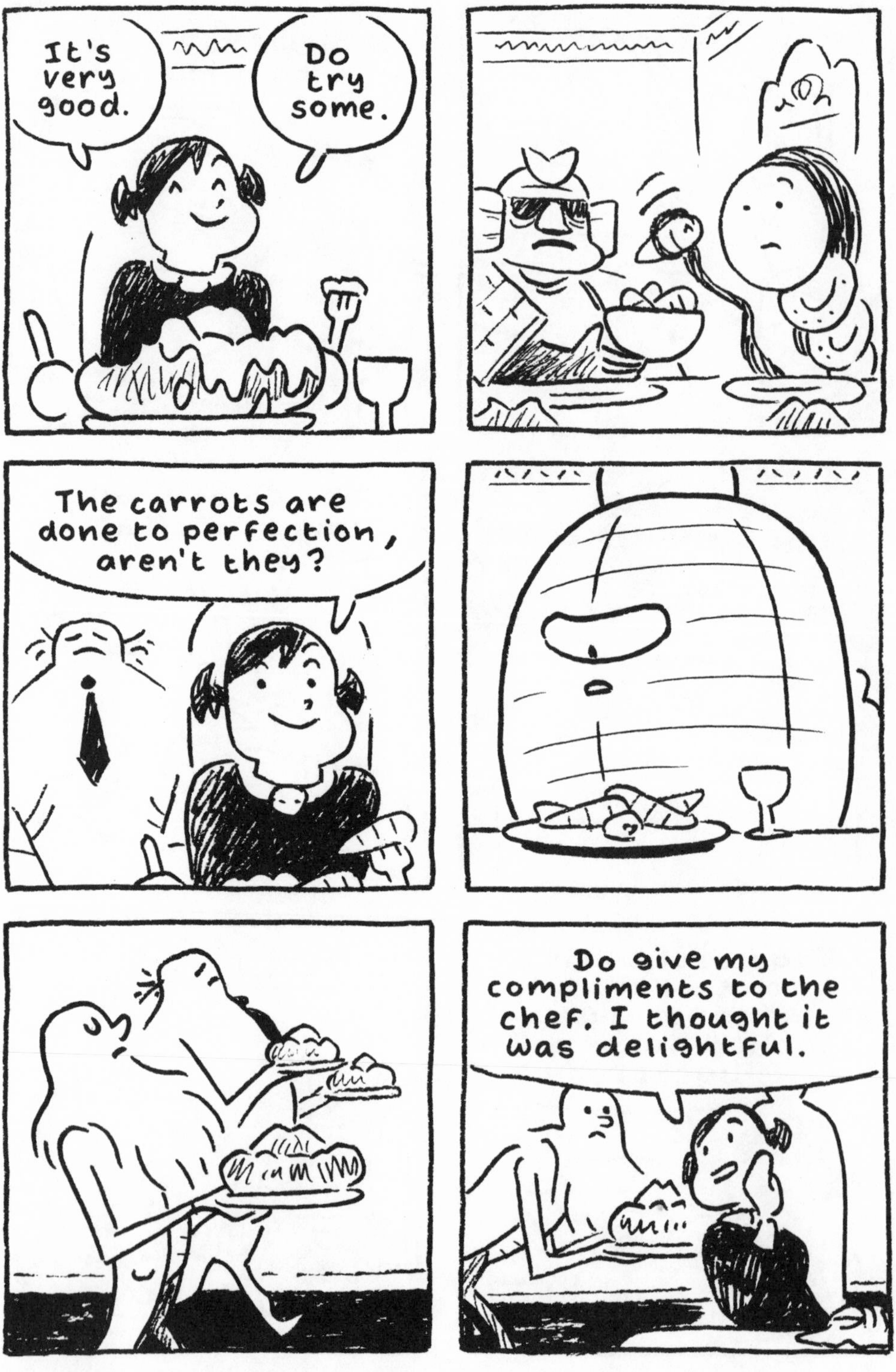

It's very good.
Do try some.
The carrots are done to perfection, aren't they?
Do give my compliments to the chef. I thought it was delightful.

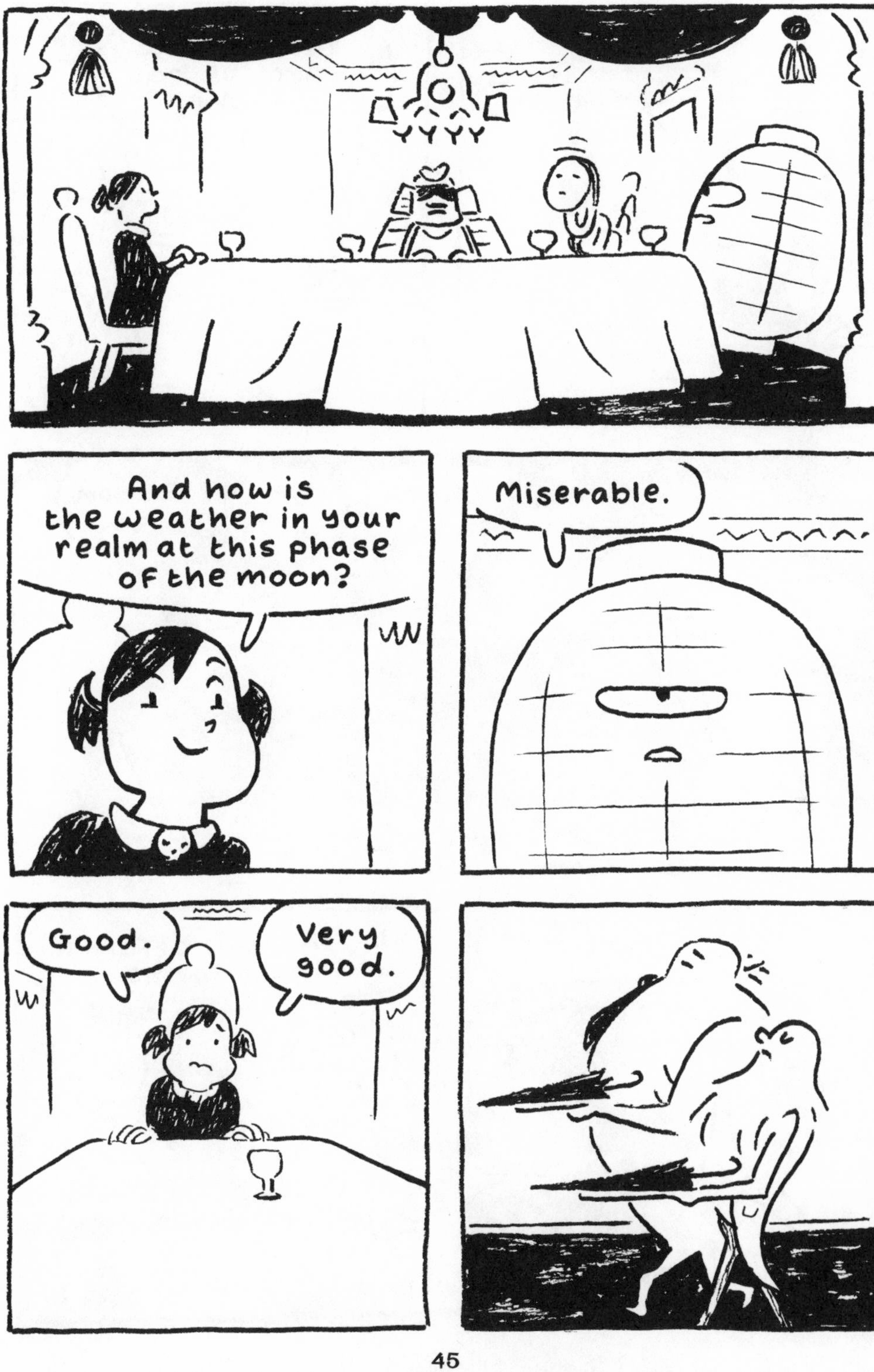
And how is the weather in your realm at this phase of the moon?
Miserable.
Good.
Very good.

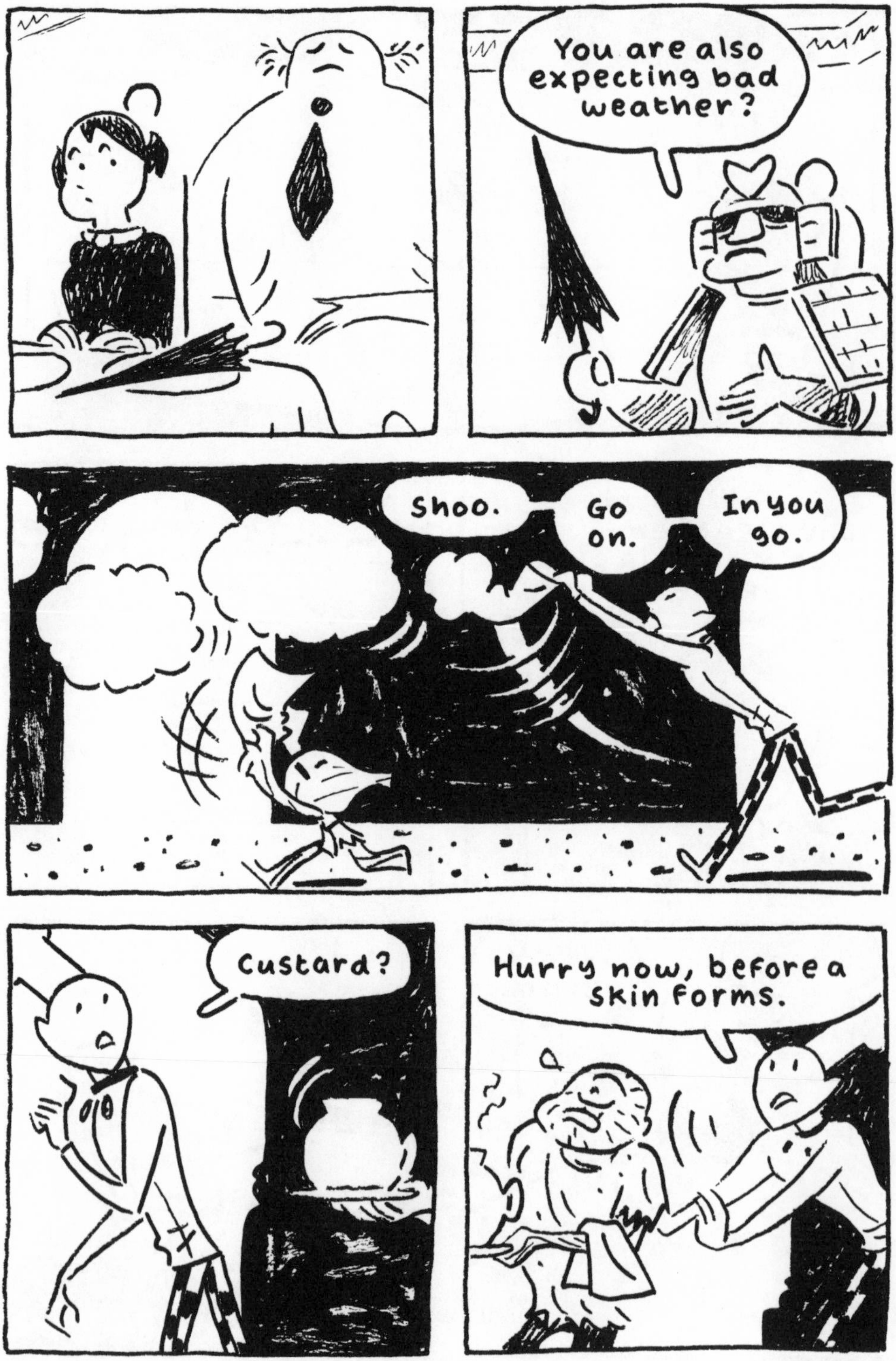
You are also expecting bad weather?
Shoo.
Go on.
In you go.
Custard?
Hurry now, before a skin forms.

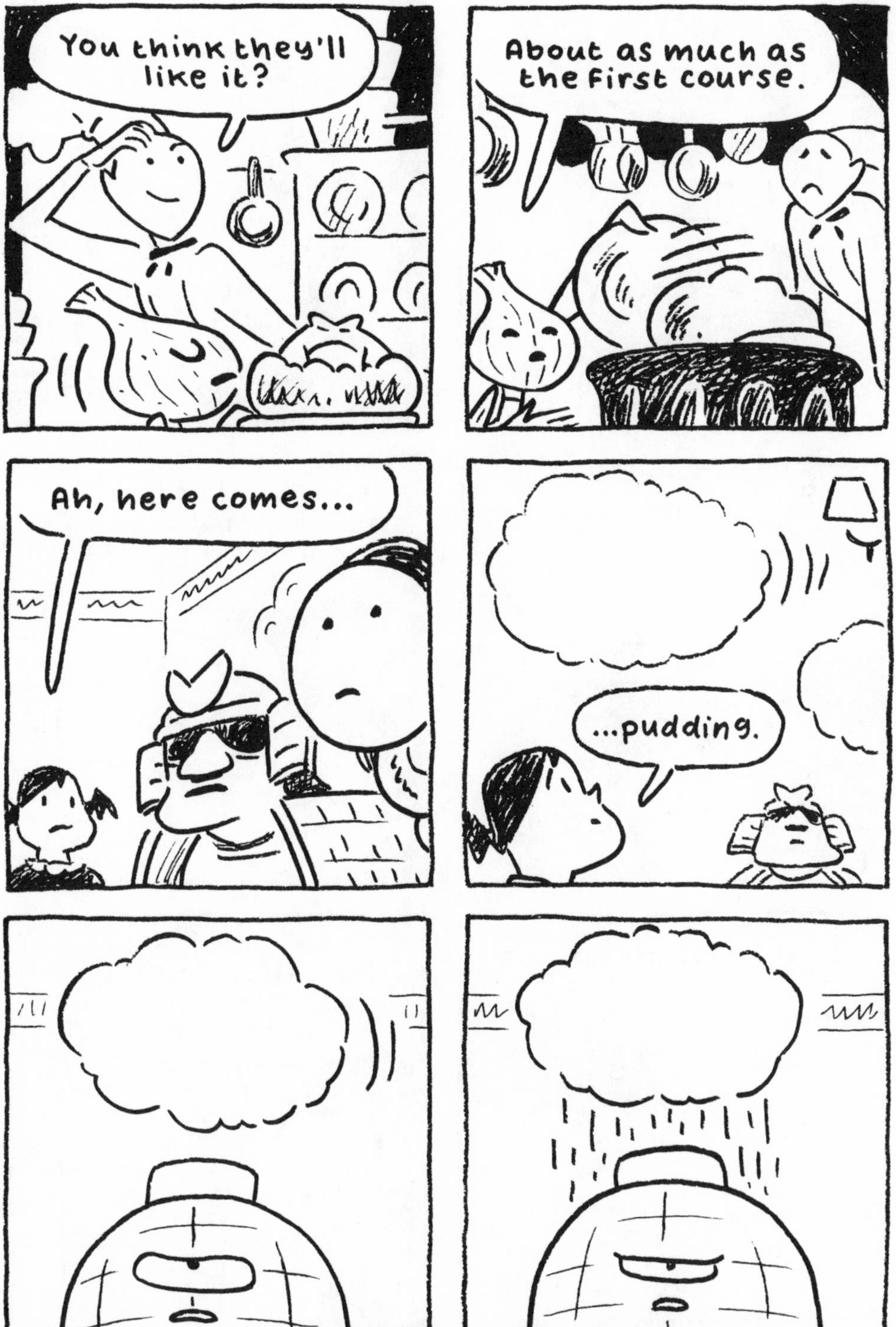
You think they'll like it?
About as much as the first course.
Ah, here comes...
...pudding.

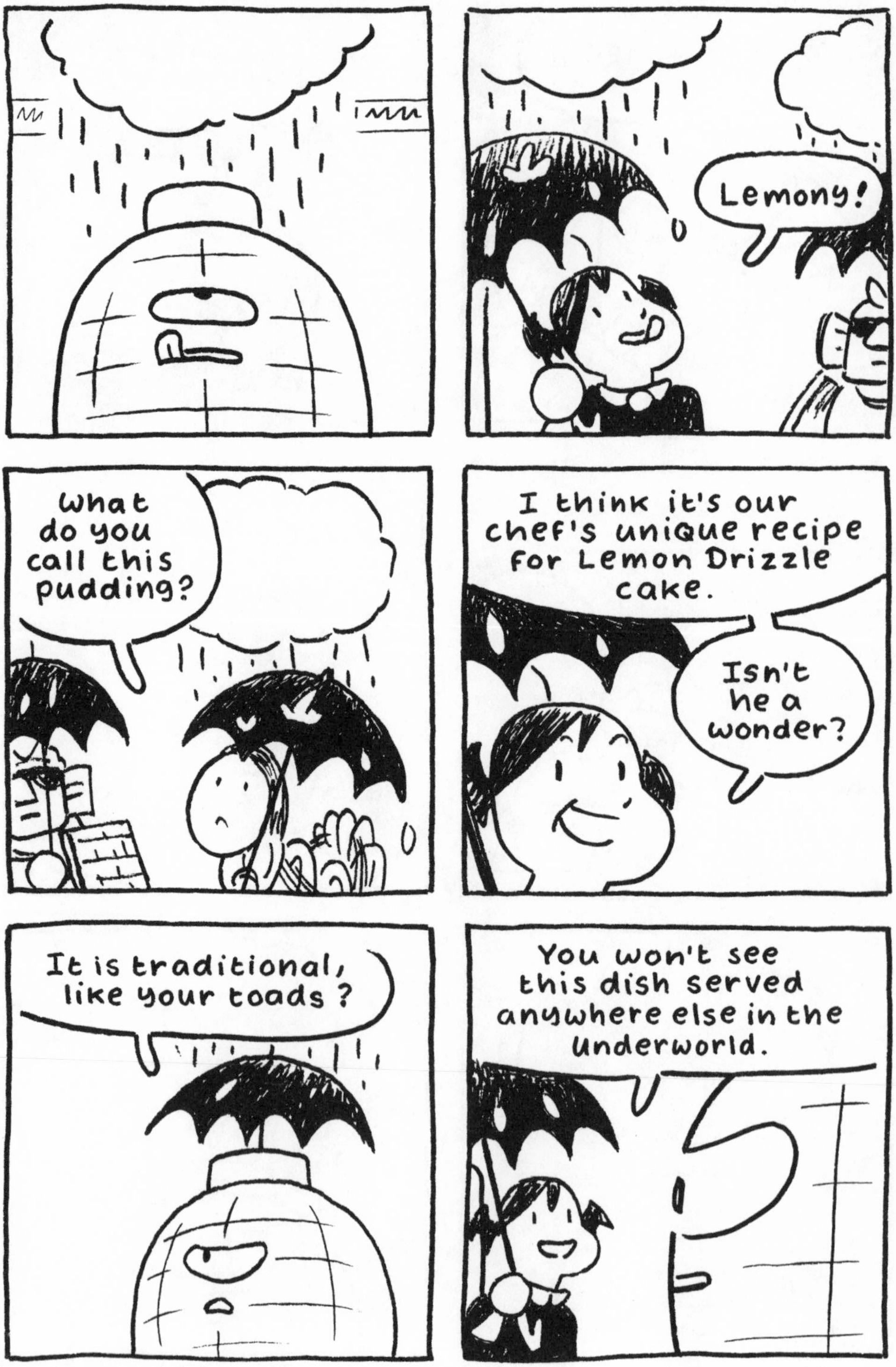
Lemony!
What do you call this pudding?
I think it's our chef's unique recipe for Lemon Drizzle cake.
Isn't he a wonder?
It is traditional, like your toads?
You won't see this dish served anywhere else in the Underworld.

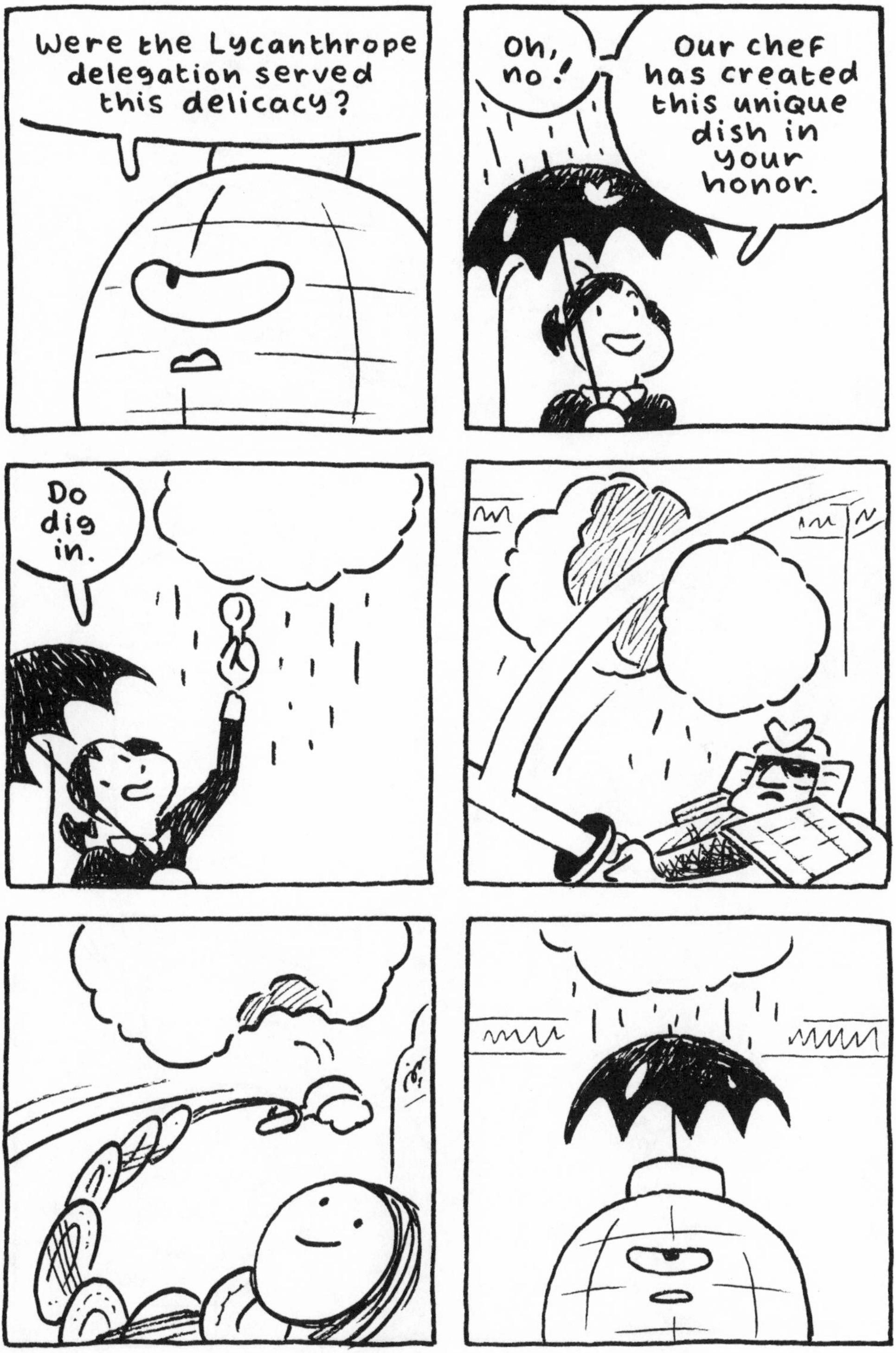
Were the Lycanthrope delegation served this delicacy?
Oh, no!
Our chef has created this unique dish in your honor.
Do dig in.

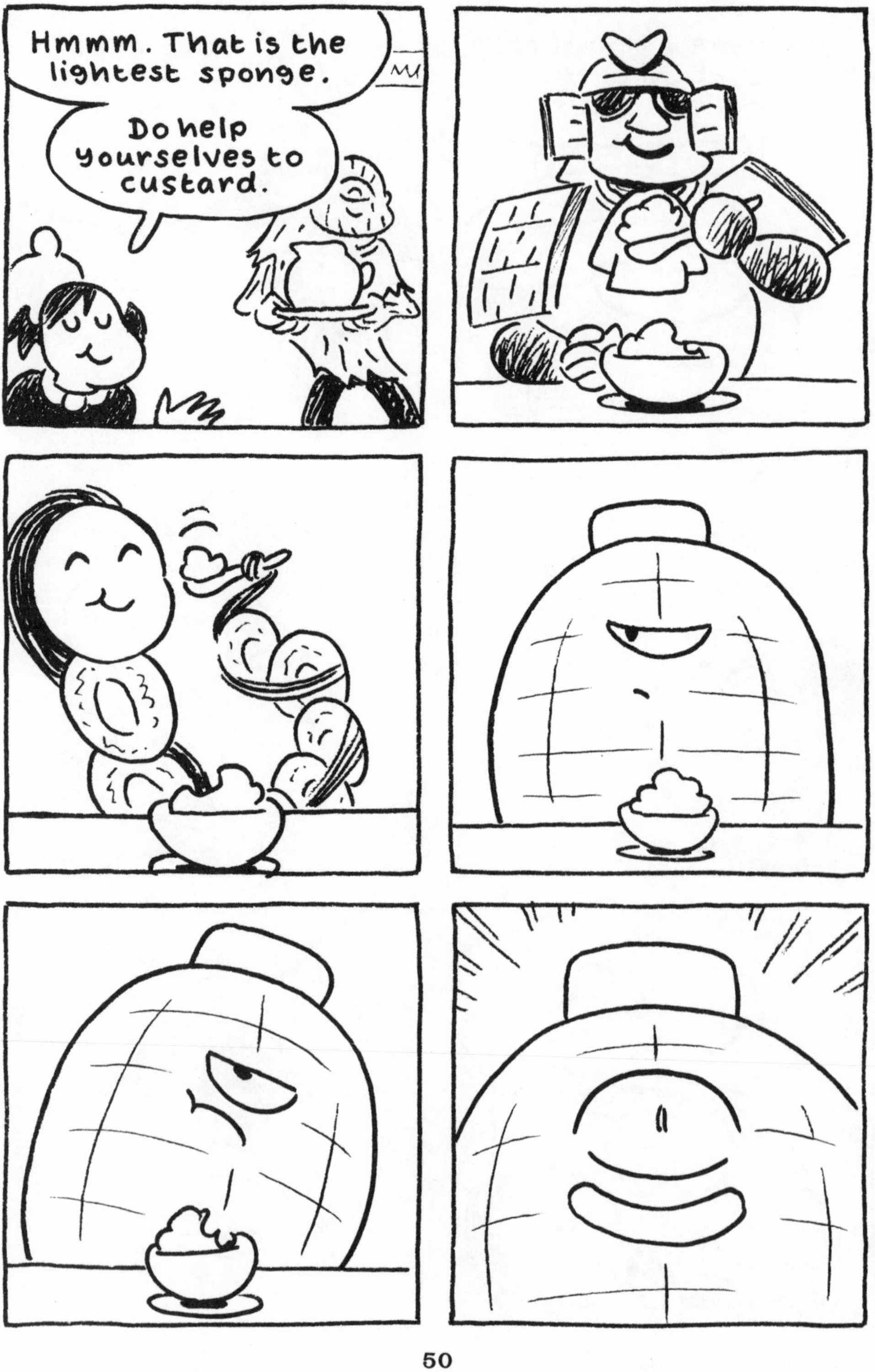
Hmmm. That is the lightest sponge.
Do help yourselves to custard.

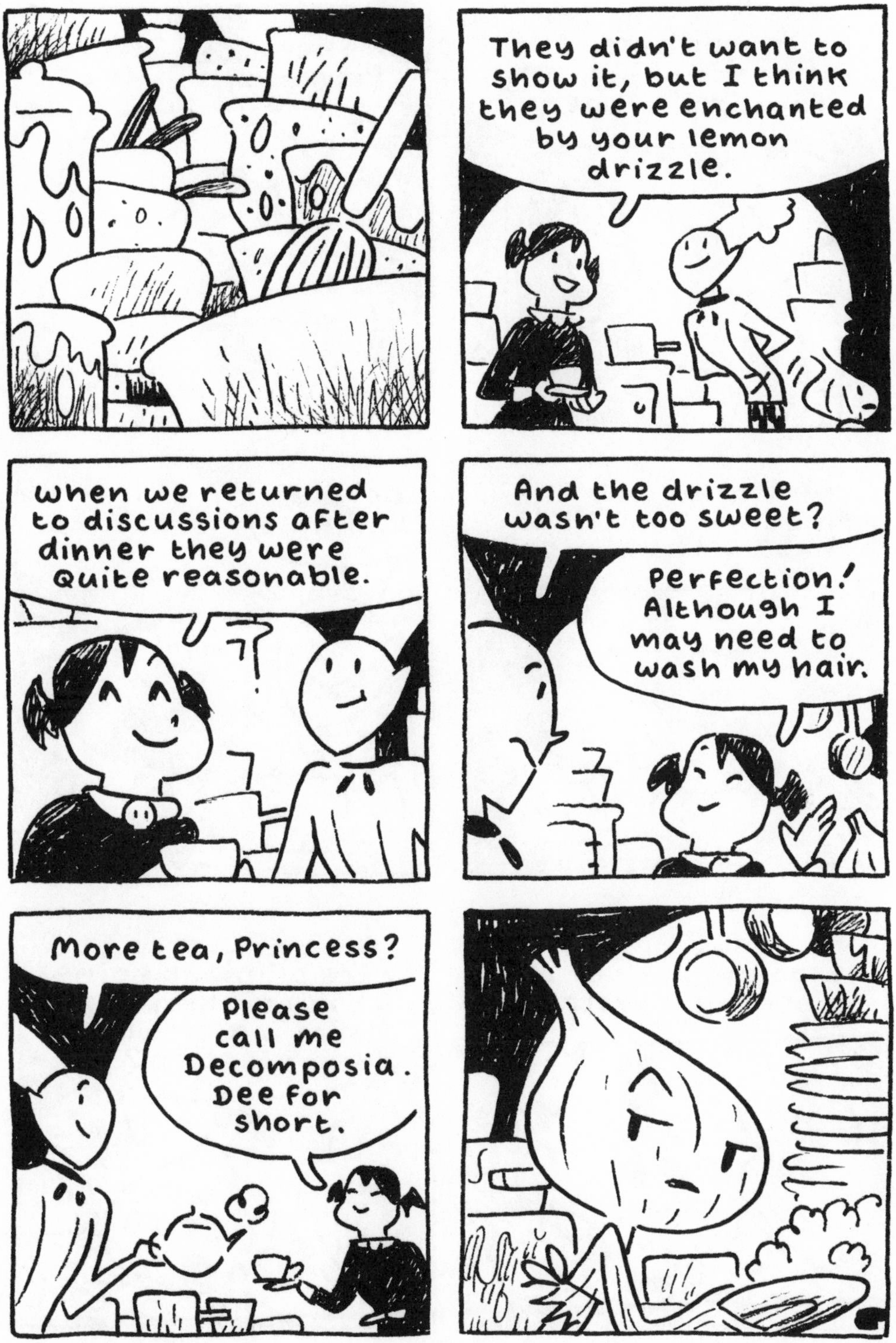
They didn't want to show it, but I think they were enchanted by your lemon drizzle.
When we returned to discussions after dinner they were quite reasonable.
And the drizzle wasn't too sweet?
Perfection! Although I may need to wash my hair.
More tea, Princess?
Please call me Decomposia. Dee for short.

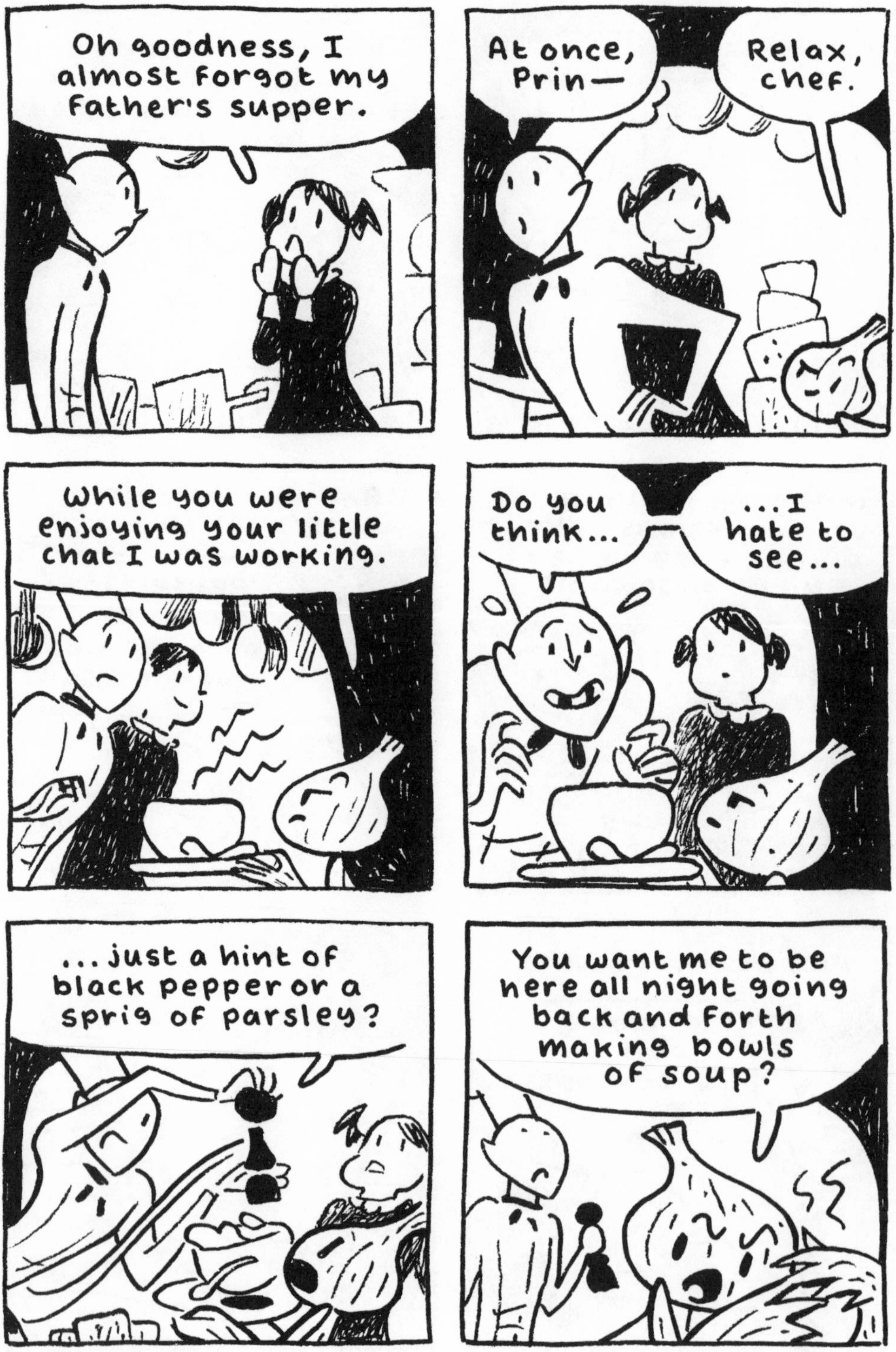
Oh goodness, I almost forgot my father's supper.
At once, Prin—
Relax, chef.
While you were enjoying your little chat I was working.
Do you think...
...I hate to see...
...just a hint of black pepper or a sprig of parsley?
You want me to be here all night going back and forth making bowls of soup?

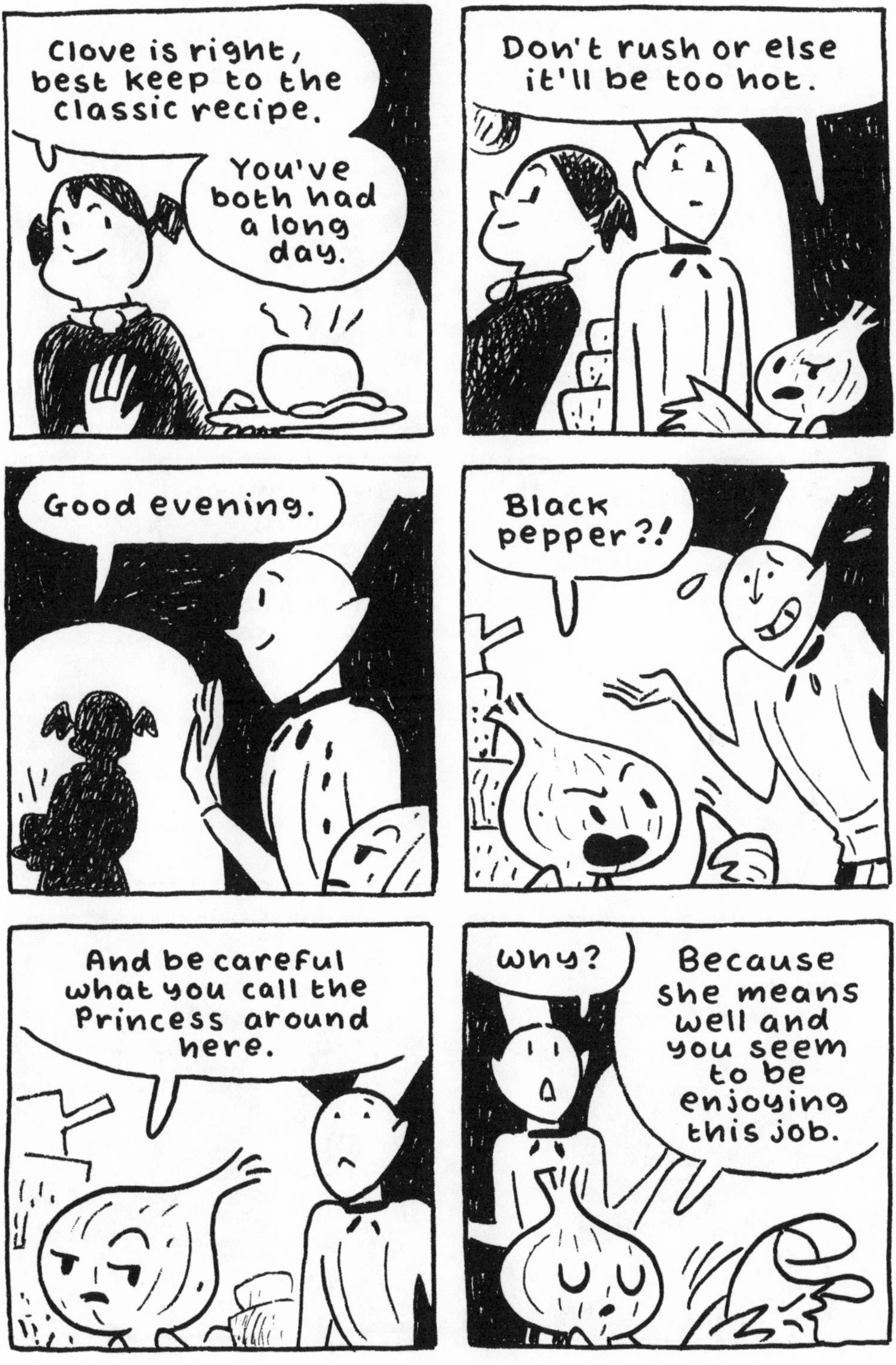
Clove is right, best keep to the classic recipe.
You've both had a long day.
Don't rush or else it'll be too hot.
Good evening.
Black pepper?!
And be careful what you call the Princess around here.
Why?
Because she means well and you seem to be enjoying this job.

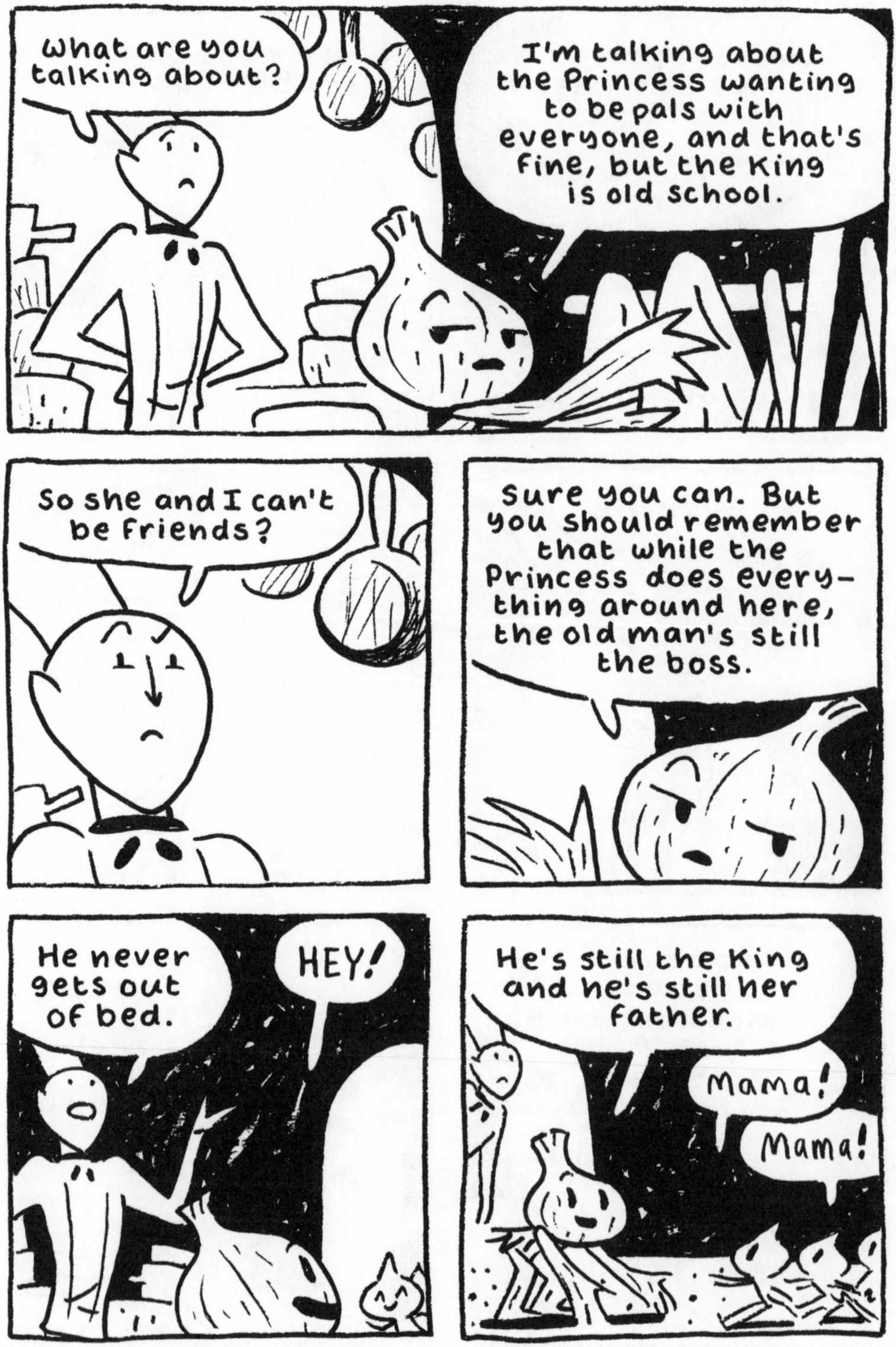

What are you talking about?
I'm talking about the Princess wanting to be pals with everyone, and that's fine, but the King is old school.
So she and I can't be friends?
Sure you can. But you should remember that while the Princess does every-thing around here, the old man's still the boss.
He never gets out of bed.
HEY!
He's still the King and he's still her father.
Mama!
Mama!

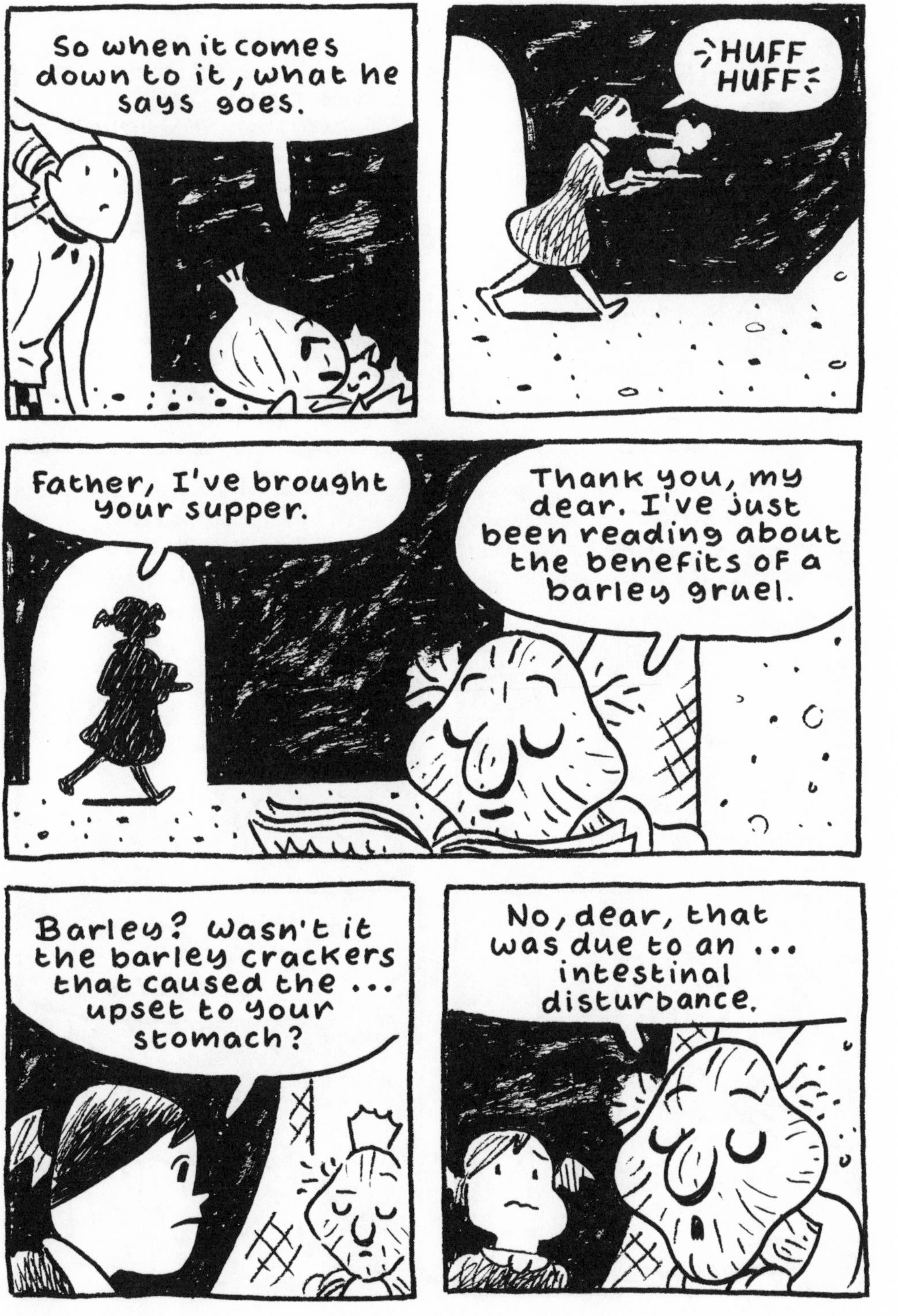
So when it comes down to it, what he says goes.
HUFF HUFF
Father, I've brought your supper.
Thank you, my dear. I've just been reading about the benefits of a barley gruel.
Barley? Wasn't it the barley crackers that caused the ... upset to your stomach?
No, dear, that was due to an ... intestinal disturbance.

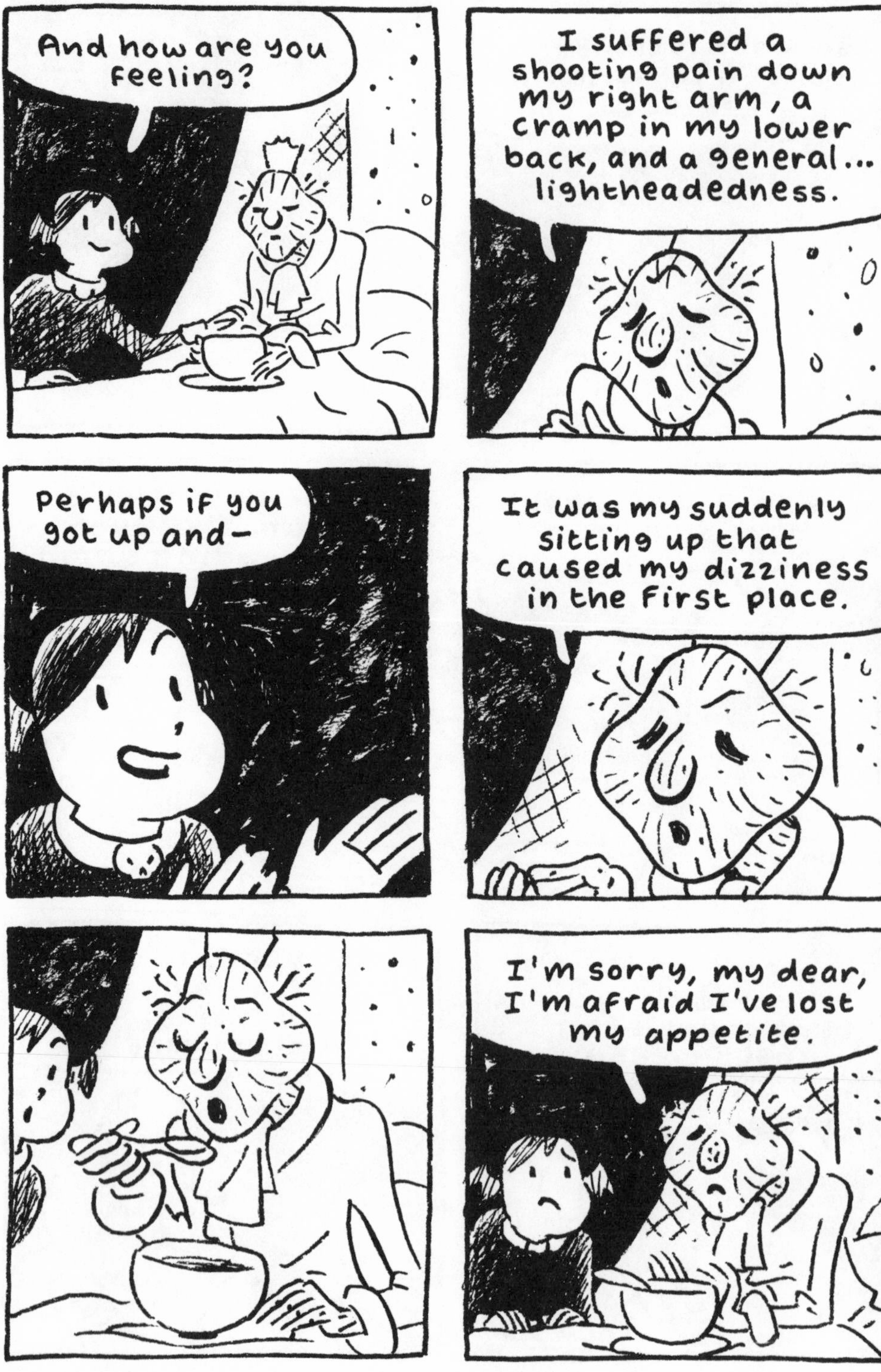
And how are you feeling?
I suffered a shooting pain down my right arm, a cramp in my lower back, and a general... lightheadedness.
Perhaps if you got up and–
It was my suddenly sitting up that caused my dizziness in the first place.
I'm sorry, my dear, I'm afraid I've lost my appetite.

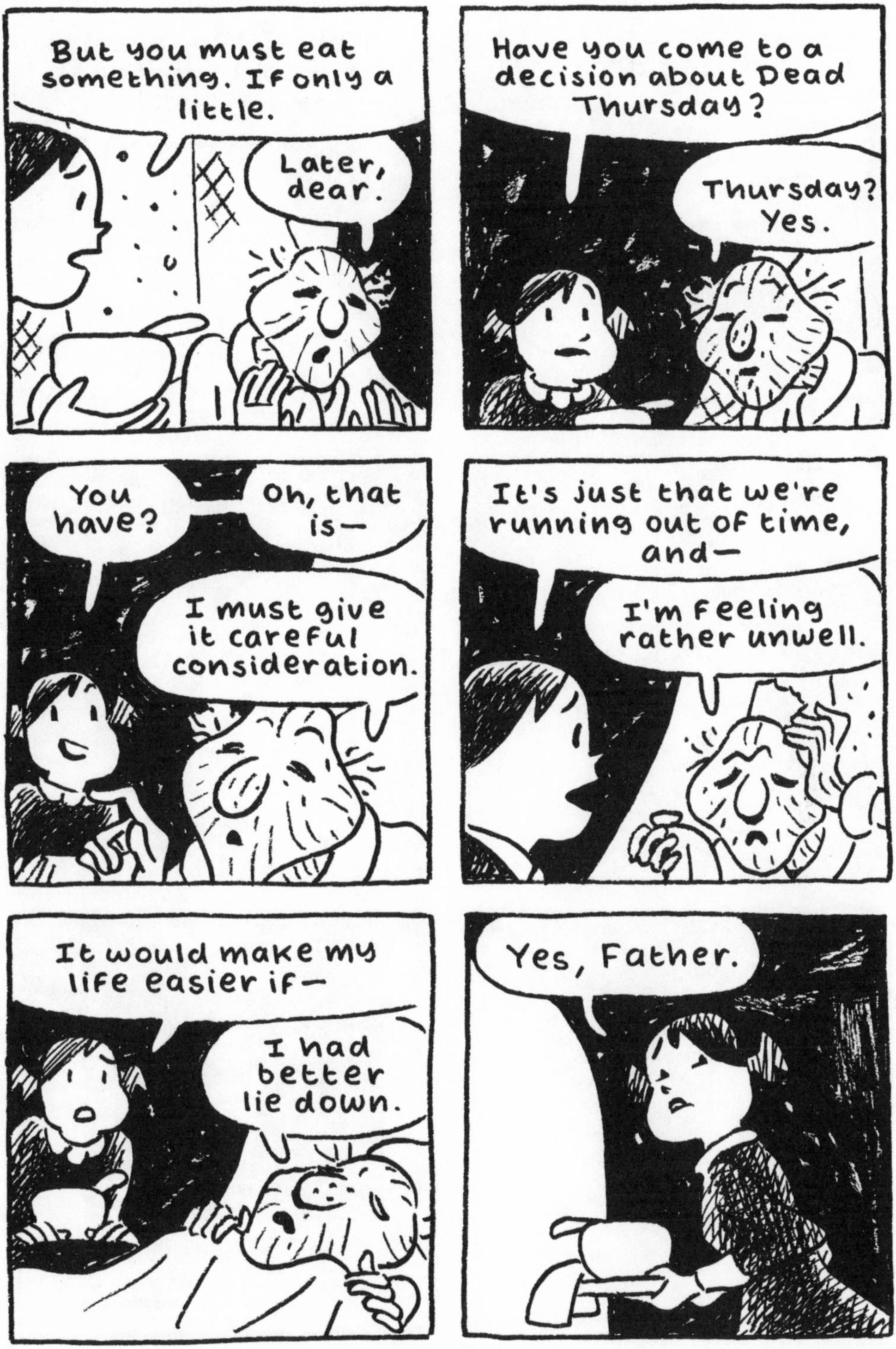

But you must eat something. If only a little.
Later, dear.
Have you come to a decision about Dead Thursday?
Thursday? Yes.
You have?
Oh, that is—
I must give it careful consideration.
It's just that we're running out of time, and—
I'm feeling rather unwell.
It would make my life easier if—
I had better lie down.
Yes, Father.

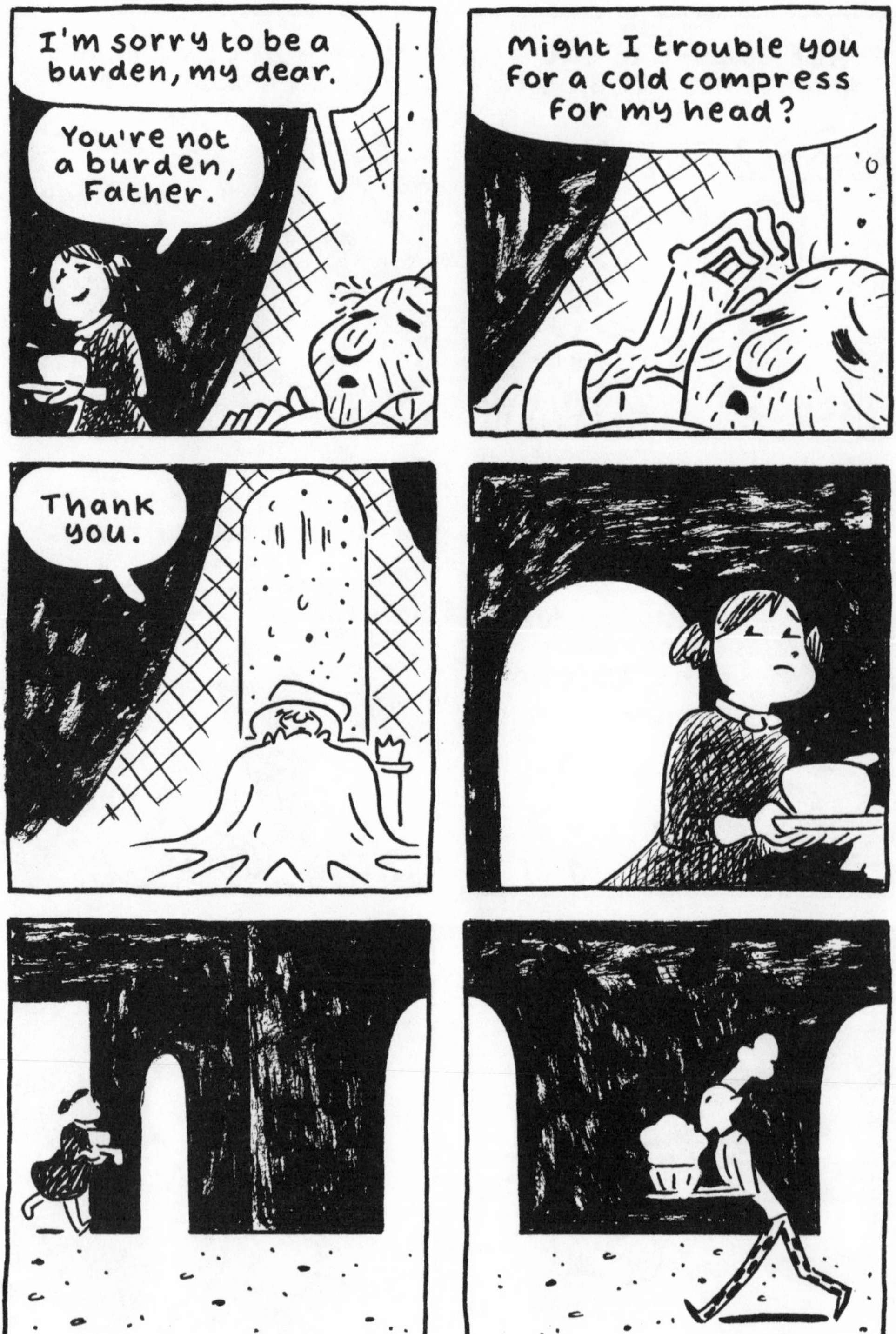
I'm sorry to be a burden, my dear.
You're not a burden, Father.
Might I trouble you for a cold compress for my head?
Thank you.

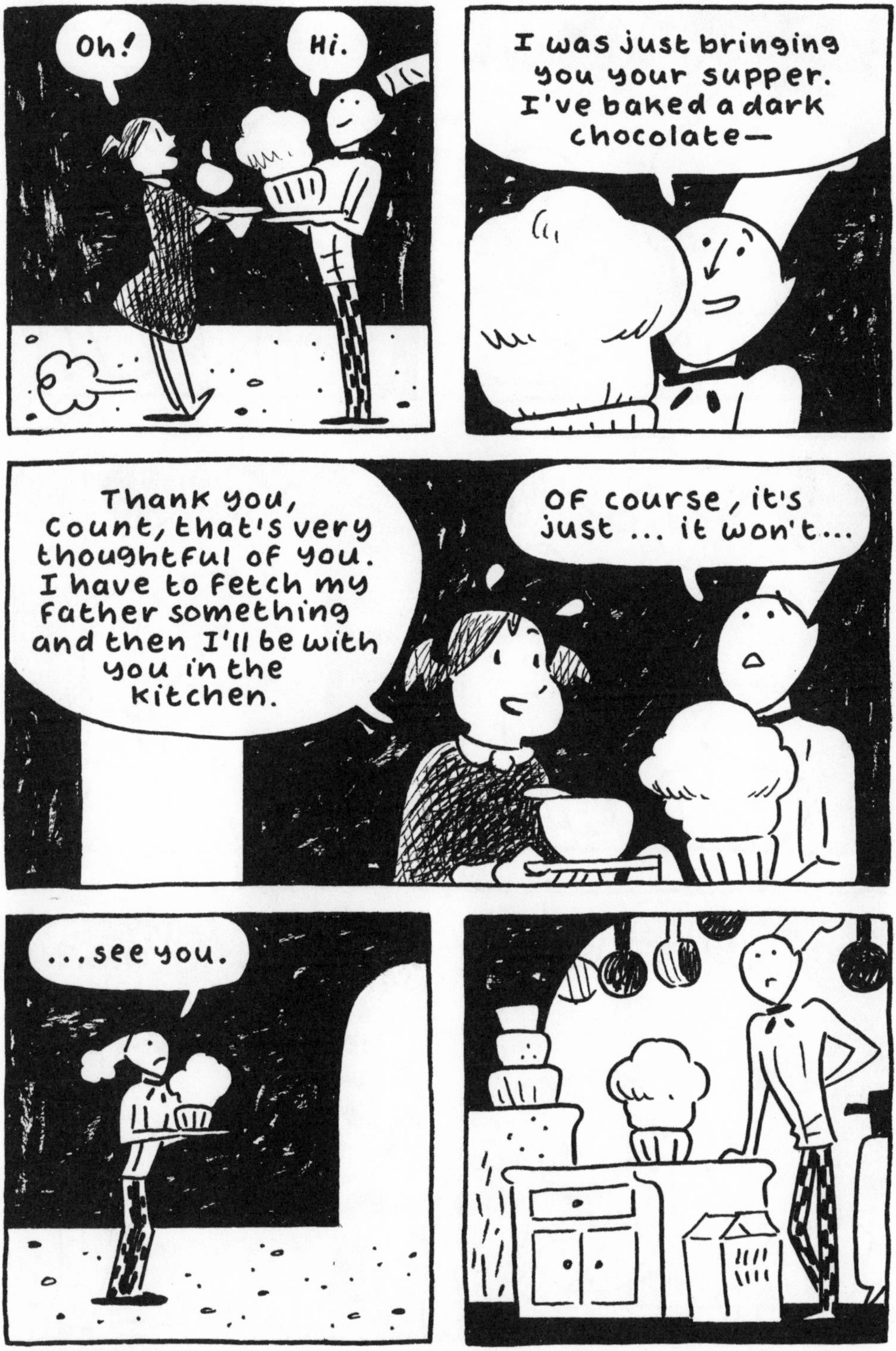
Oh!
Hi.
I was just bringing you your supper. I've baked a dark chocolate—
Thank you, Count, that's very thoughtful of you. I have to fetch my father something and then I'll be with you in the kitchen.
Of course, it's just ... it won't...
...see you.

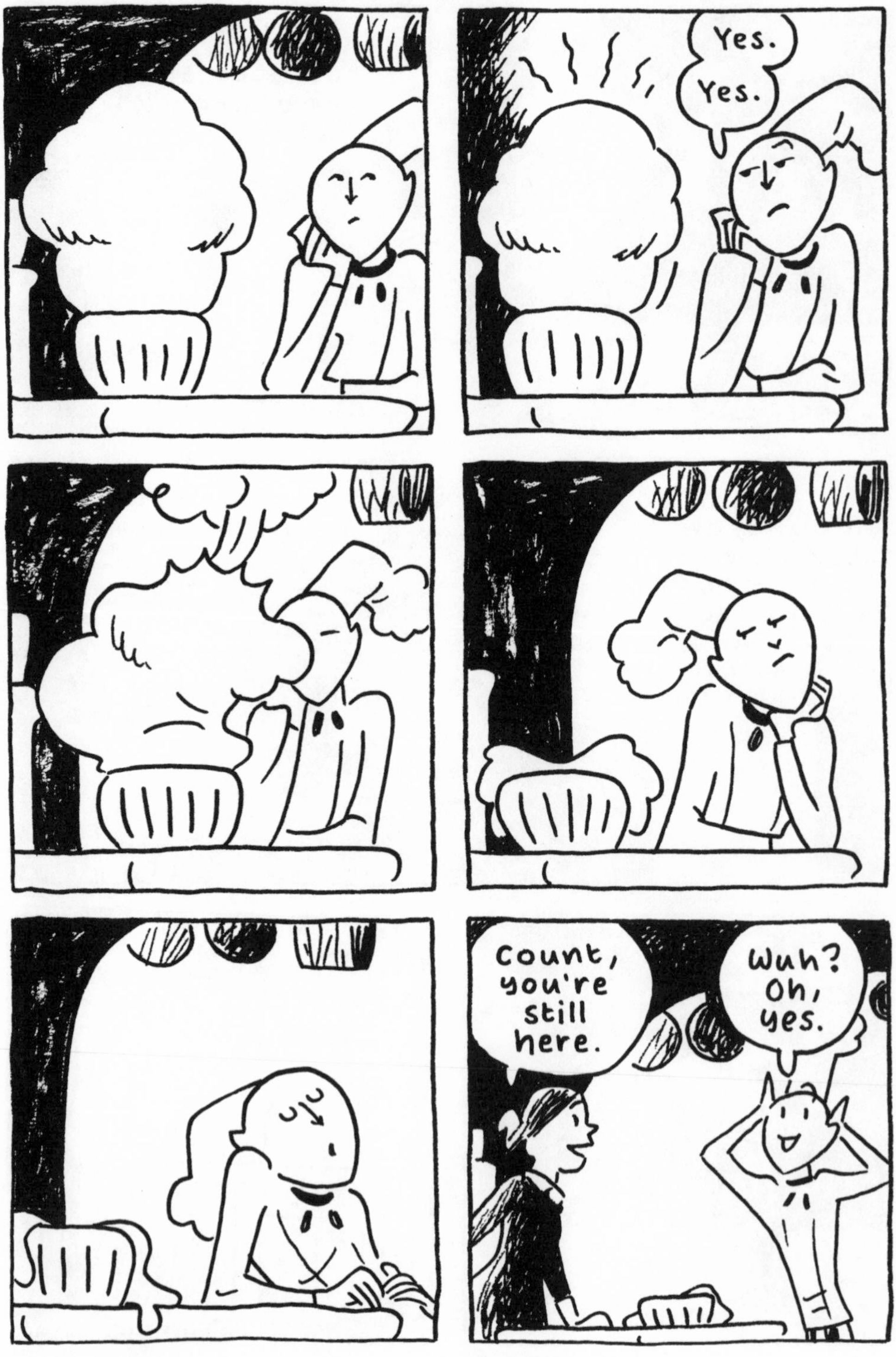
Yes.
Yes.
Count, you're still here.
Wuh? Oh, yes.

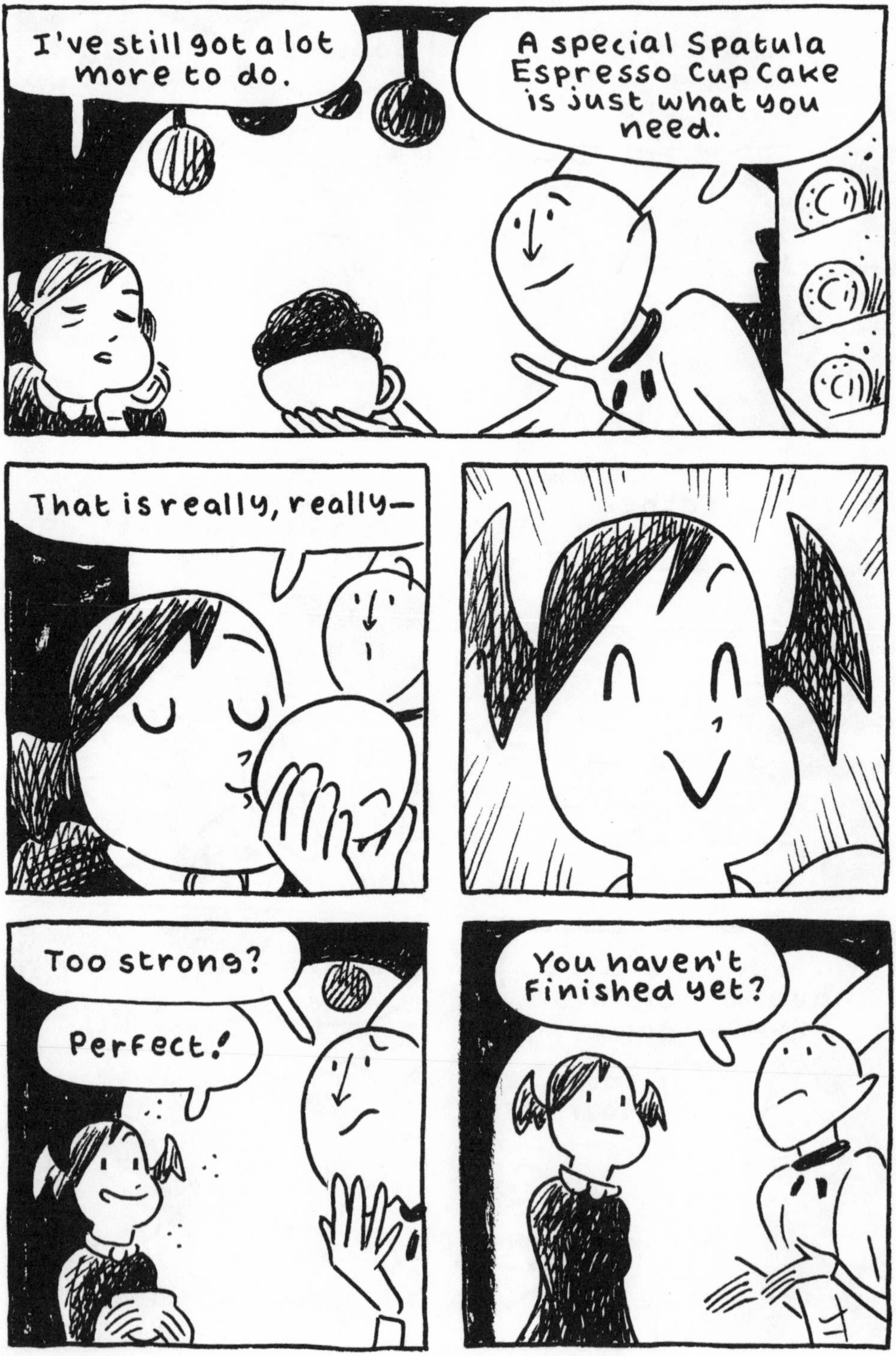

I've still got a lot more to do.
A special Spatula Espresso CupCake is just what you need.
That is really, really—
Too strong?
Perfect!
You haven't Finished yet?

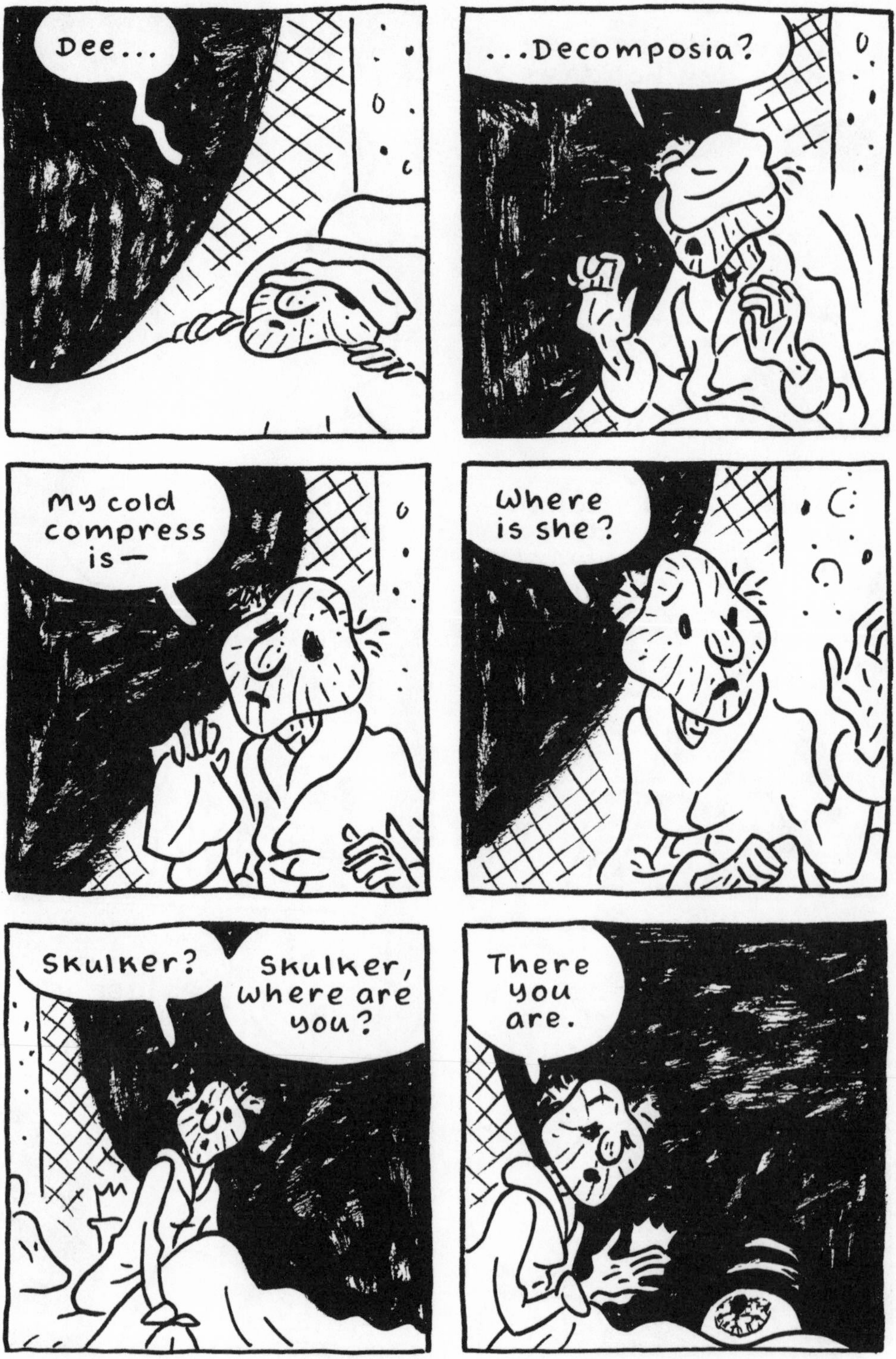

Dee...
...Decomposia?
My cold compress is—
Where is she?
Skulker?
Skulker, where are you?
There you are.

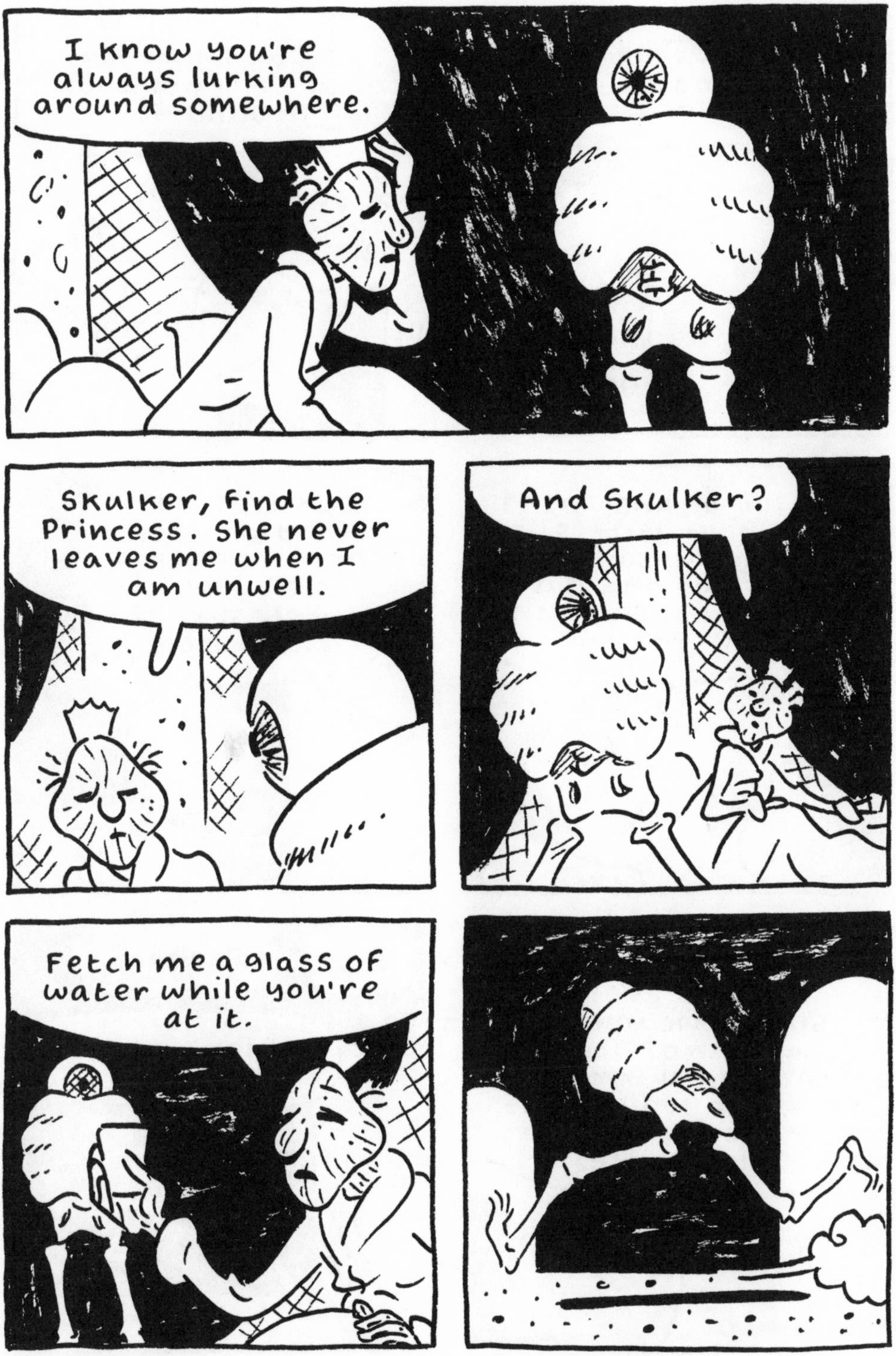

I know you're always lurking around somewhere.
Skulker, find the Princess. She never leaves me when I am unwell.
And Skulker?
Fetch me a glass of water while you're at it.

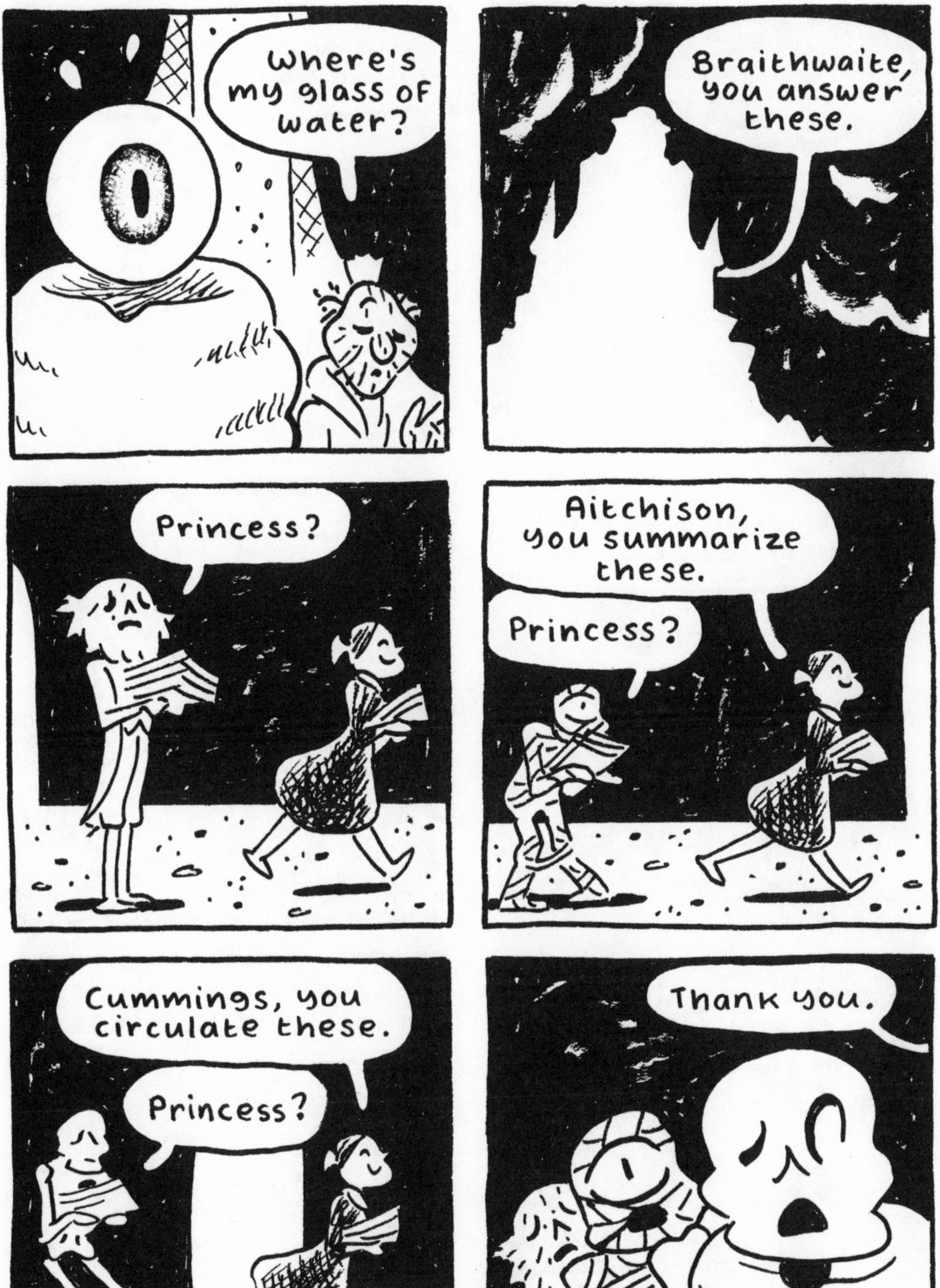
Where's my glass of water?
Braithwaite, you answer these.
Princess?
Aitchison, you summarize these.
Princess?
Cummings, you circulate these.
Princess?
Thank you.

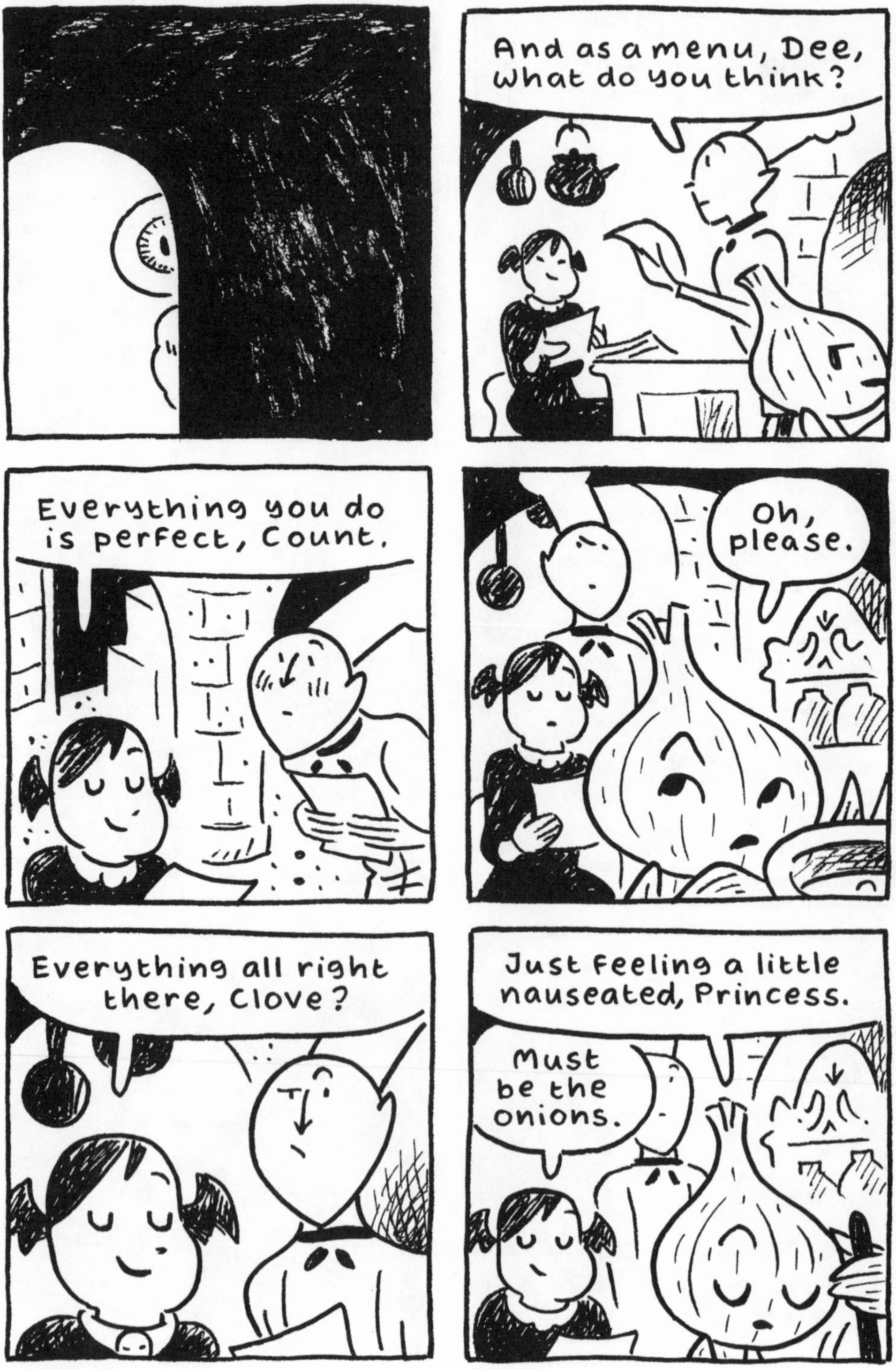
And as a menu, Dee, what do you think?
Everything you do is perfect, Count.
Oh, please.
Everything all right there, Clove?
Just feeling a little nauseated, Princess.
Must be the onions.

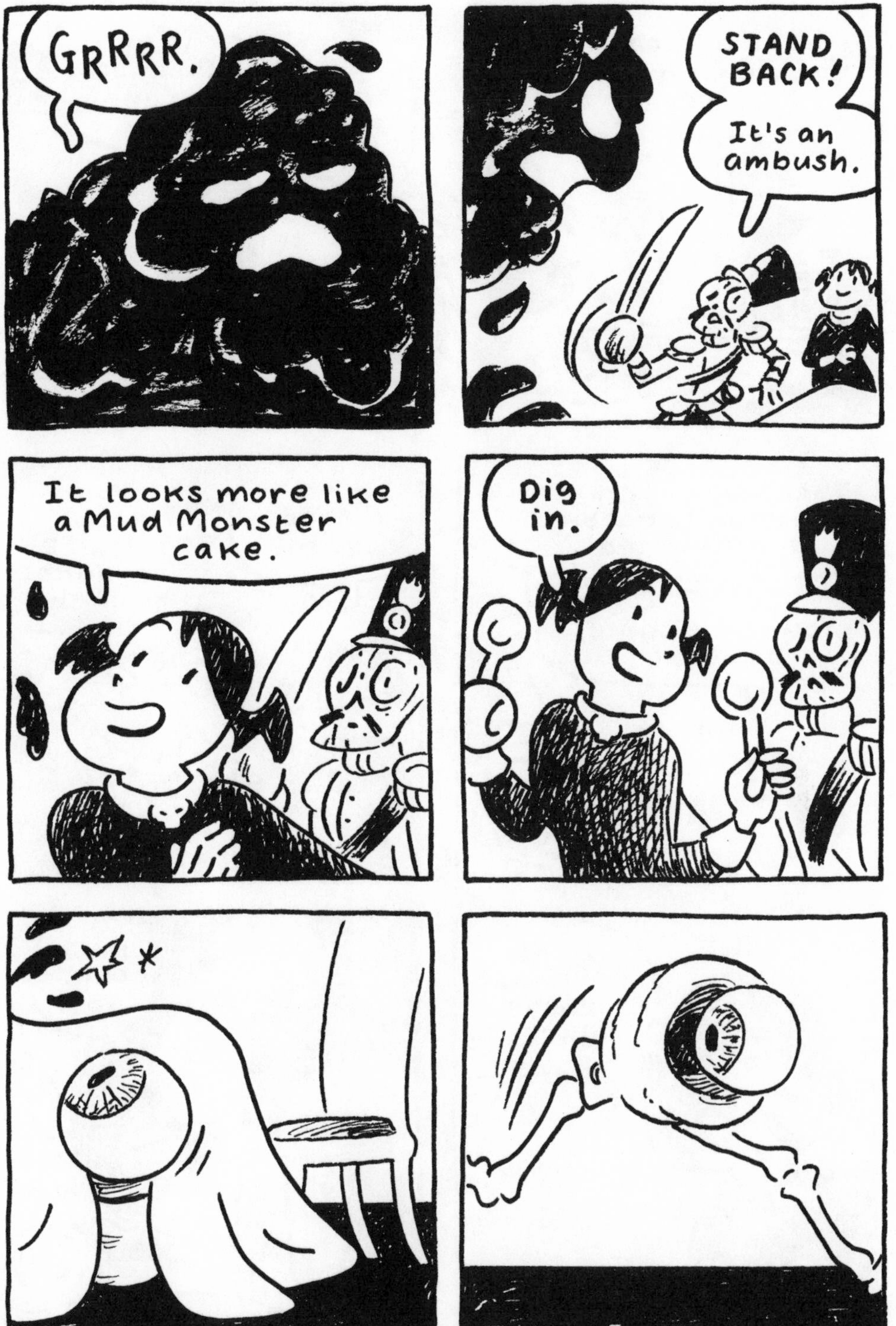
GRRRR.
STAND BACK!
It's an ambush.
It looks more like a Mud Monster cake.
Dig in.

76

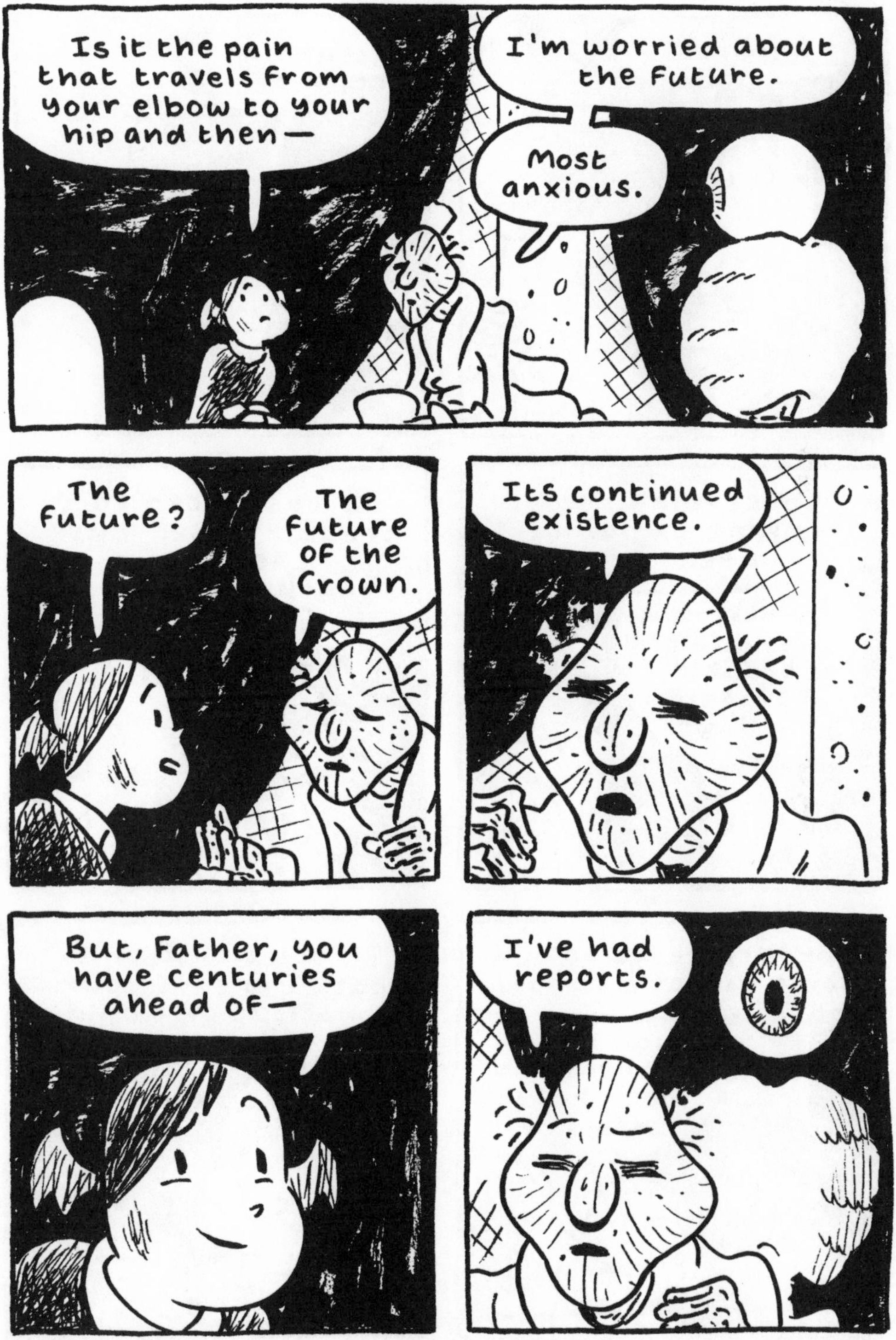
Is it the pain that travels from your elbow to your hip and then—
I'm worried about the future.
Most anxious.
The future?
The future of the Crown.
Its continued existence.
But, Father, you have centuries ahead of—
I've had reports.

"Reports"?

Disturbing reports.

Concerning the running of palace affairs.

Father, you shouldn't trouble yourself with—

I was forced to trouble myself due to the serious nature of the concerns.

Any problems should come directly to me.

You know my health is not what it should be.

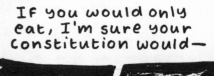

If you would only eat, I'm sure your constitution would—

85

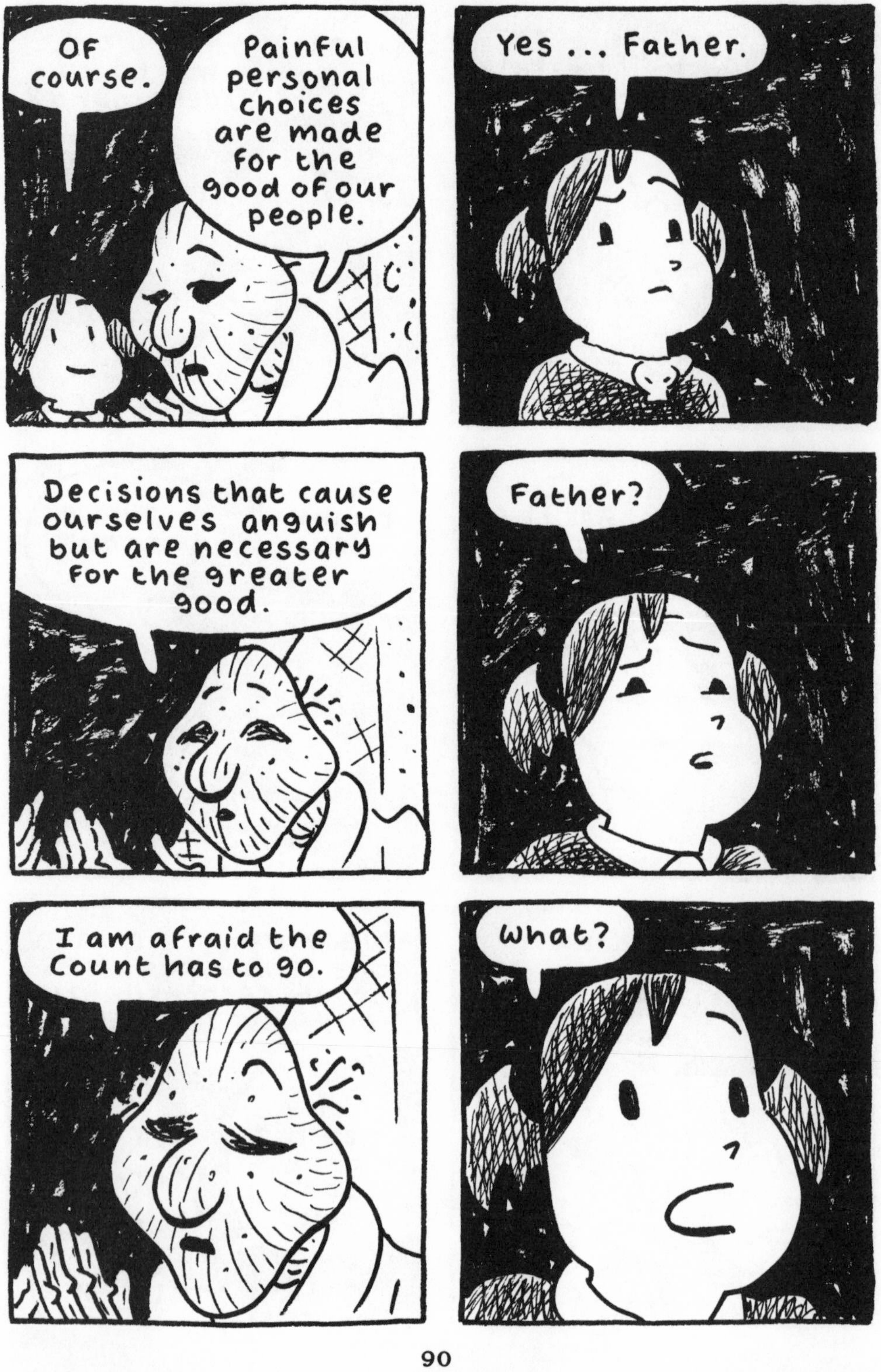
Of course.
Painful personal choices are made for the good of our people.
Yes ... Father.
Decisions that cause ourselves anguish but are necessary for the greater good.
Father?
I am afraid the Count has to go.
What?

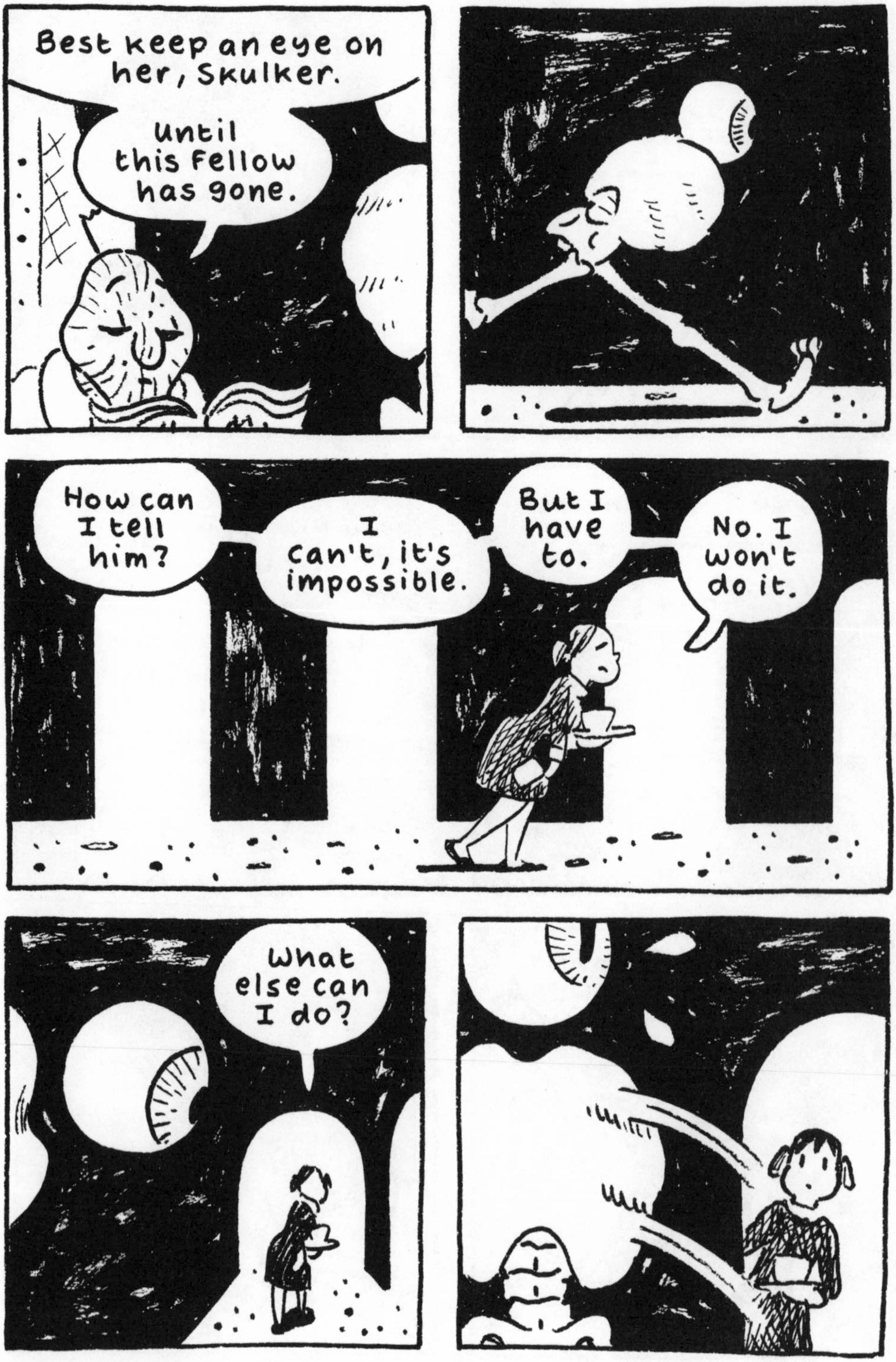
Best keep an eye on her, Skulker.
Until this fellow has gone.
How can I tell him?
I can't, it's impossible.
But I have to.
No. I won't do it.
What else can I do?

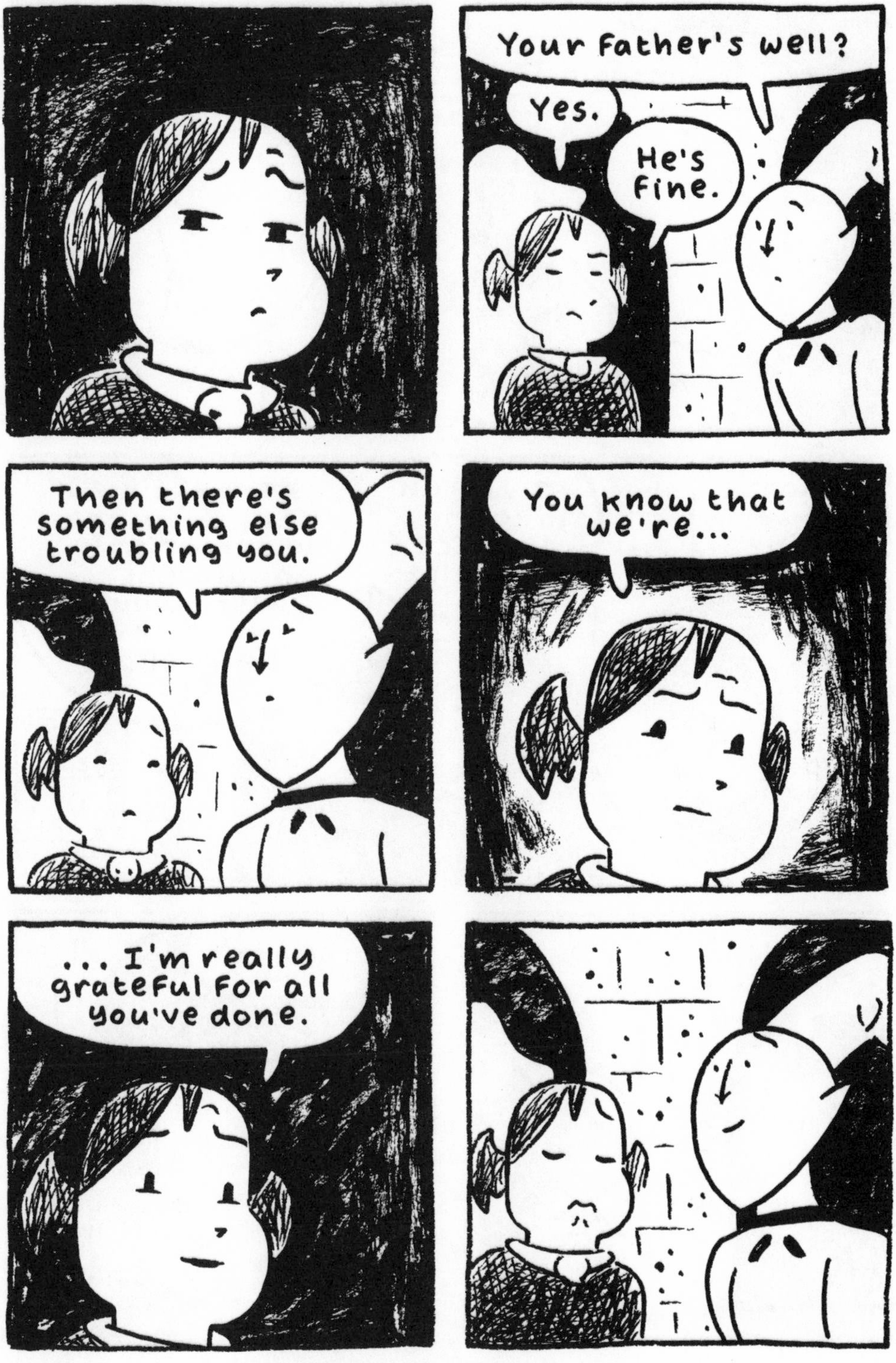
Your father's well?
Yes.
He's fine.
Then there's something else troubling you.
You know that we're...
... I'm really grateful for all you've done.

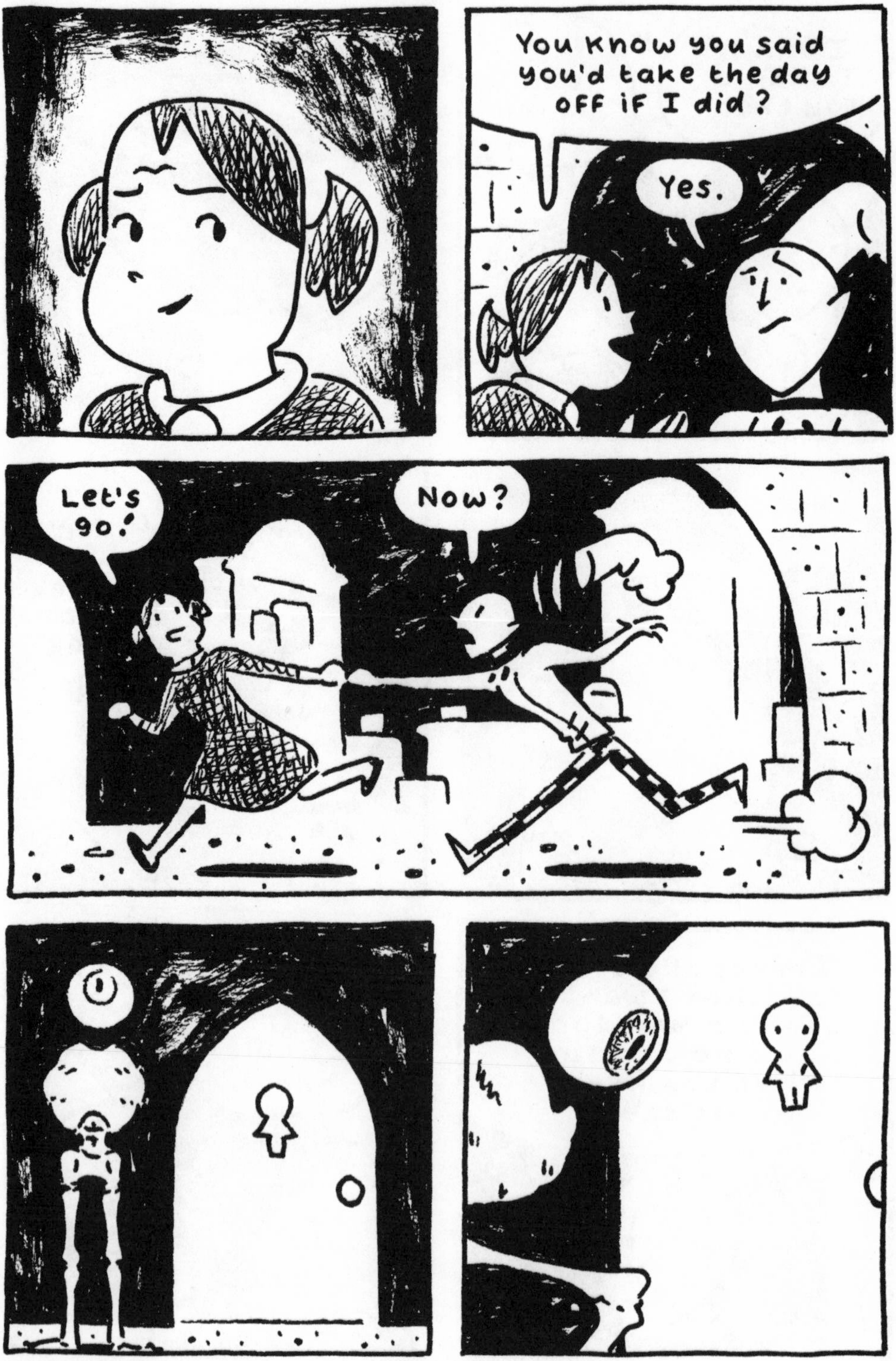
You know you said you'd take the day off if I did?
Yes.
Let's go!
Now?

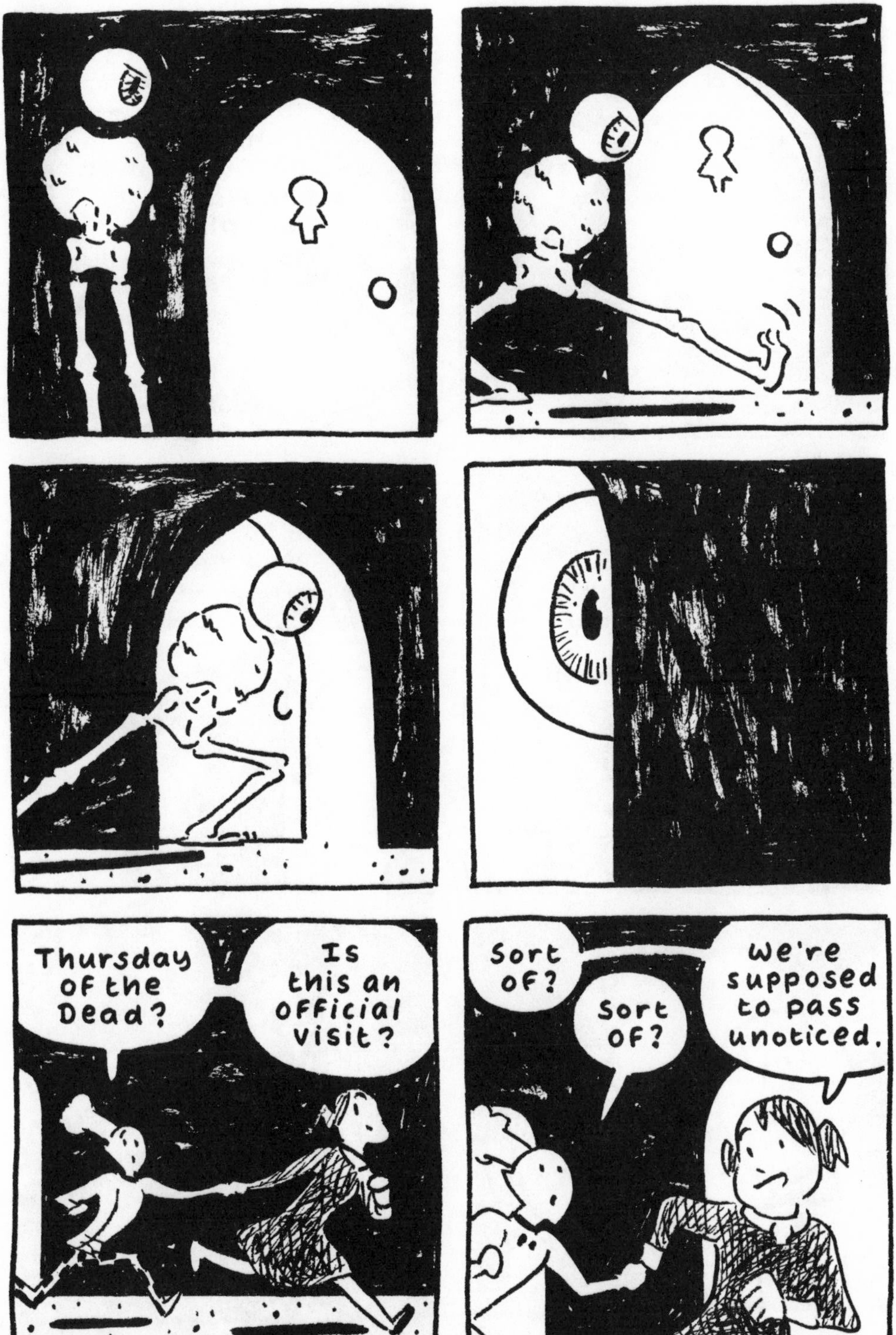
Thursday of the Dead?
Is this an official visit?
Sort of?
Sort of?
We're supposed to pass unoticed.

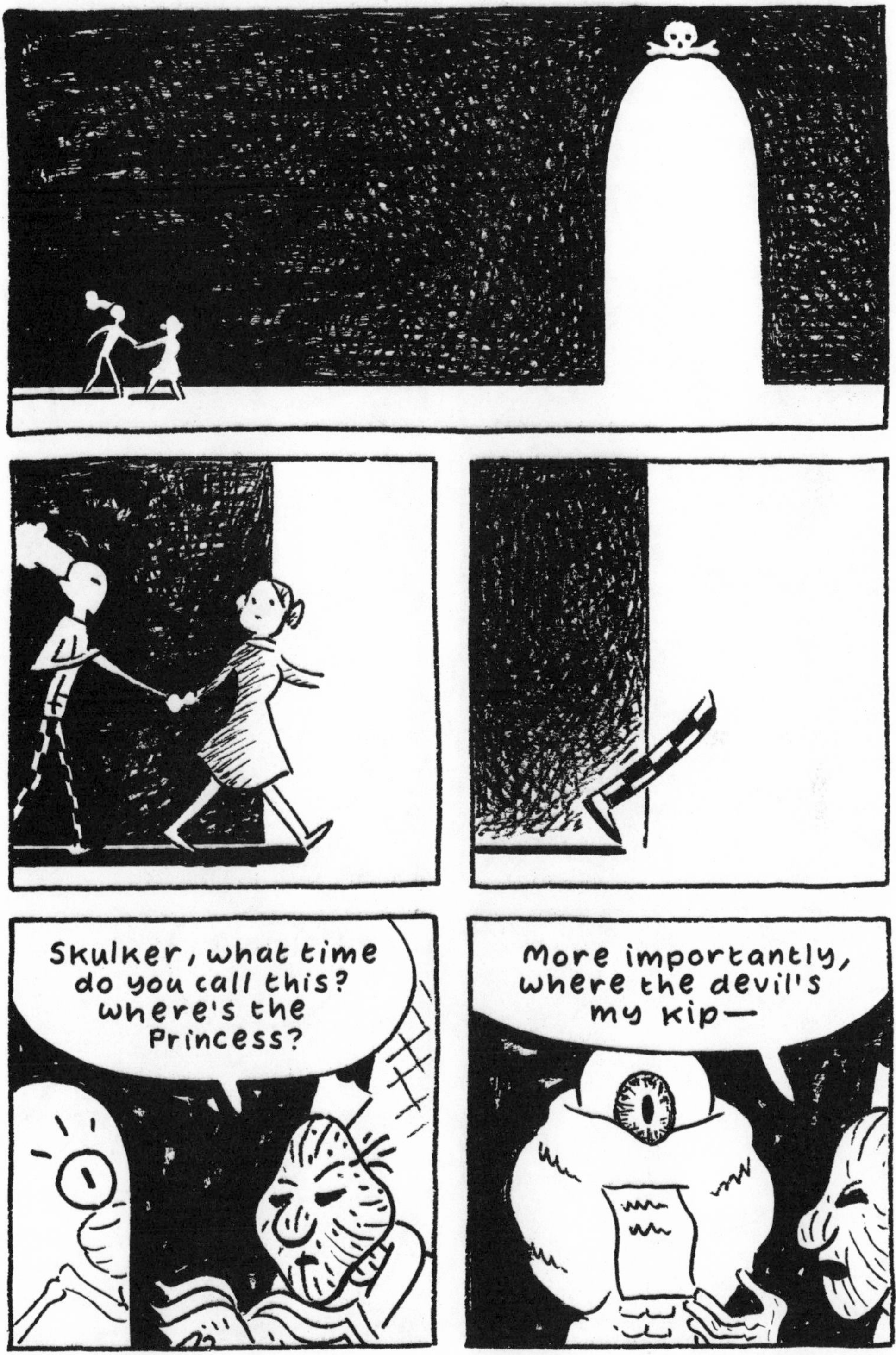
Skulker, what time do you call this? Where's the Princess?
More importantly, where the devil's my kip—

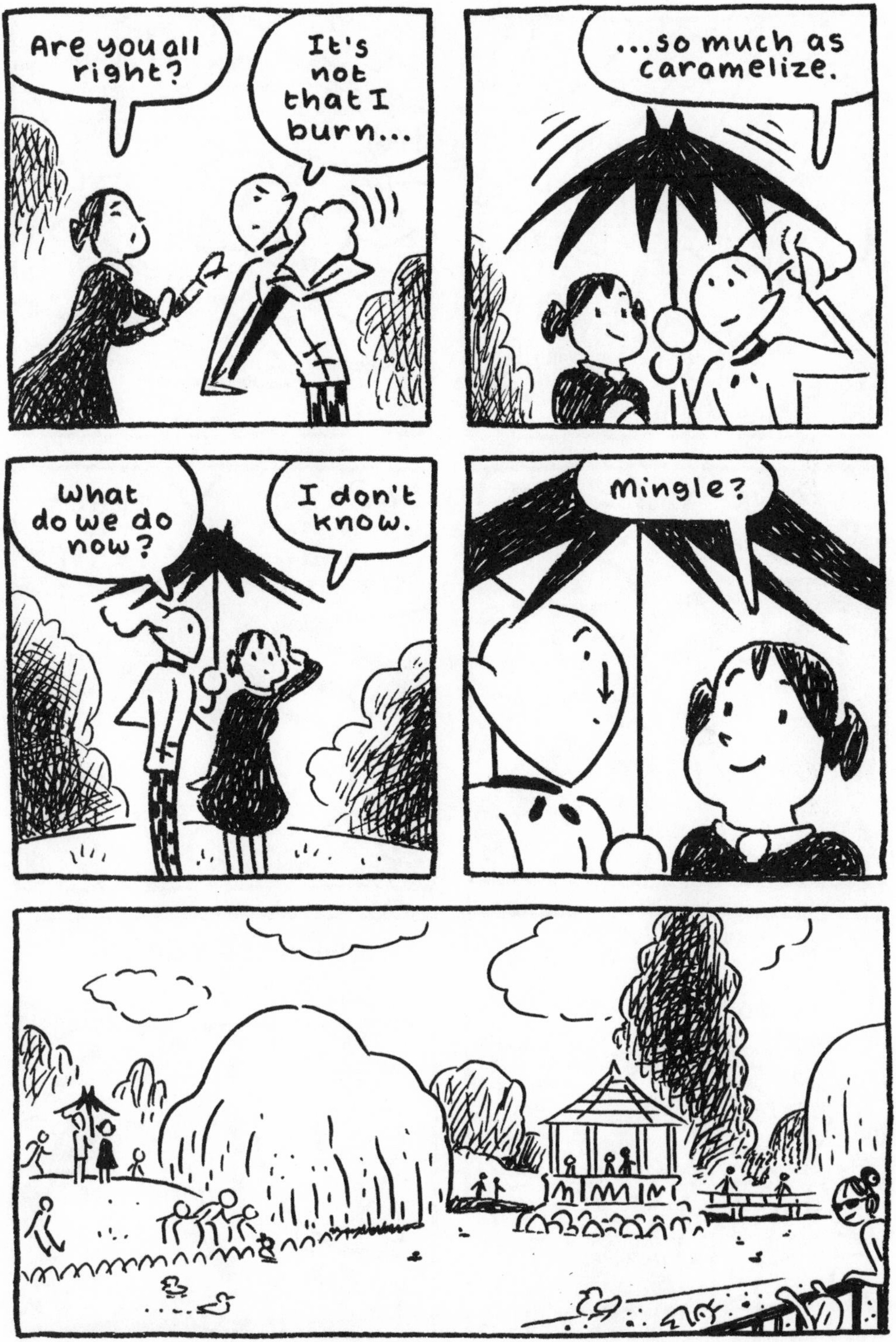
Are you all right?
It's not that I burn...
...so much as caramelize.
What do we do now?
I don't know.
Mingle?

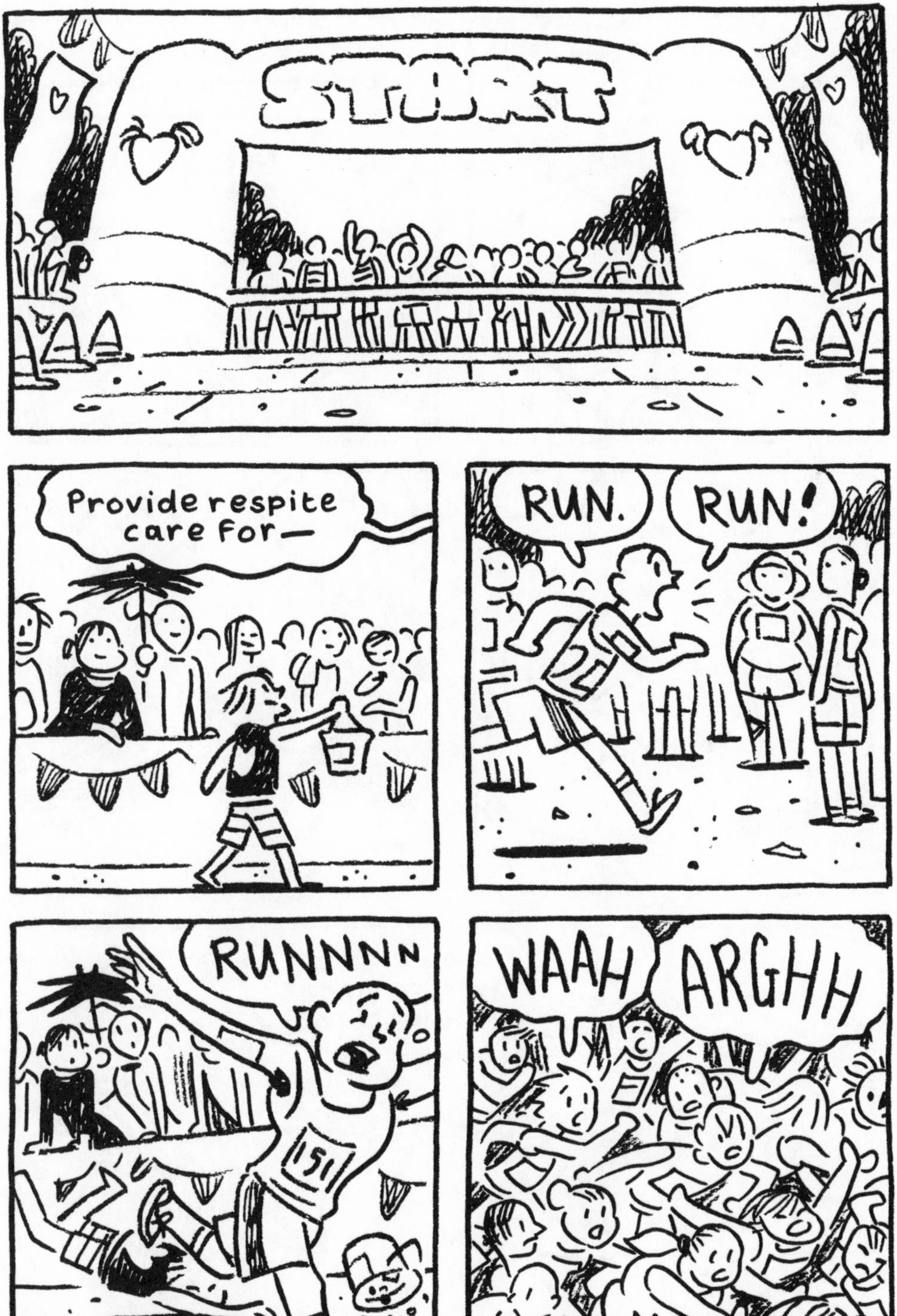
START
Provide respite care for—
RUN.
RUN!
RUNNNN
151
WAAH
ARGHH

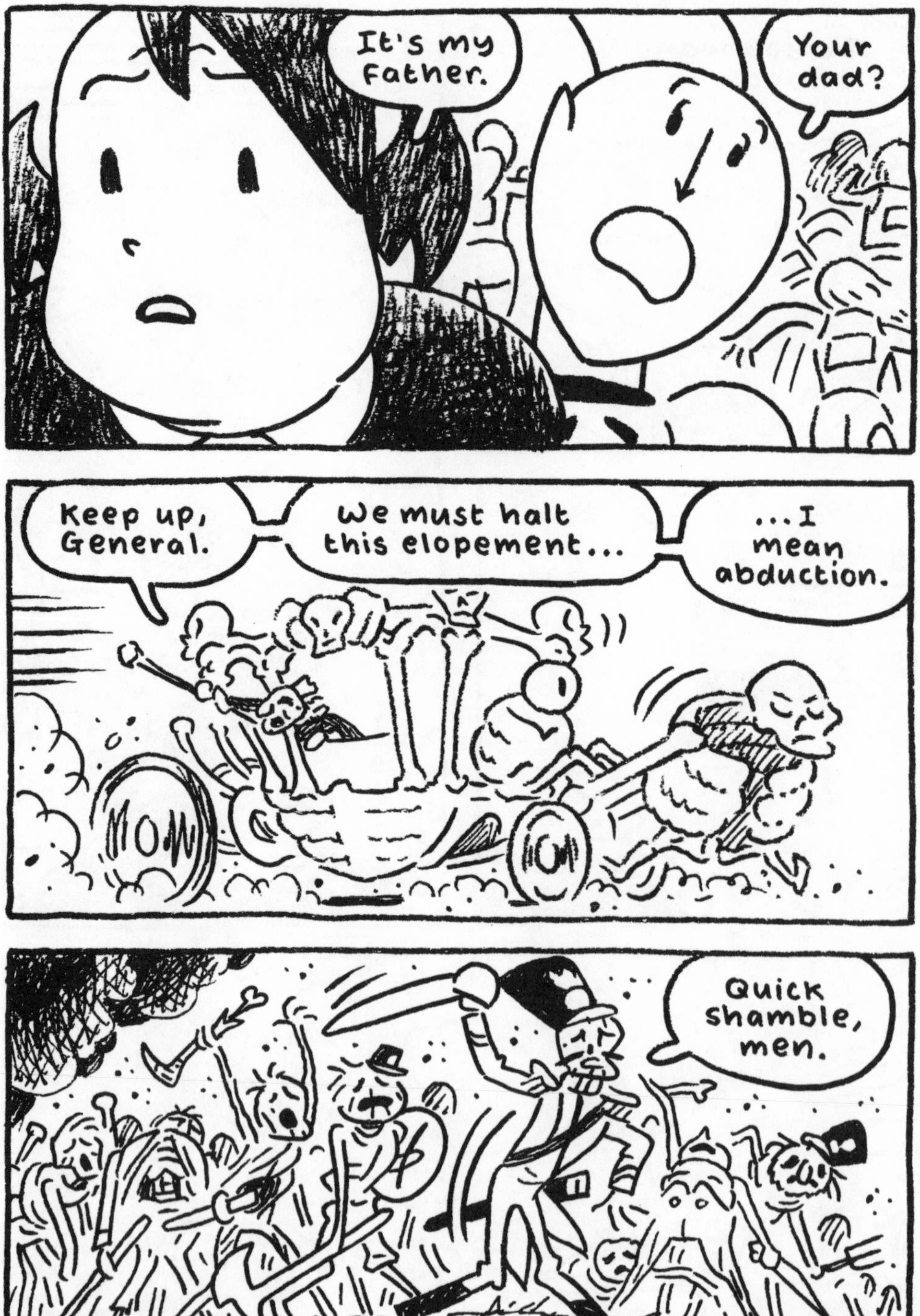
It's my father.
Your dad?
Keep up, General.
We must halt this elopement...
...I mean abduction.
WOW
Quick shamble, men.

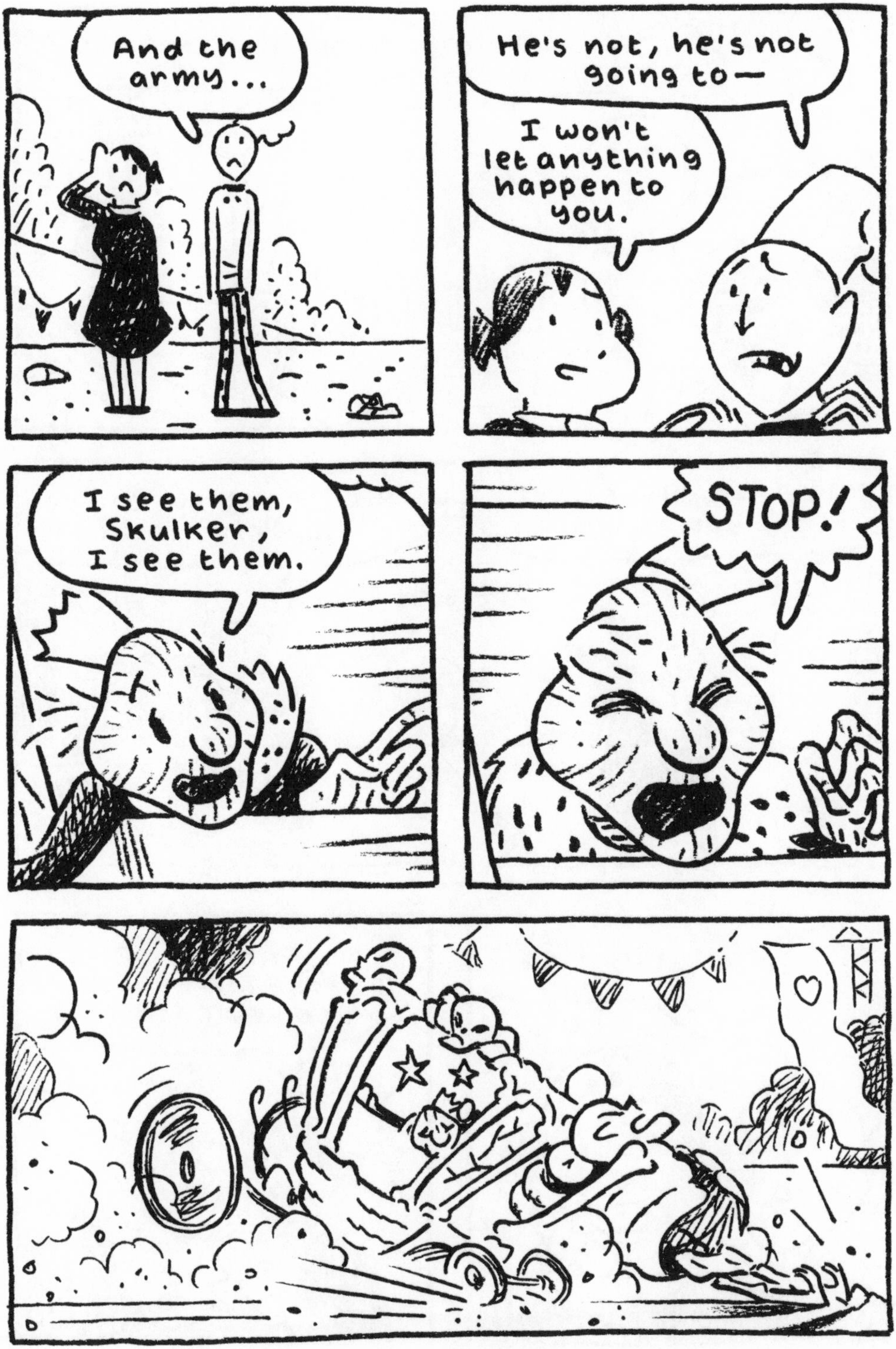

And the army...
He's not, he's not going to—
I won't let anything happen to you.
I see them, Skulker, I see them.
STOP!

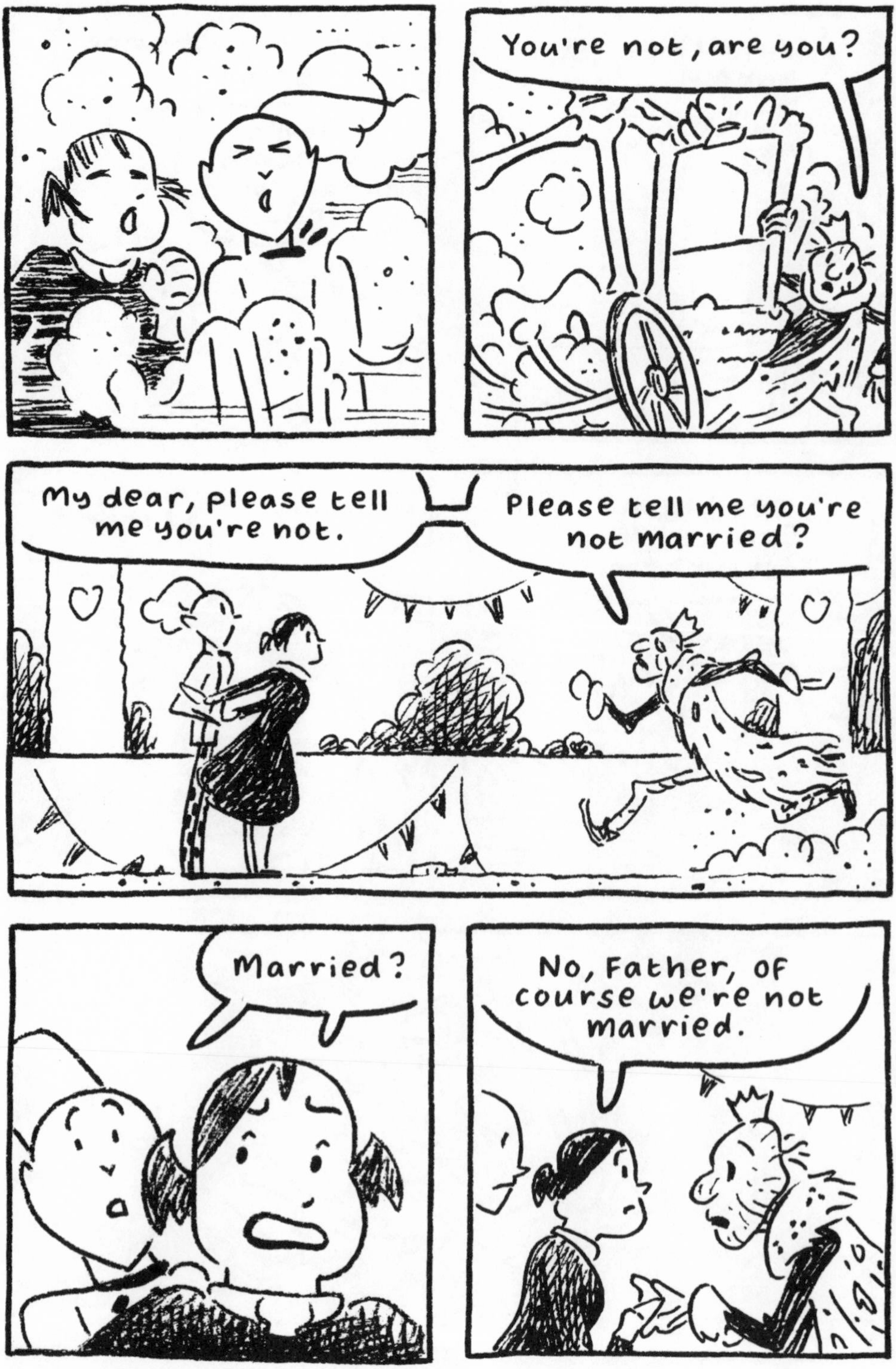
You're not, are you?
My dear, please tell me you're not.
Please tell me you're not married?
Married?
No, Father, of course we're not married.

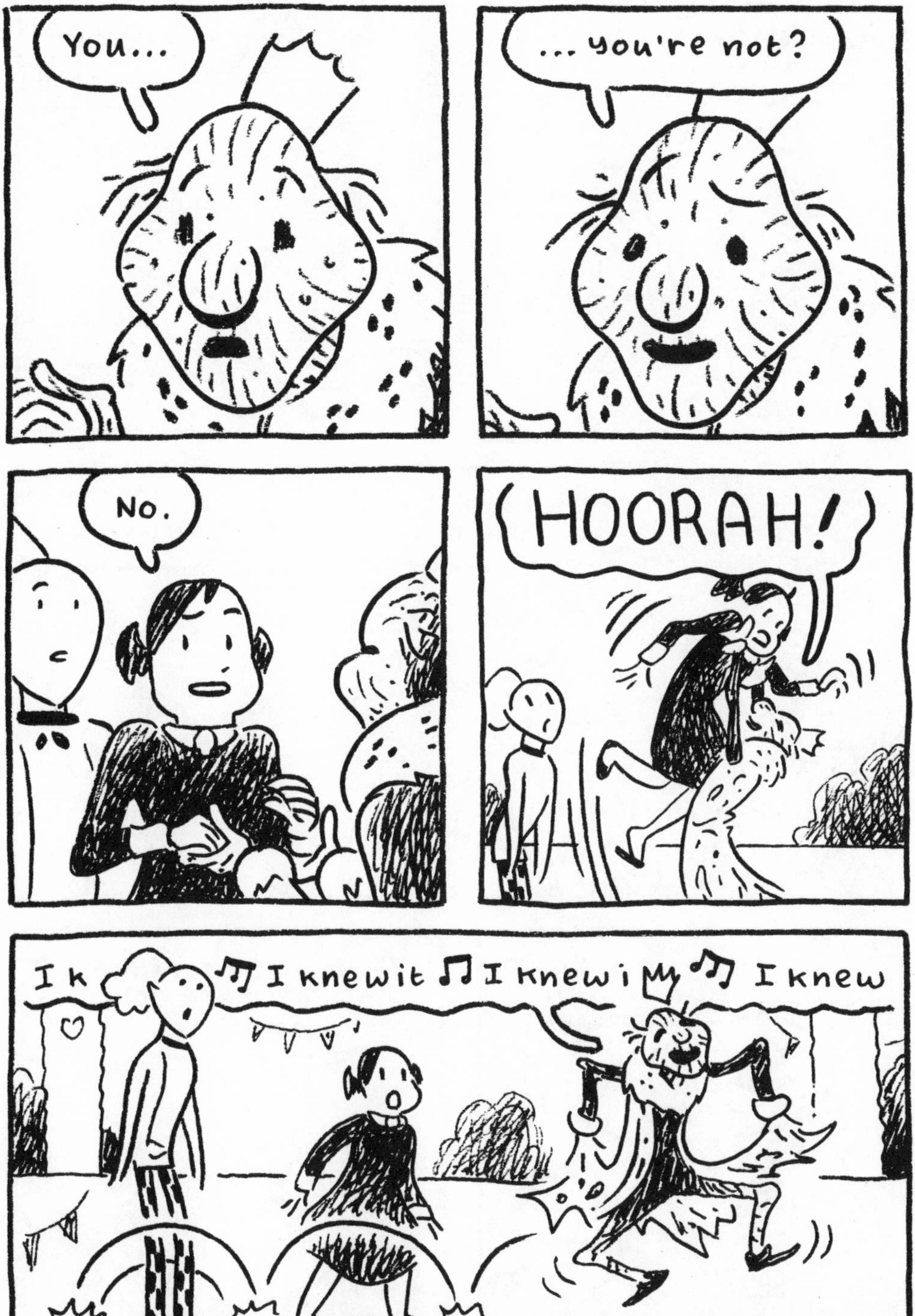
You...
... you're not?
No.
HOORAH!
I k ♫ I knewit ♫ I knewi ♫ I knew

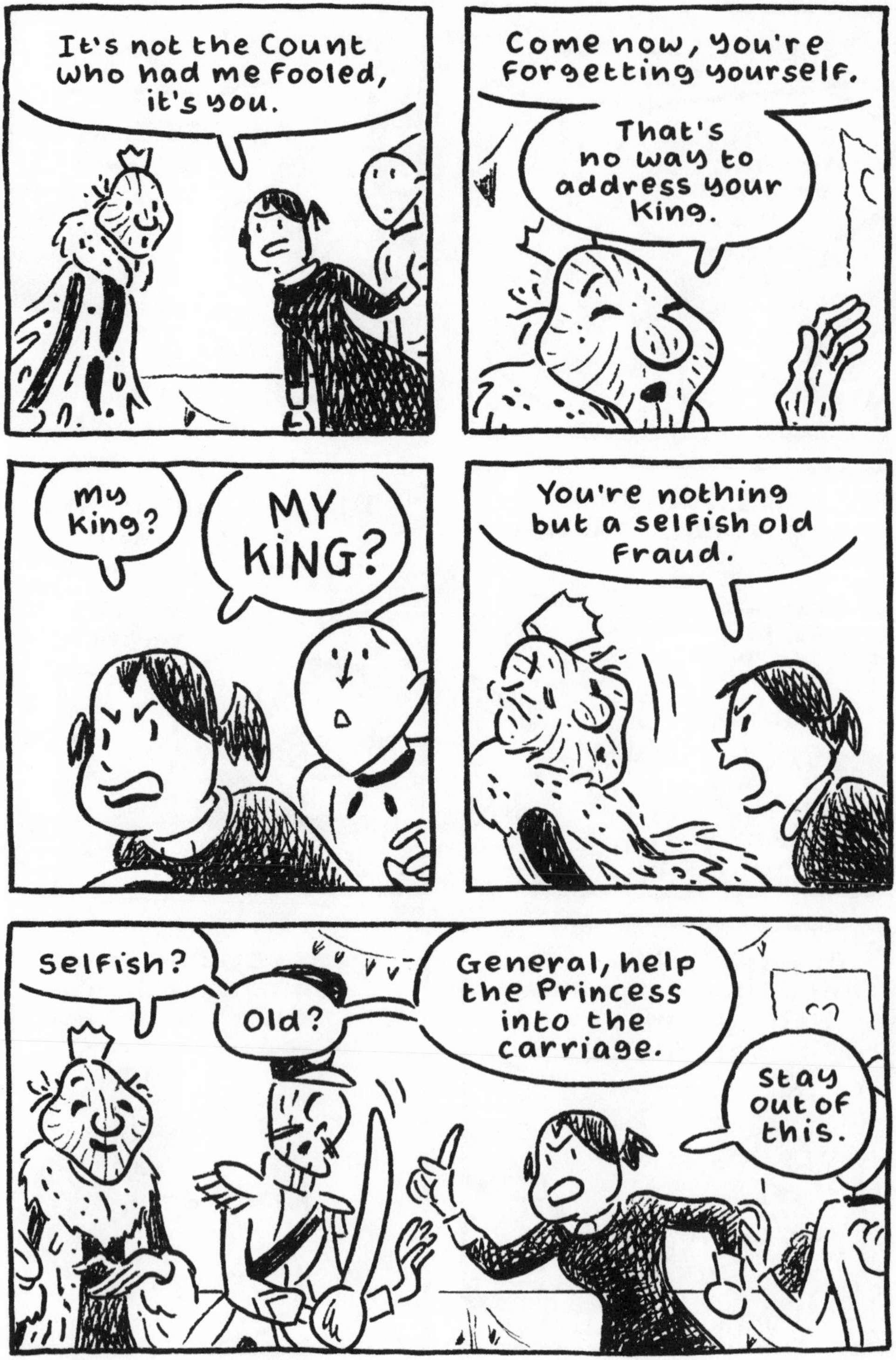
It's not the Count who had me fooled, it's you.
Come now, you're forgetting yourself.
That's no way to address your King.
My King?
MY KING?
You're nothing but a selfish old Fraud.
Selfish?
Old?
General, help the Princess into the carriage.
Stay out of this.

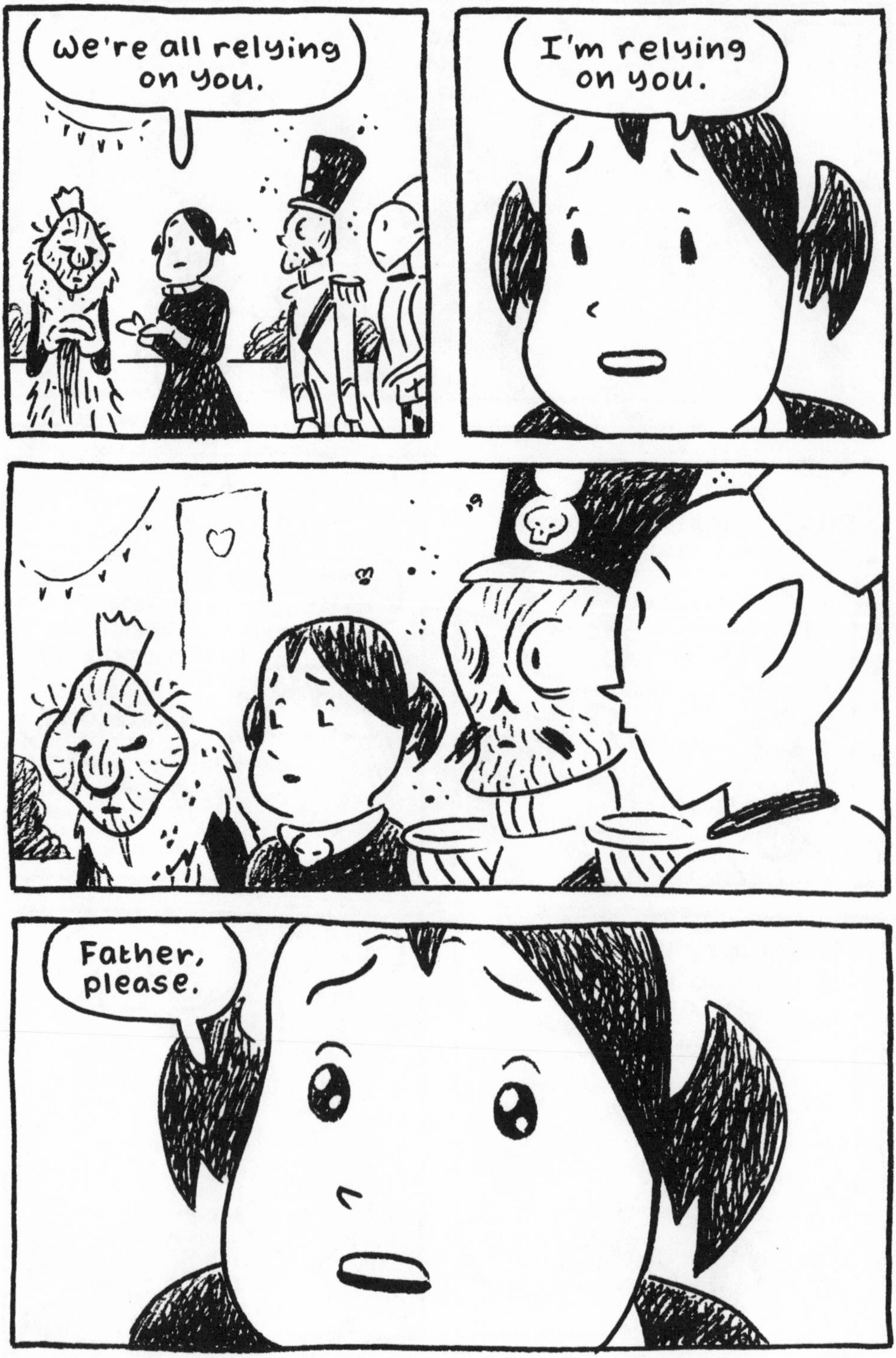
We're all relying on you.
I'm relying on you.
Father, please.

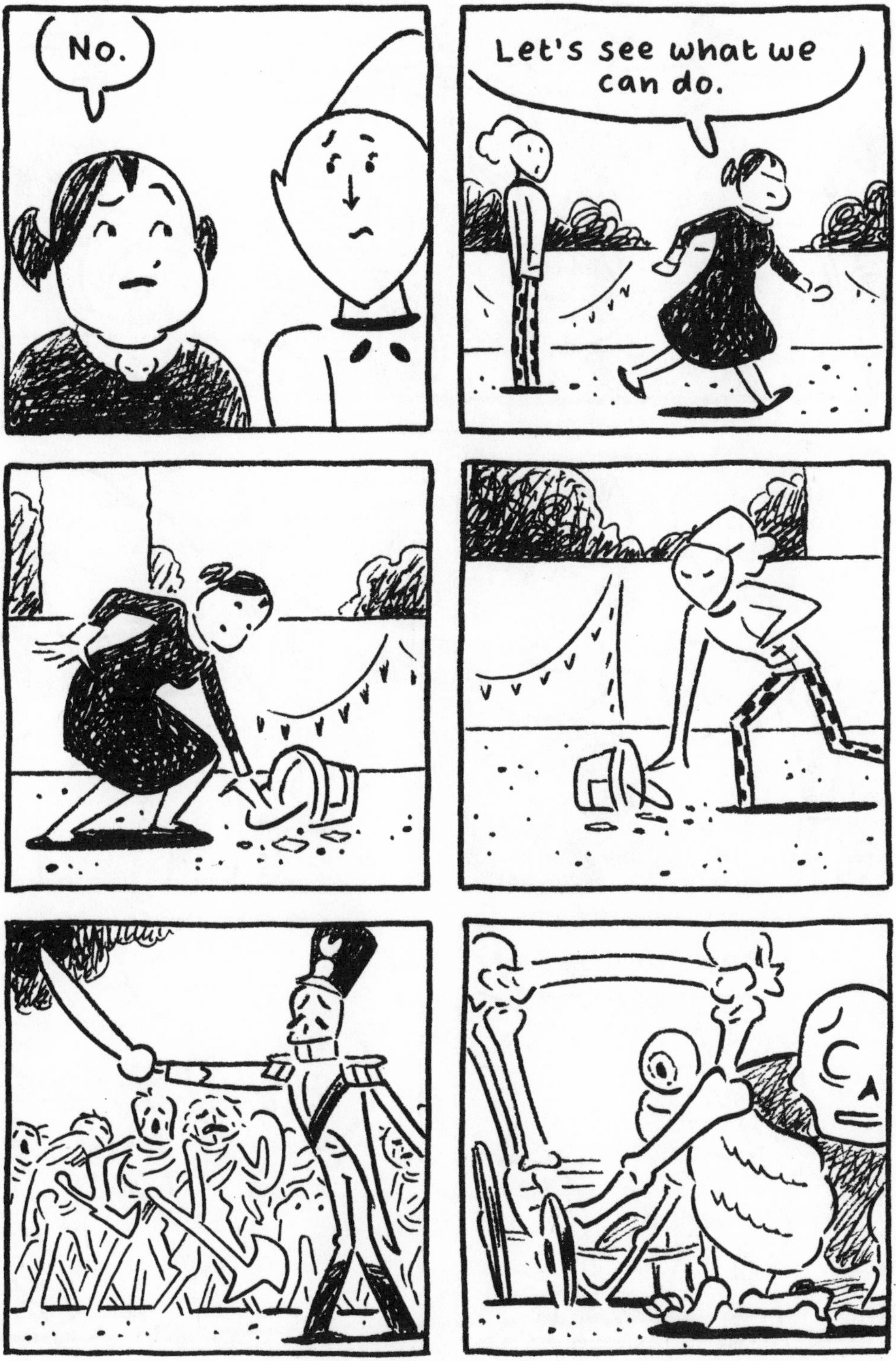
No.
Let's see what we can do.

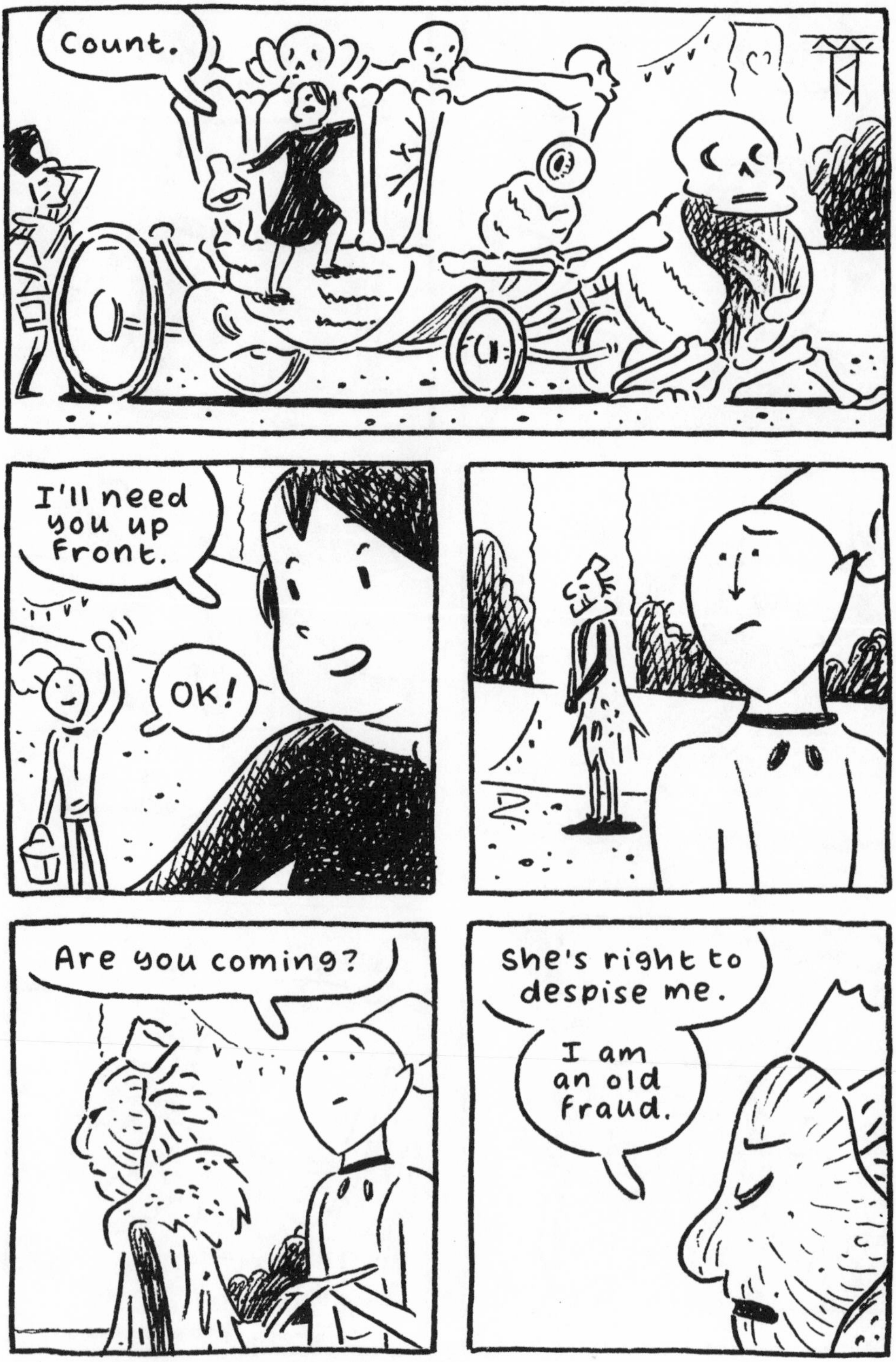
Count.
I'll need you up front.
OK!
Are you coming?
She's right to despise me.
I am an old fraud.

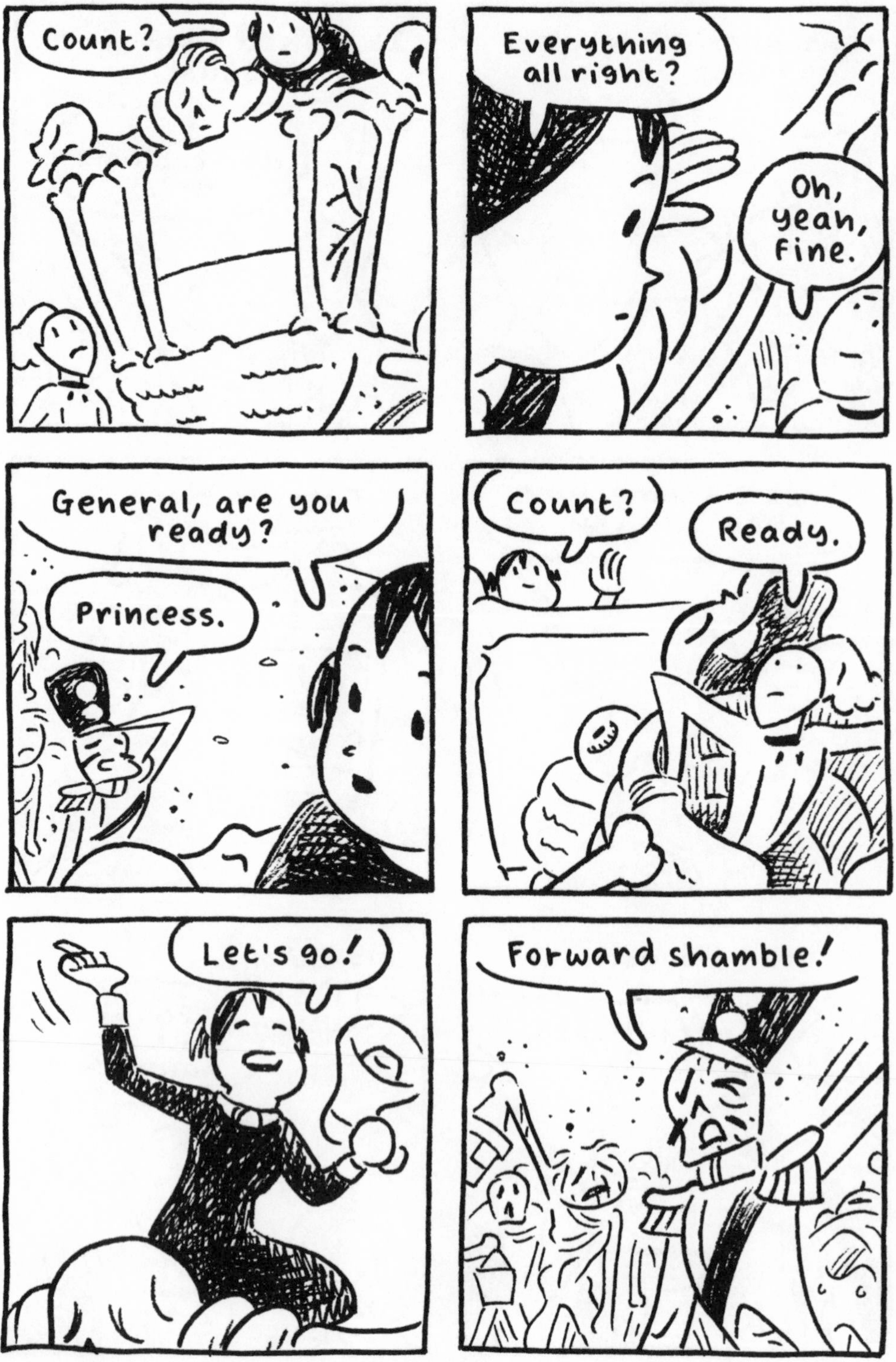
Count?
Everything all right?
Oh, yeah, fine.
General, are you ready?
Princess.
Count?
Ready.
Let's go!
Forward shamble!

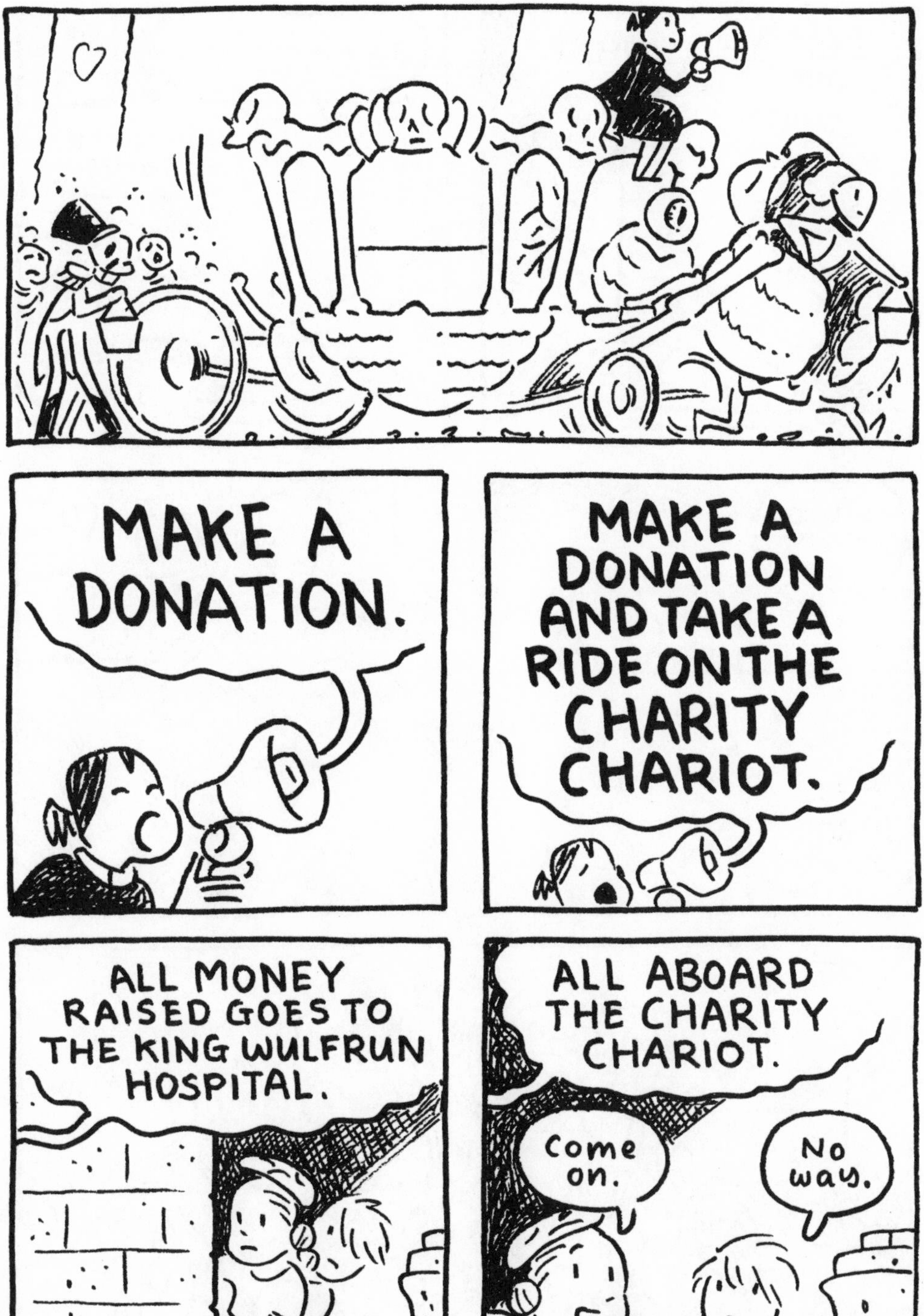
MAKE A DONATION.
MAKE A DONATION AND TAKE A RIDE ON THE CHARITY CHARIOT.
ALL MONEY RAISED GOES TO THE KING WULFRUN HOSPITAL.
ALL ABOARD THE CHARITY CHARIOT.
Come on.
No way.

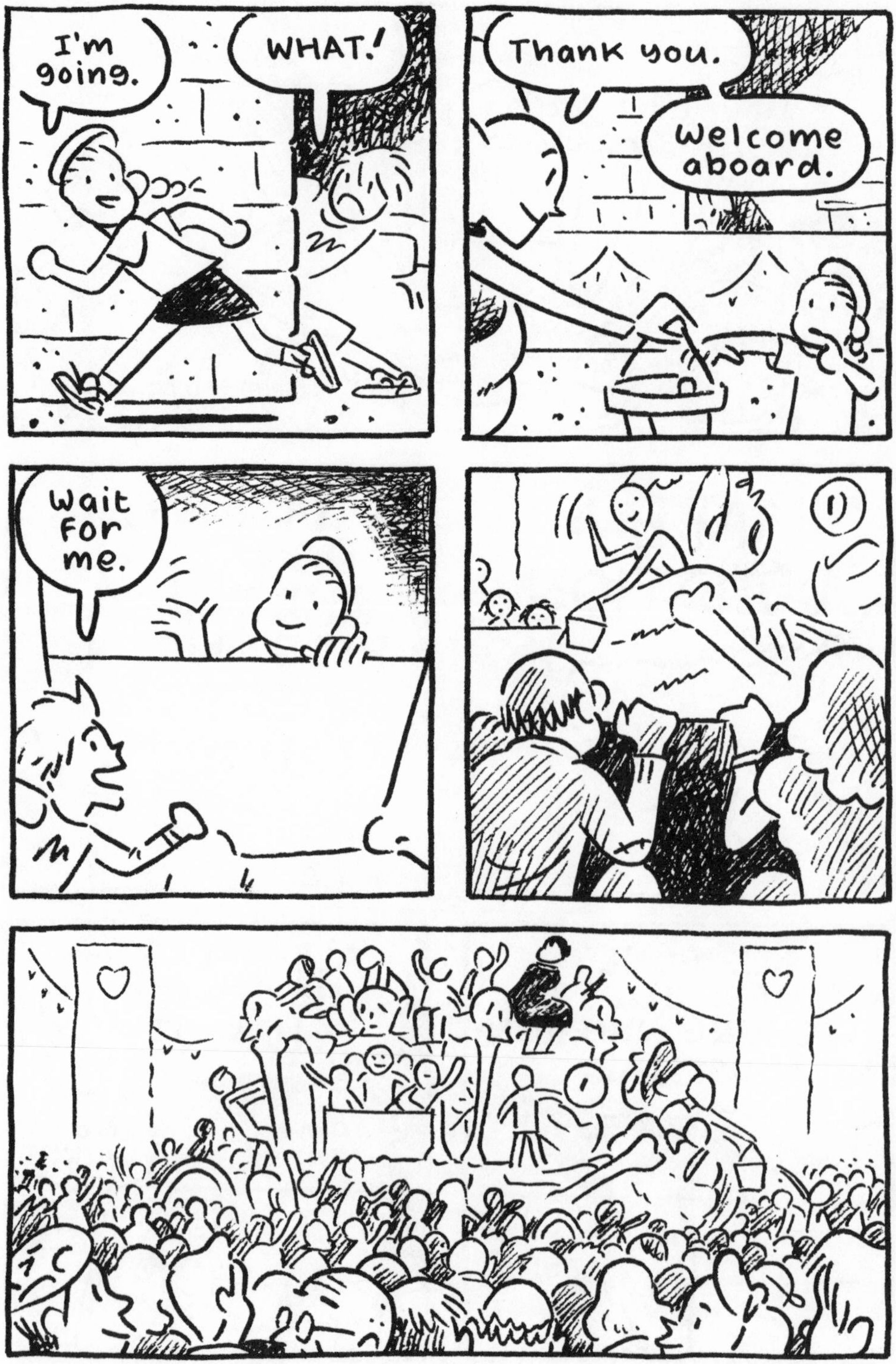
I'm going.
WHAT!
Thank you.
Welcome aboard.
Wait for me.
!!

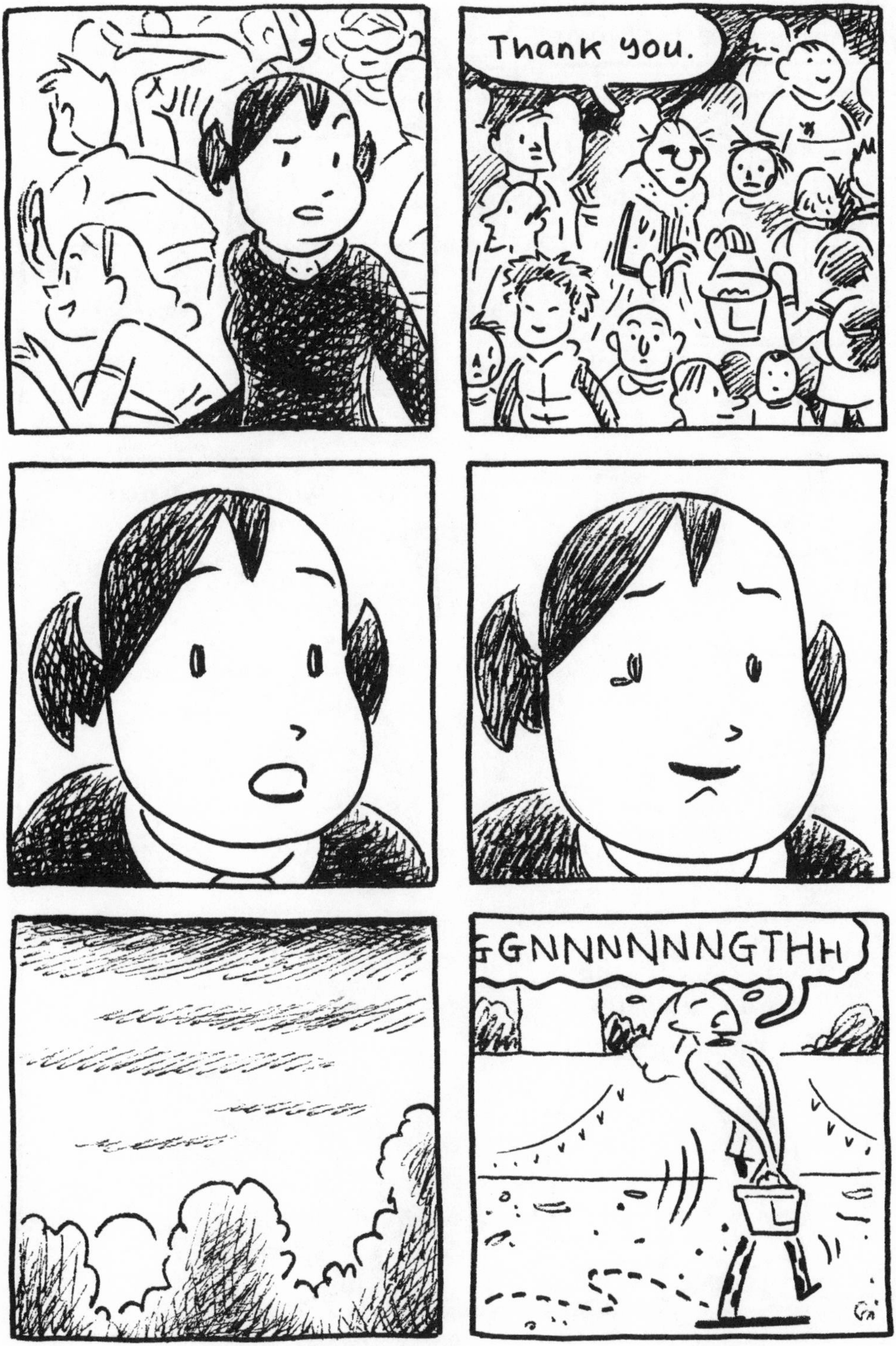
Thank you.
GGNNNNNNGTHH

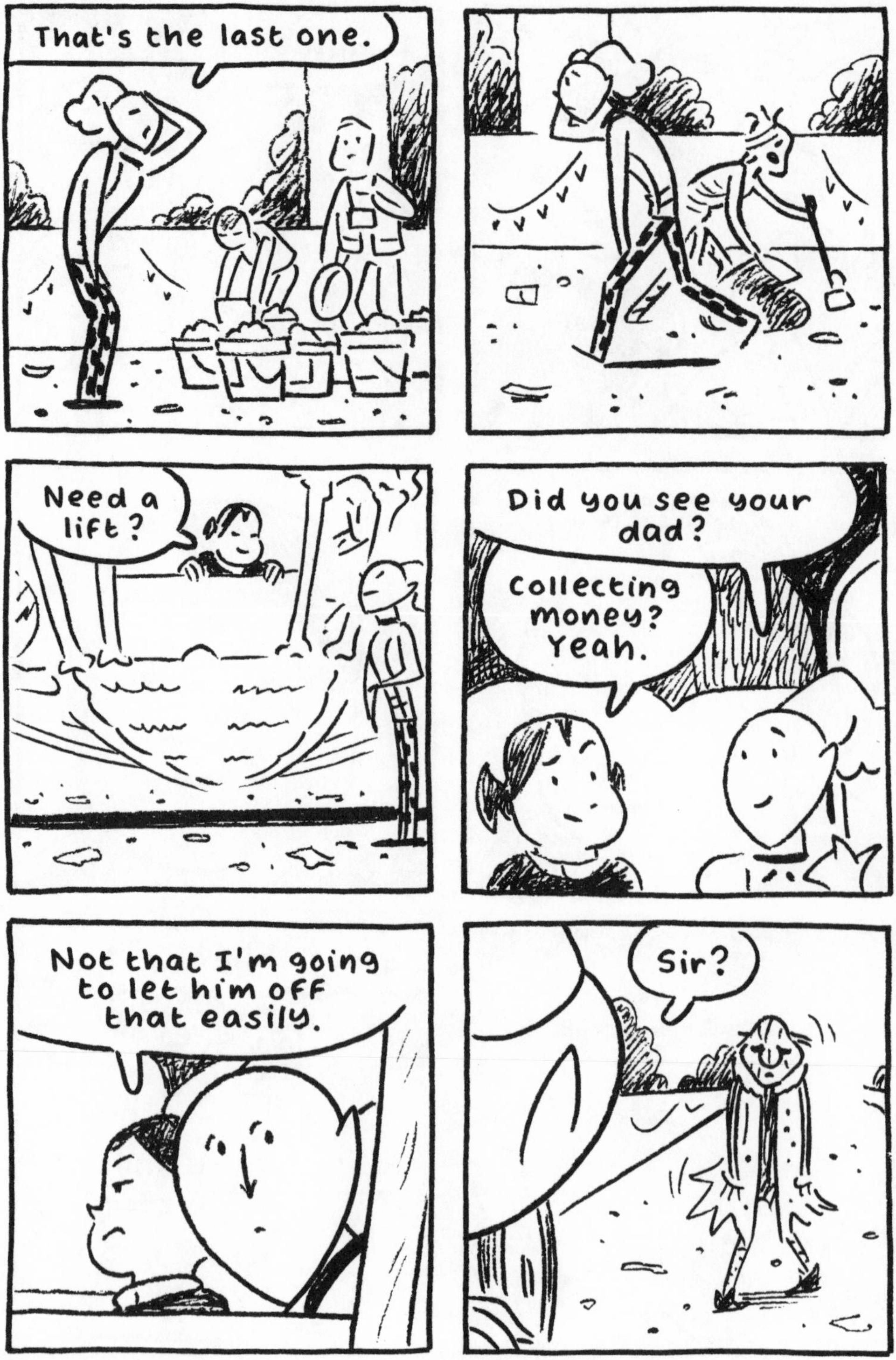
That's the last one.
Need a lift?
Did you see your dad?
Collecting money? Yeah.
Not that I'm going to let him off that easily.
Sir?

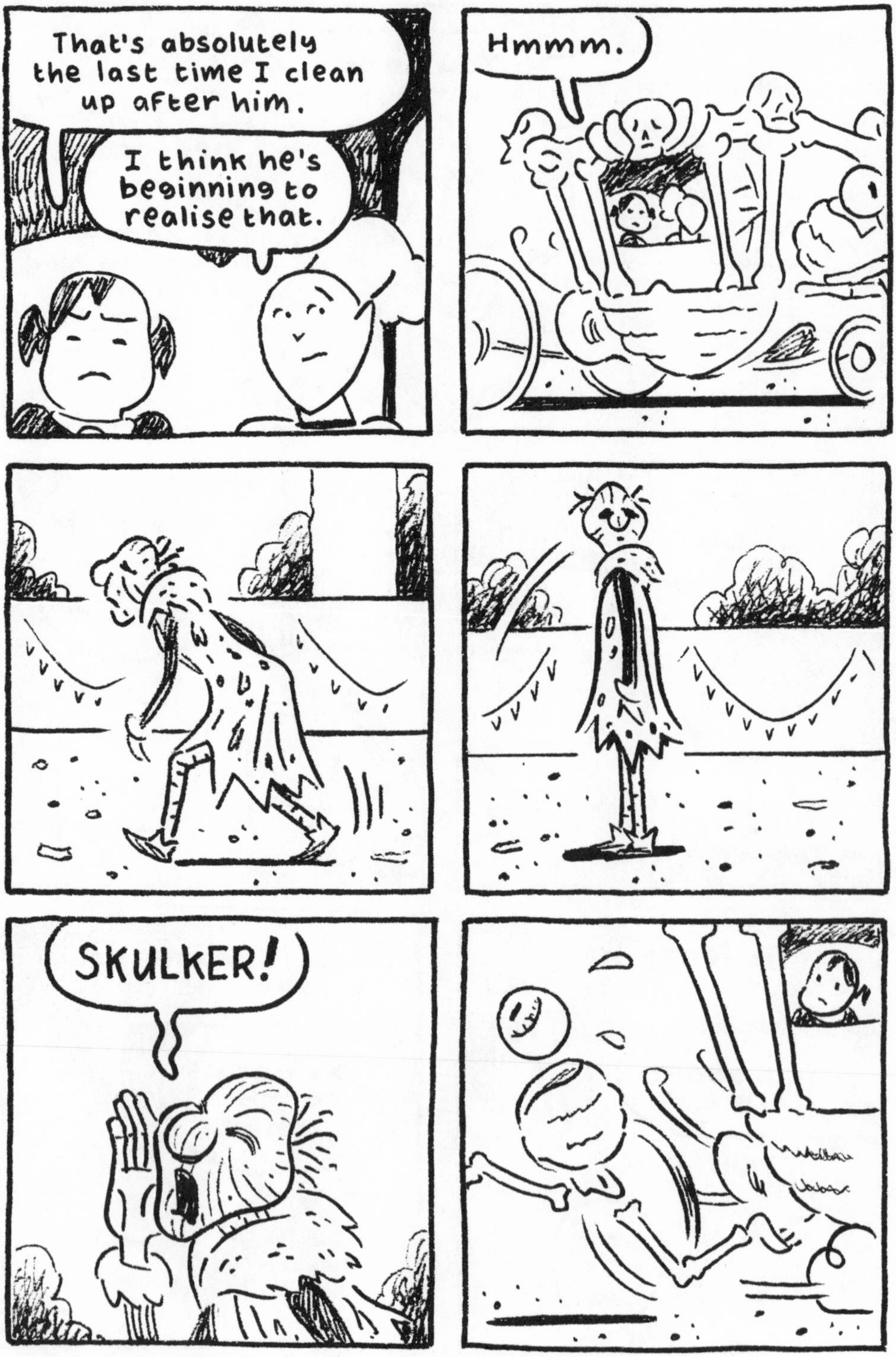
That's absolutely the last time I clean up after him.
I think he's beginning to realise that.
Hmmm.
SKULKER!

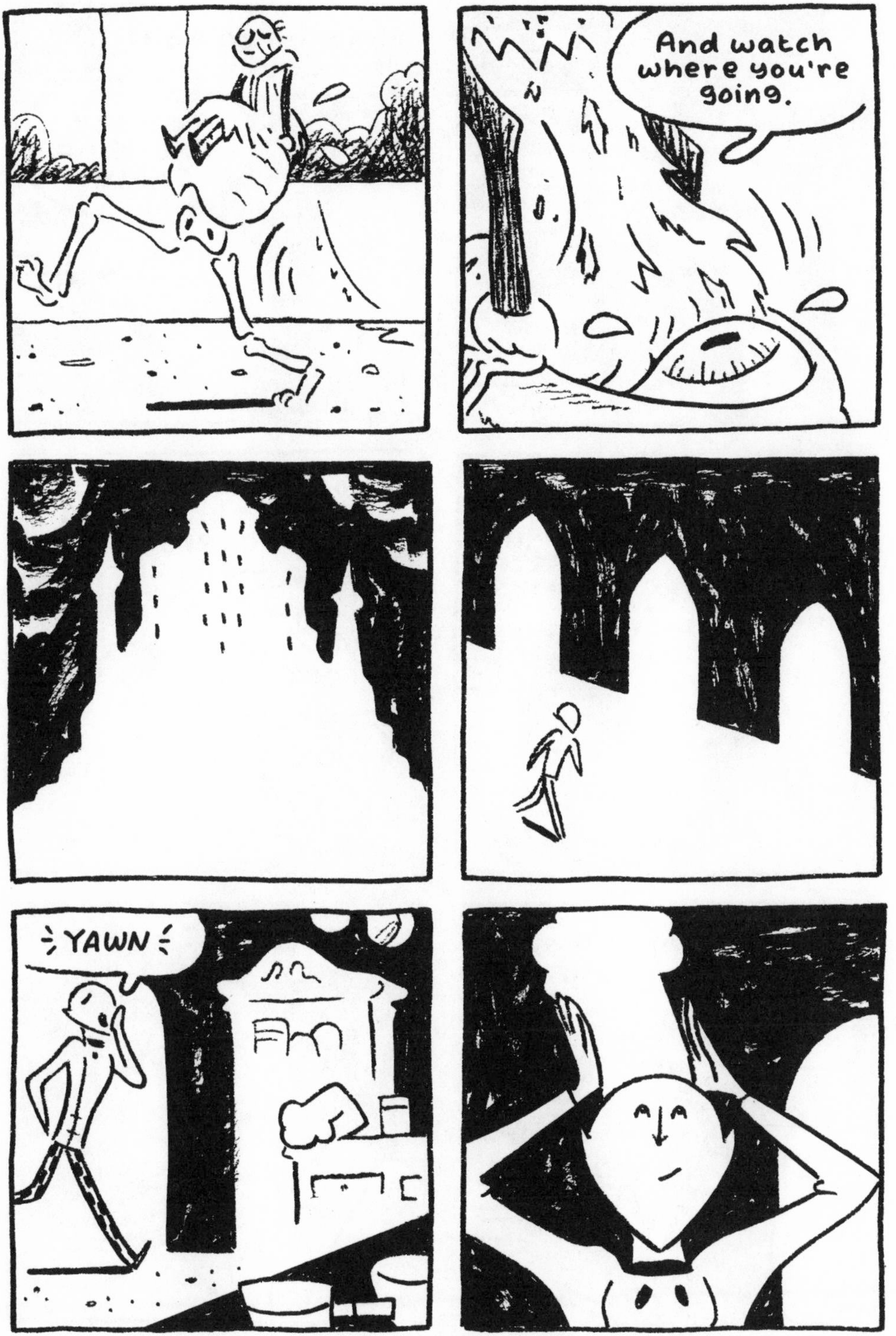
And watch where you're going.
YAWN

146

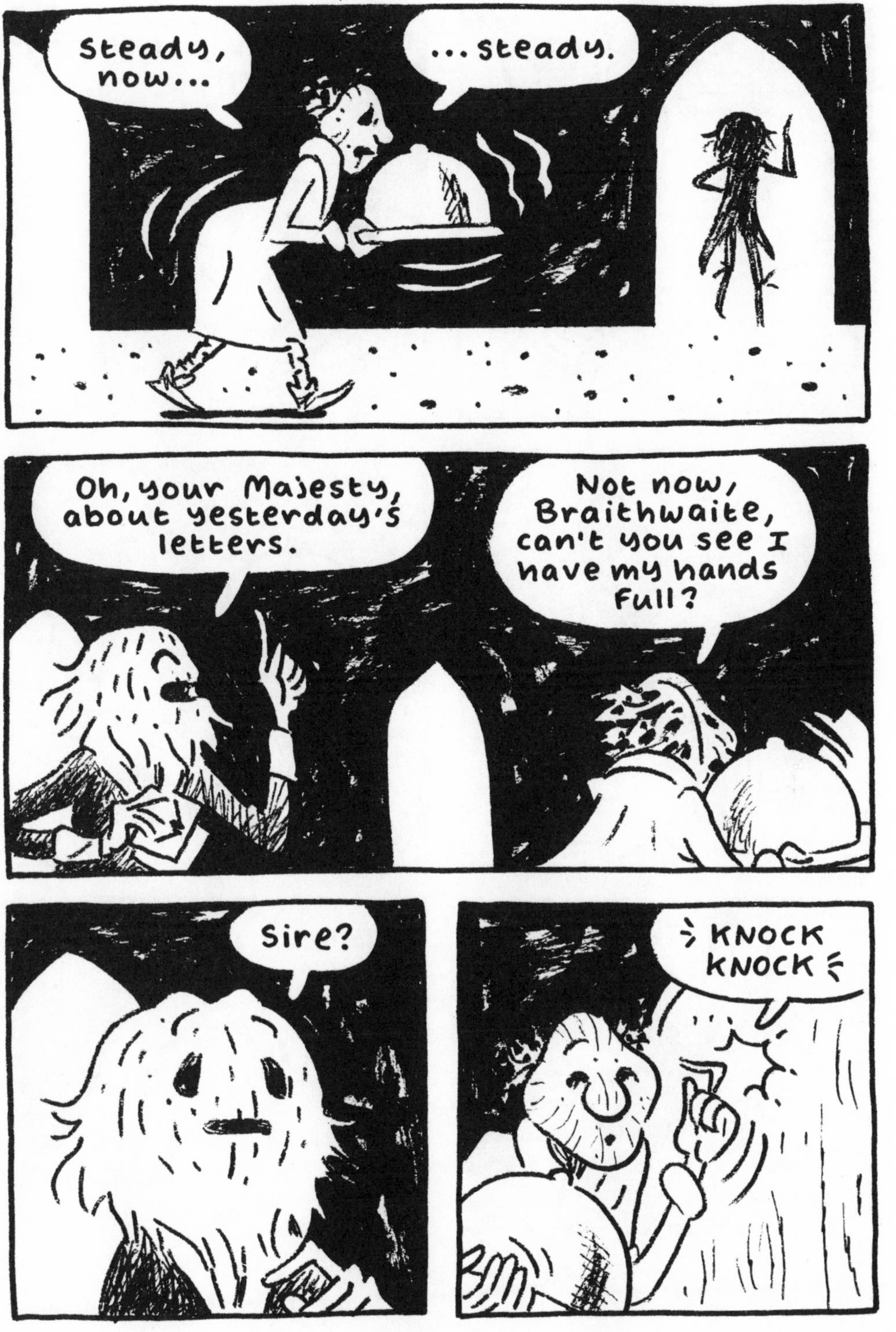
Steady, now...
...steady.
Oh, your Majesty, about yesterday's letters.
Not now, Braithwaite, can't you see I have my hands full?
Sire?
KNOCK KNOCK

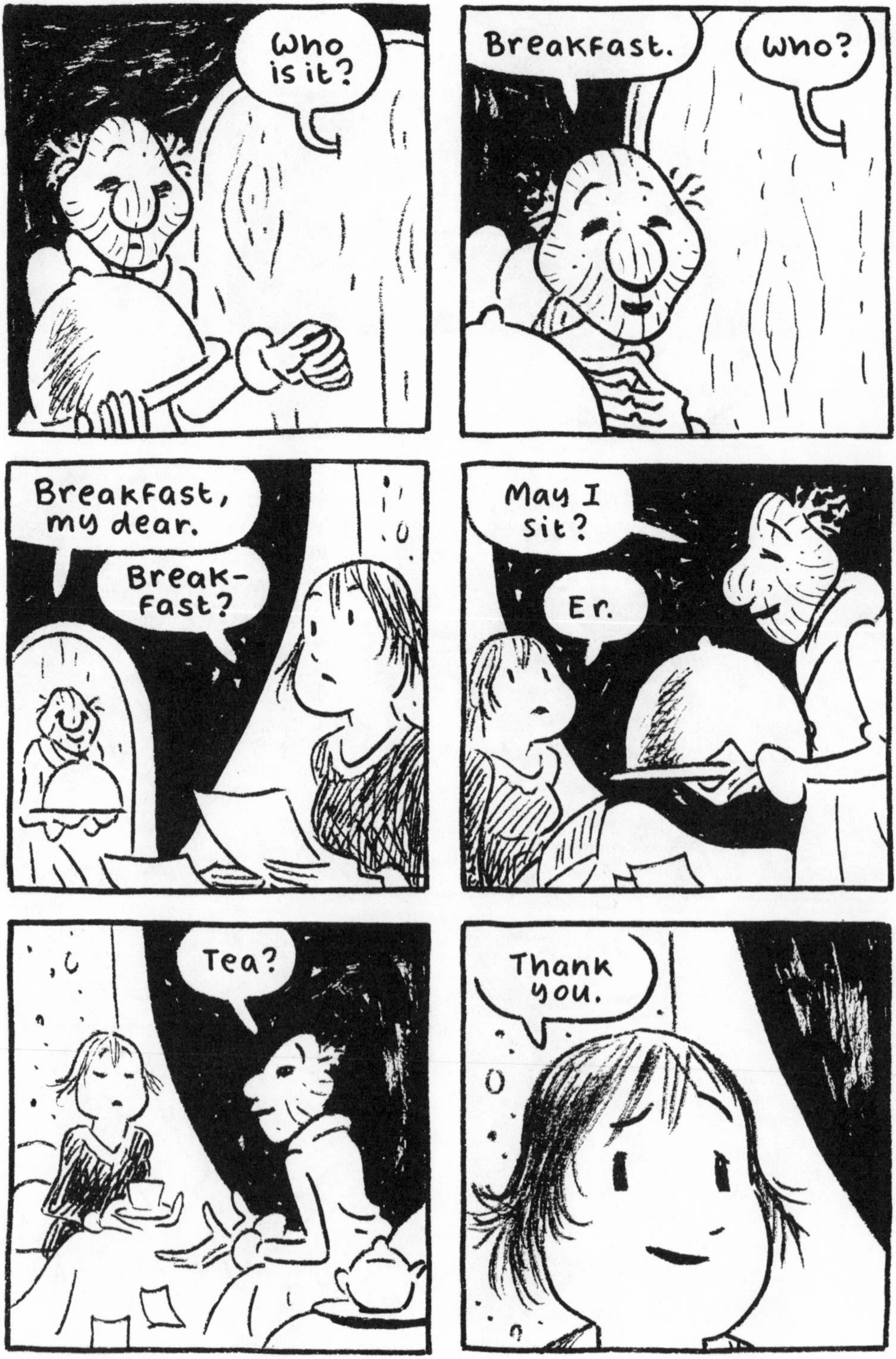
Who is it?
Breakfast.
Who?
Breakfast, my dear.
Break-fast?
May I sit?
Er.
Tea?
Thank you.

149

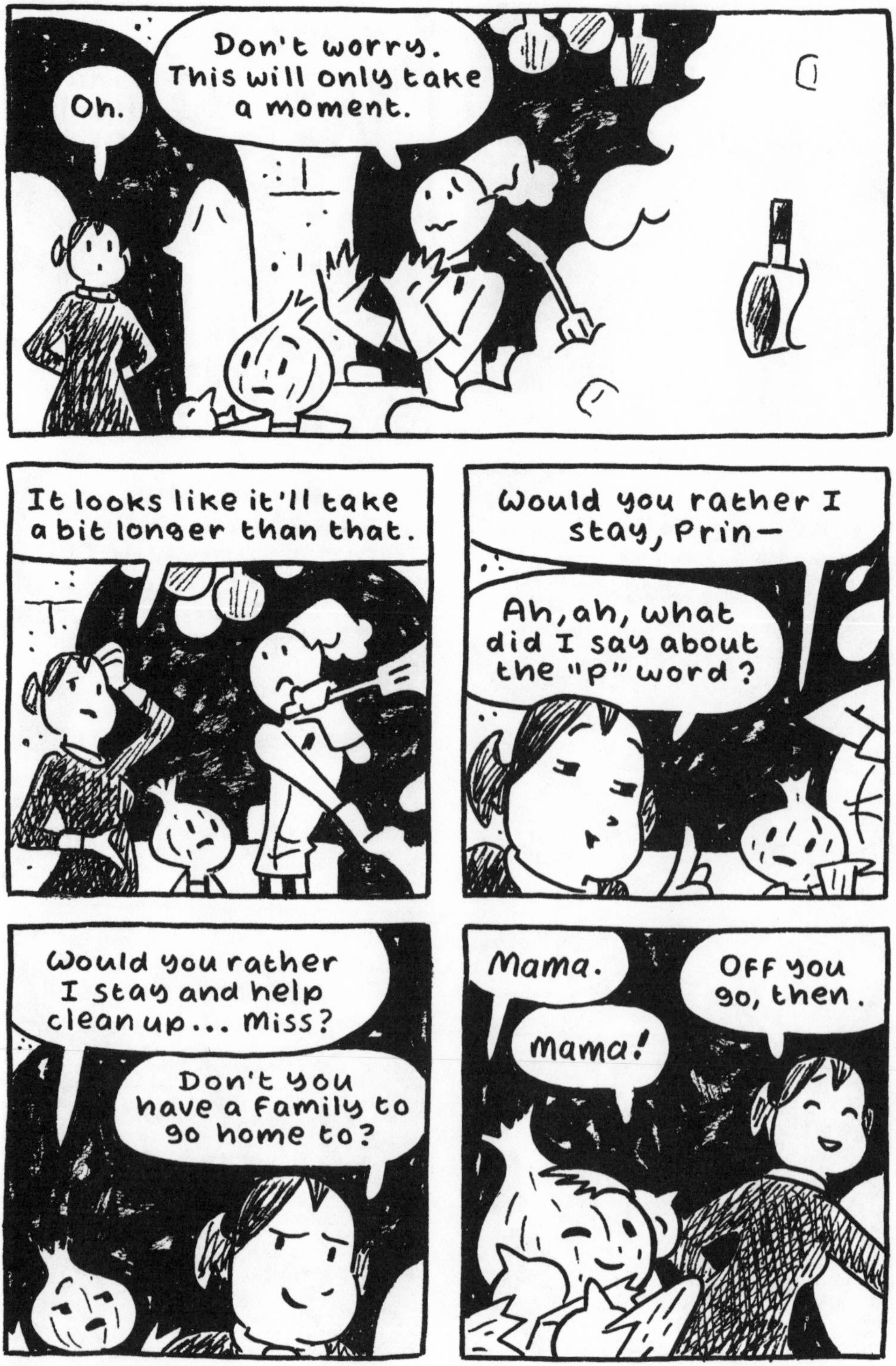
Oh.
Don't worry. This will only take a moment.
It looks like it'll take a bit longer than that.
Would you rather I stay, Prin—
Ah, ah, what did I say about the "p" word?
Would you rather I stay and help clean up... Miss?
Don't you have a family to go home to?
Mama.
Mama!
Off you go, then.

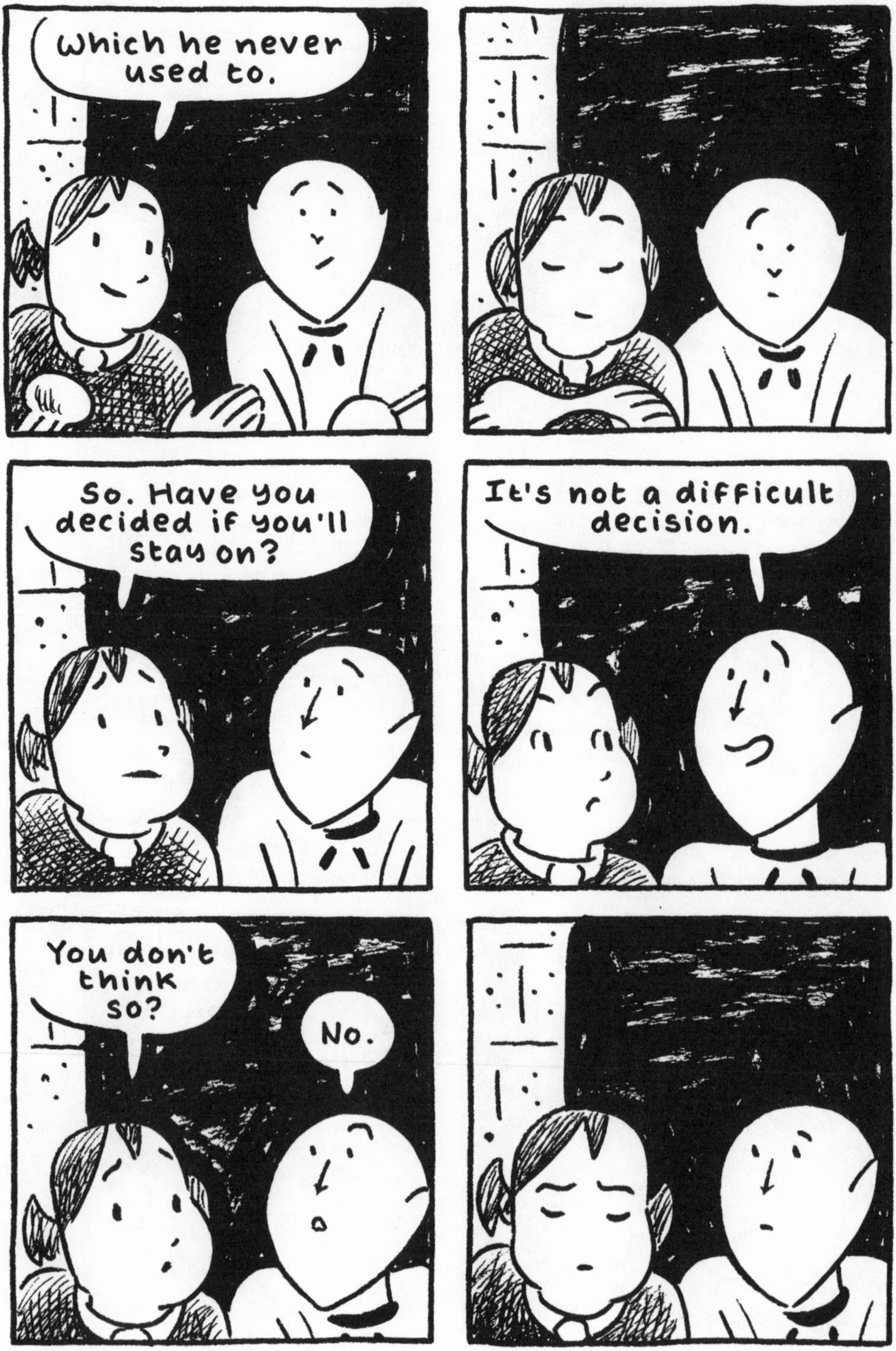
Which he never used to.
So. Have you decided if you'll stay on?
It's not a difficult decision.
You don't think so?
No.

158

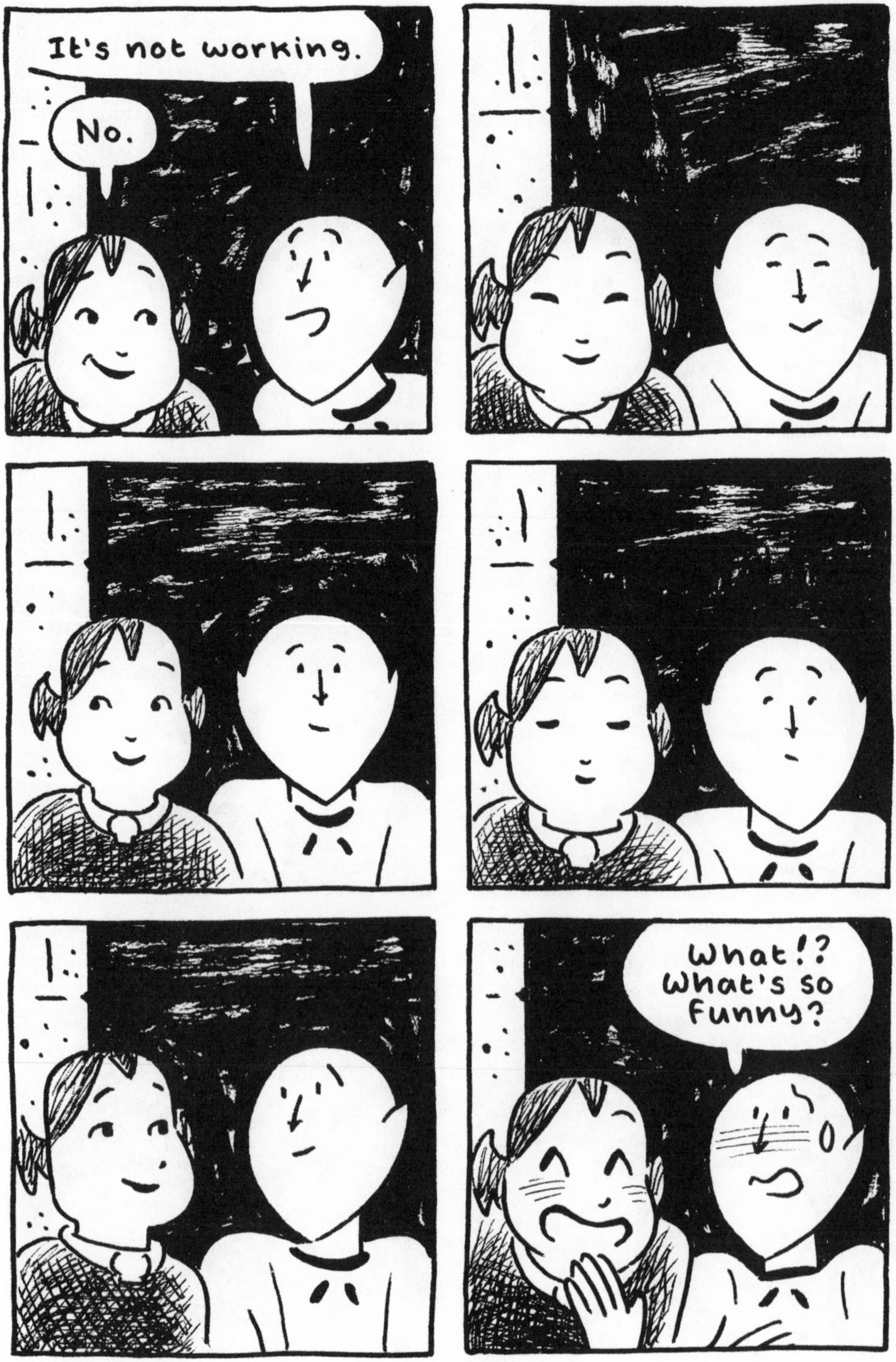
It's not working.
No.
What!? What's so funny?

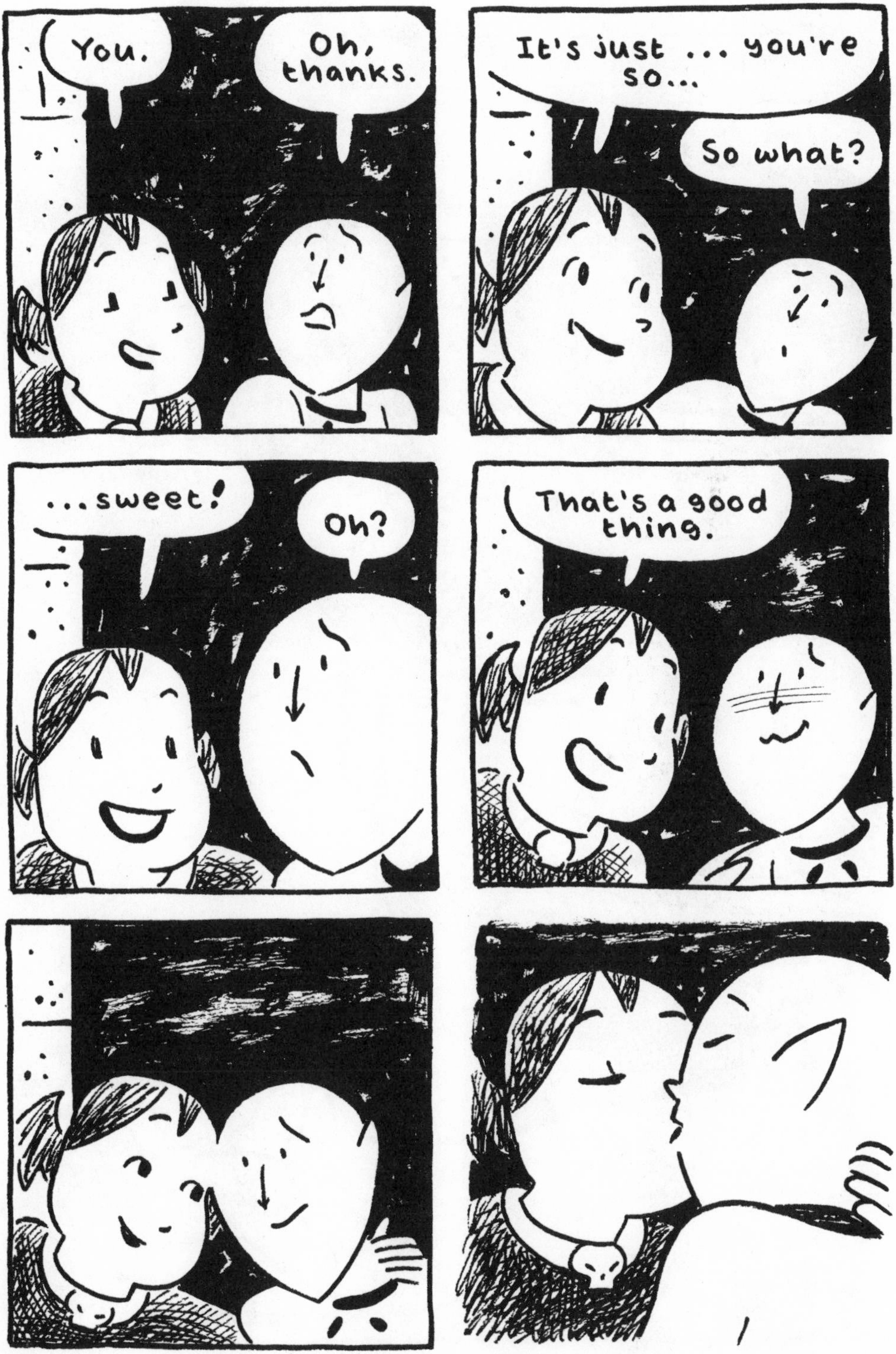
You.
Oh, thanks.
It's just ... you're so...
So what?
...sweet!
Oh?
That's a good thing.

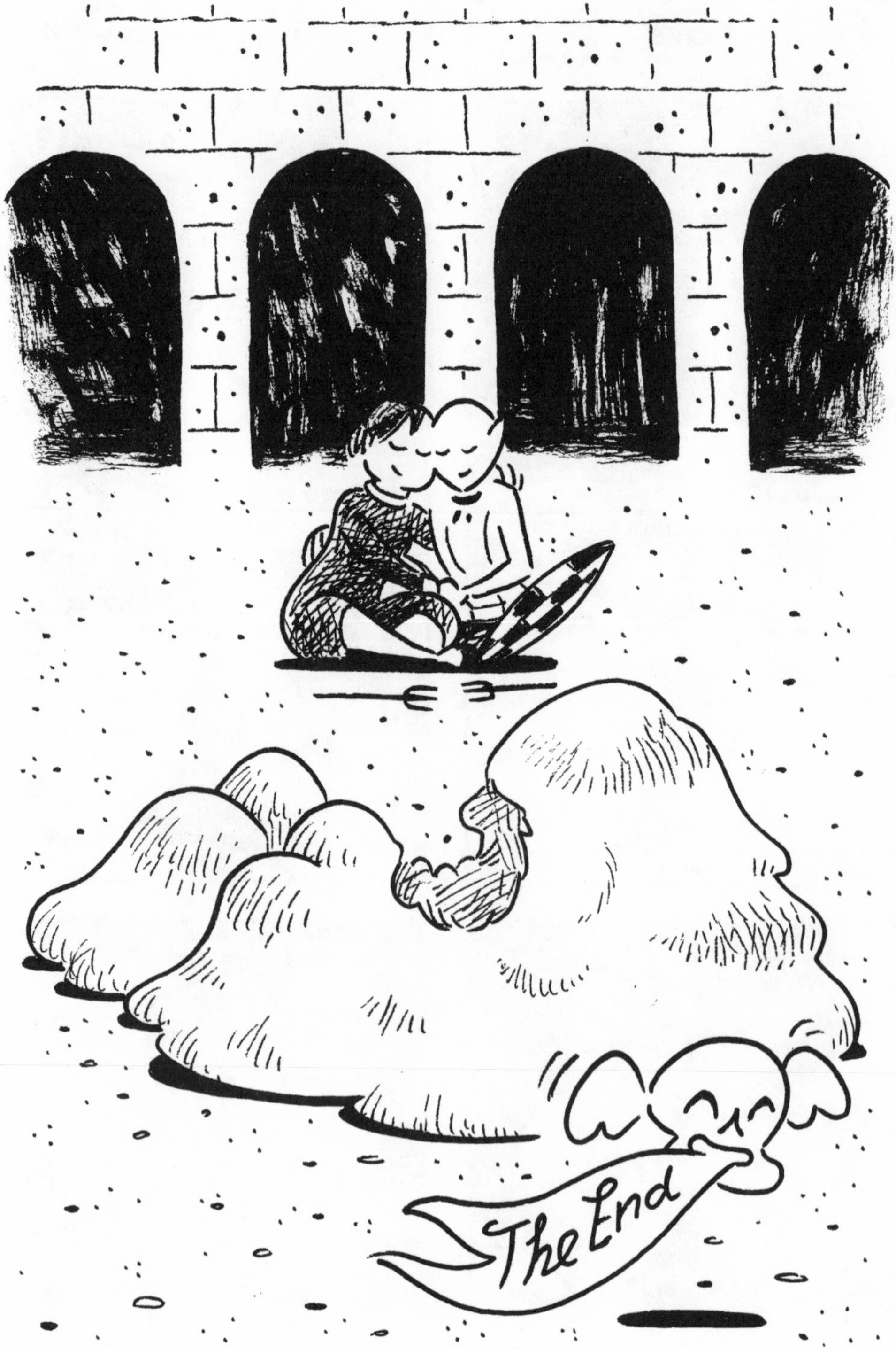
The End

Sketches

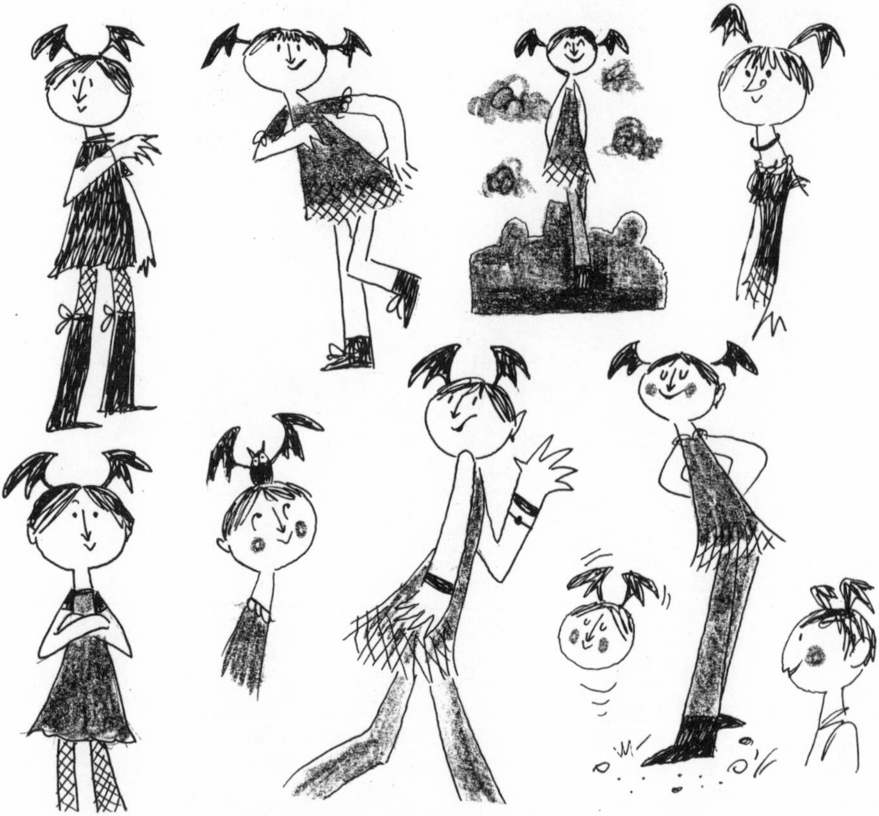

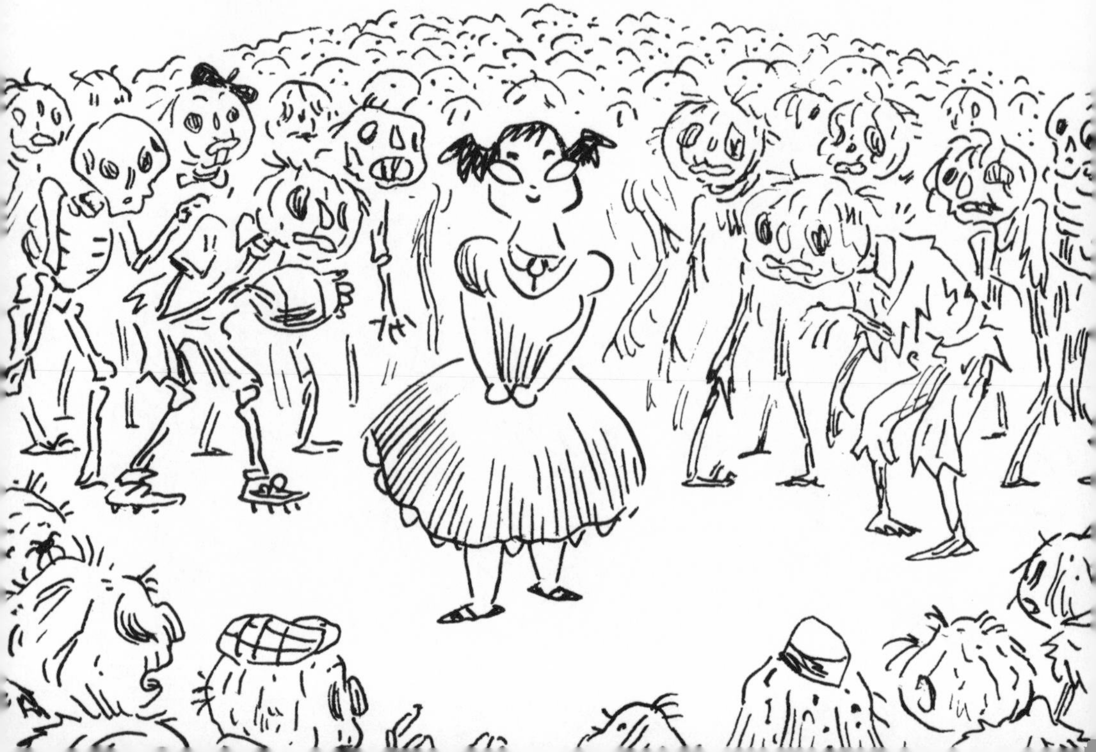

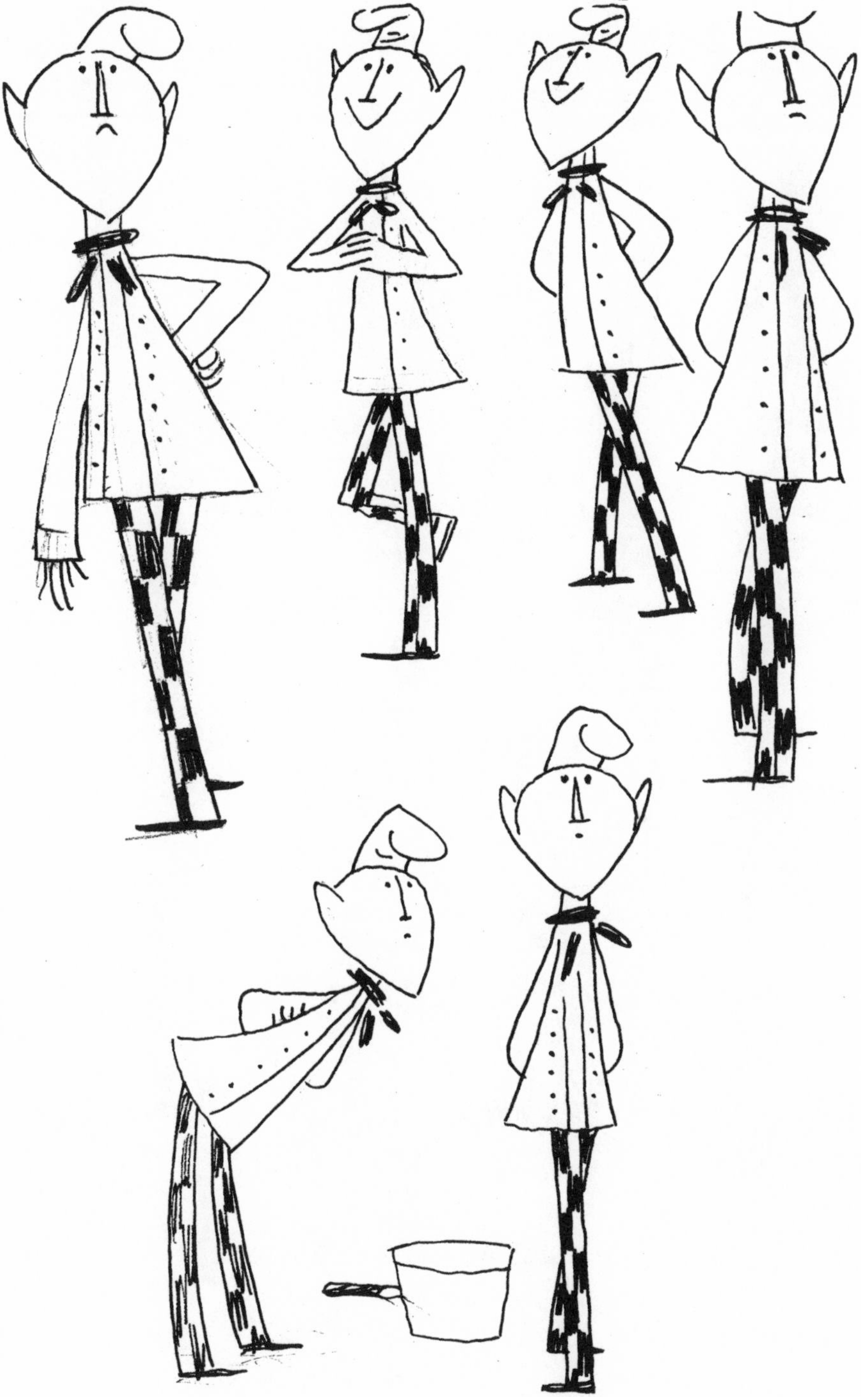

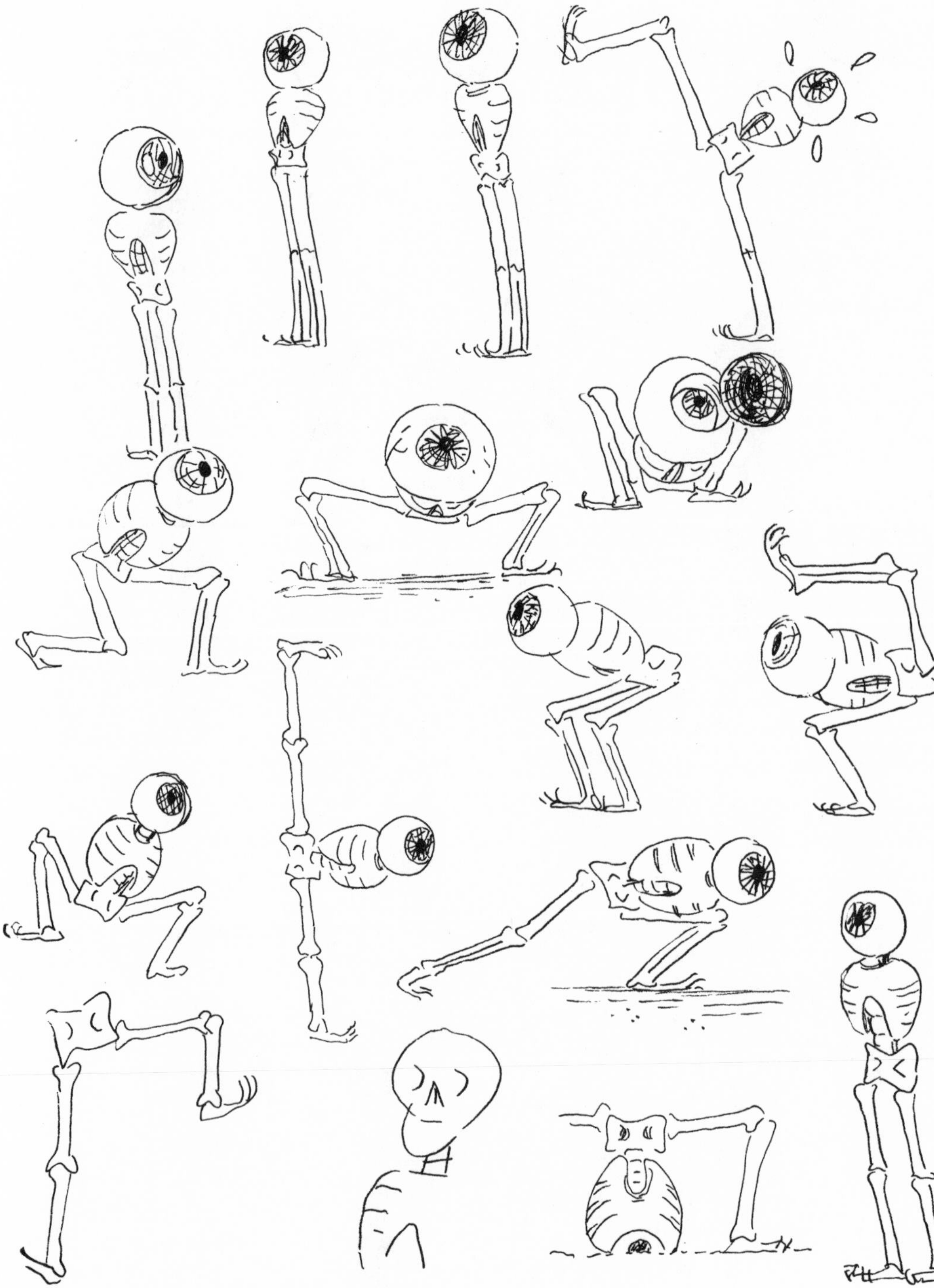

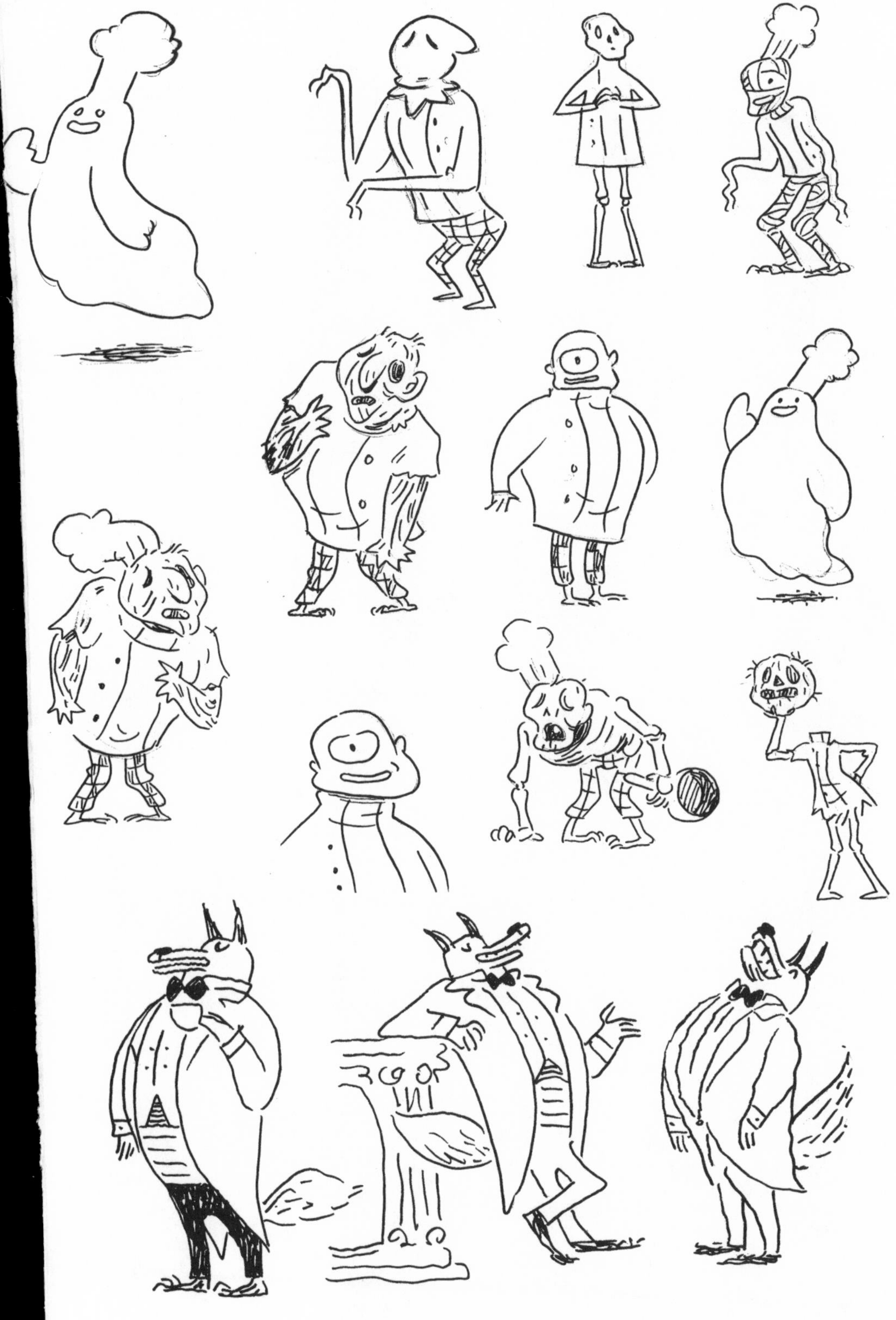

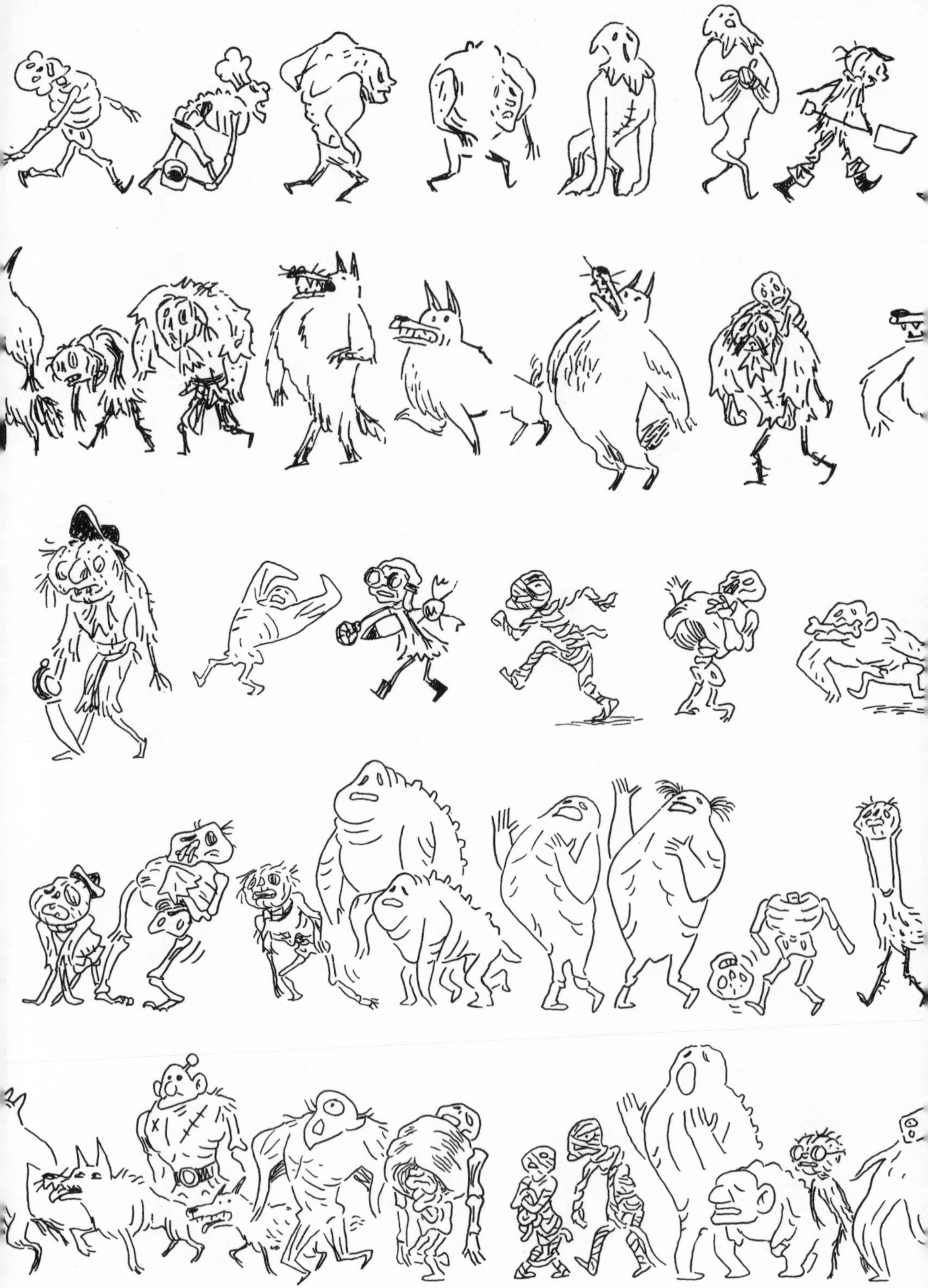